Ruined Stones

Books by Eric Reed

The Guardian Stones
Ruined Stones

Ruined Stones

Eric Reed

Poisoned Pen Press

Copyright © 2017 by Eric Reed

First Edition 2017

10 9 8 7 6 5 4 3 2 1

Library of Congress Catalog Card Number: 2016961973

ISBN: 9781464208348   Trade Paperback
      9781464208355   Ebook

Poisoned Pen Press
4014 N. Goldwater Boulevard, #201
Scottsdale, Arizona 85251
www.poisonedpenpress.com
info@poisonedpenpress.com

Printed in the United States of America

To Geordies everywhere

Chapter One

The young woman waited beside the ruins in the freezing December night.

While she waited she smoked. To someone watching from a short distance, she would have presented a barely perceptible thickening in the unbroken darkness of the blackout. Anyone in the street—and there were few about at this late hour—would have seen nothing more than the red blinking demon eye at the end of her cigarette.

During the day Benwell's Roman temple was not impressive. The remains of the walls were less than knee-high. Two carved altars sat at one end. That was all. Tonight, though she couldn't see the ruins, the idea she was standing where the ancients had worshiped strange gods chilled the woman more than the biting wind off the River Tyne.

Why, she couldn't say. It wasn't as if she hadn't loitered here before. The place was a customary place of business for professional women. Located in a green space between houses, it offered privacy, everyone knew where it was, and a copper couldn't very well move you along if you were only admiring a local landmark.

Which, truth to tell, suited both working girls and over-worked coppers.

Where was he?

She checked her watch. The dial glimmered ghost-like in the smothering darkness.

It would be Christmas before long. Her mam had always taken her to church on Christmas Eve. What would she say if she saw her daughter now, waiting at a pagan temple for…?

But she couldn't know. Her daughter had left home long before and never gone back.

Maybe next Christmas, if things worked out. Maybe she'd be able to return as a respectable woman, as her mam would put it. She could almost smell the turkey, taste the mince pies, see the Christmas pudding. She wouldn't resist eating Brussels sprouts. Not that there'd be much of the traditional meal if rationing was still in effect.

Could you even find Christmas crackers these days? The family was always startled by the bangs when they pulled them, even though they knew what was coming. Her dad had always balked at putting on the paper hat from his cracker. Finally he'd agree and pull it down to his ears, looking silly. All for the amusement of the kids, as they realized when they were older.

When she left she hadn't guessed she'd ever miss such ordinary things. She'd been wrong, especially when Christmas brought back memories.

A footstep crunched on frozen grass behind her.

Chapter Two

"Welcome to Newcastle, Miss Baxter." Sergeant Joe Baines sounded less than enthusiastic. "Come to bring the woman's touch to our station, have you?"

It was not the sort of big-city police station Grace had expected. During peace time it had been a corner shop, some distance along Carter Street from the maisonette where she was lodging. The sergeant's office had been the shopkeeper's kitchen.

She hoped her duties did not involve the kettle on the cooker behind the table the sergeant was using for a desk.

Baines must have noticed her looking around. "We're still in a bit of shambles," he explained. "The authorities thought it safer to move the station further from the river and so here we are."

He removed his spectacles, rubbed his reddened eyes, and then his wide forehead. He was prematurely balding. There was a doughy look to his features. Grace was used to men with weathered faces. She was dark-haired and dark-eyed with a broad face, the face of a country woman. She still had the rosy complexion of youth.

"Got a bit of a headache," Baines continued. "And speaking of headaches, I want to make it plain right away I do not believe women should be involved in police work. It's nothing personal, you understand."

"But I was told—"

"Never mind what you were told. For a start you're not strong enough to deal with violent drunks. As we would say in Glasgow, comes chucking out time and fights with broken bottles break out in the gutters—and that's the women!"

Grace bit her tongue. Not strong enough? She'd grown up assisting in cleaning out barns and baling hay.

"However," Baines continued, "if we must work with women, and it would appear that we must, I will admit they can deal with certain situations better than men. Apart from filing and answering the phone, your official duties will also involve assisting refugees, keeping an eye on young girls and kids likely to get into trouble, moving nymphs of the pavement along, and settling domestic disputes. You'll be on the day shift, though with the manpower shortages our schedules are usually erratic. Any questions?"

"None, sir," She had plenty of questions but was afraid of losing her temper at the answers she might get.

"Good. I hope you're up to learning on the job. We can't spare men for training. You have to get to know the locals, so today I'm sending you out to take statements about an incident last night. Women like to gossip and are more likely to talk to another woman. Constable Wallace will give you a tour of the neighborhood, show you where it took place, and leave you to it." He got up, revealing himself to be shorter than Grace, who thought she could certainly handle him if he were an unruly drunk.

Which was not what she should be thinking about her commanding officer at their first meeting.

Baines poked his head around the kitchen door. "Wallace, a minute if you would."

The white-haired officer who entered the kitchen looked well past retirement age.

"Wallace, show Miss Baxter the file on that dead woman, will you, and get me a headache powder."

Grace followed the older man back into the former shop. The shelves held a wireless, stacks of forms, steel helmets, and gas masks rather than tinned food and jars of sweets. The young constable at the desk, once the shop counter, looked at Grace as if he'd never seen a woman in a police uniform before.

Perhaps he hadn't.

"Constable Wallace, let me introduce myself properly. I'm Grace Baxter."

"I'm Arthur Wallace. Do you mind if I call you Grace? We're an informal lot here."

Already annoyed by Baines' attitude, Grace looked at the man in bemusement. Didn't he take her seriously either?

He went on, apparently oblivious. "I don't belong here any more than you do. There I was, good and retired from police work and then the war broke out. All the young officers were being called up. So here I am again, doing my bit."

"My father was the village constable before he joined up. That's how I got involved in police work."

"Where are you from?"

"Noddweir."

"Noddweir? Can't say the name's familiar."

"I'm not surprised. It's a tiny place in Shropshire, near the Welsh border."

"Is that so? We have a different class of crime here in the city. No stolen cows. This is a working-class area. A lot of the residents are employed at the Vickers factory along Scotswood Road. They work hard and drink hard. Unfortunately, the blackout's made Newcastle a playground for criminals. Now some have guns. Before the war it was knives, broken bottles, and lead pipes. And we're relying on inexperienced officers and old-timers like myself. The war's also given us a black market to deal with."

"I'm here to help. If I'm allowed to."

"Don't worry, you will be. We need all the help we can get. Don't let Sergeant Baines bother you. He's been distracted. Going through a bad time. He's a good sort, normally. But these headaches of his…" He rummaged in a drawer under the counter. "Where the hell are those powders?"

"Look on the shelf behind you," Grace suggested.

"What? Oh, yes, I see them." He straightened up with a grunt. "Bloody arthritis." He found a folder on a shelf and handed it to her. "Glance over it while I have a couple of words with the sergeant. A woman was found dead earlier this morning in the ruins of the local Roman temple. An accident, apparently. Scanty details at present, of course, so we haven't yet reached the point where we can claim, as Baines would no doubt say in his quaint Scottish way, many a mickle has made a muckle. Which translated means there are very few facts to be gathered together into a lump representing a definite solution."

A Roman temple, here? That struck Grace as strange. She drew a stool up to the counter. The young officer manning it kept glancing at her from the corner of his eye. She turned slightly to show him her Women's Auxiliary Police Corps badge and opened the folder.

The first item she saw was a rough sketch of a rectangular foundation. A pair of small squares labeled as altars stood inside the structure in front of a semi-circular wall at one end. The woman's body was roughly sketched, arms and legs awkwardly positioned.

Grace read on. The cause of death appeared to be a severe injury caused by the woman falling and striking her head on the nearest altar. She carried no identity card or handbag and was described as dark-haired, slight of build, about five-feet-four, with an estimated age in the mid twenties. She wore a green skirt and overcoat, white blouse, low-heeled shoes, and what was described as the usual undergarments.

"I'll bet you don't find dead bodies beside ancient Roman temples in that little country village of yours," the returning Wallace remarked.

She remembered the deaths associated with another ancient religious site—the stone circle on Guardians Hill overlooking Noddweir. She kept the thought to herself. "The dead woman is unidentified?"

"Aye, a mystery woman. Stu McPherson notified us. Lives in this street. He was on the way to school when he found her. She was probably a tart. That grassy bit where the ruins sit is well-known as a perfect place for such ladies to meet clients at night."

"I wouldn't expect to find a Roman temple sitting in the middle of houses on a city street."

"There's not much left of it, mind. Not surprising, seeing how it was built almost two thousand years ago, or so they told us at school. The altar she hit her head on isn't the original, though. Apparently it's a cast. Not that it mattered to the poor woman's skull. If she wasn't a tart, it may be she was drunk, wandering around in the blackout, tripped, and hit her head."

"Might have been a robbery and the assailant knocked her down."

"It's possible." Wallace shrugged. "All sorts of things could have happened, but until I have reason to think otherwise, my opinion is it was an accident."

"It says here that judging from the body's condition she died in the evening. That means she would have been lying out there all night."

"It's dark as the pit there with the blackout. Anyone crossing that open area would have had to trip over the body to notice it."

Grace ran her gaze down the typed report. "What do you make of the comment of the boy who found her, about the way the woman was posed?"

"You mean like a swastika? Rubbish. She accidentally wound up sprawled that way when she fell. Kids that age have good imaginations."

Grace examined the artist's sketch again. "Was the body really lying there like this?"

"Oh, I didn't notice anything so exaggerated. Artistic license." He stood up. "Now I'm supposed to show you around the neighbourhood before you start your interviews." He held the door open for her. "And, Miss Baxter, here in Newcastle we aren't a superstitious lot. Don't get carried away with any swastika nonsense."

She said nothing, but as they left the station she thought it wasn't simply that the sketch showed the woman's limbs laid out in the shape of a swastika. Being a country woman, one filled by her grandmother with folk wisdom, she recognized the arrangement of the victim's bent arms and legs into that of an ancient symbol of good fortune—and, incidentally, one that was the reverse of the Nazi swastika.

Chapter Three

Grace stepped over an eroded stone wall lower than her knees and stood in the middle of what had once been a temple. On three sides, fences and the backs of houses enclosed the open patch of ground occupied by the ruins. On the remaining side ran a street lined with terraced houses facing the temple. Chandler Street, she had noted, trying to orient herself.

The tour Constable Wallace gave her had been brief, mostly of smoke-blackened flat-fronted maisonettes and high-walled backyards containing outdoor privies and small shed-like lean-sot or under-staircase niches—coal holes—where the precious fuel was stored whose burning added to a constant pall of smoke generated by factories and foundries. As the year advanced to a close, the air was further obscured by the fog of December.

Then he'd quite abruptly left her to it. She had the impression Wallace expected she could handle herself while Sergeant Baines expected her to flounder, and rather hoped that she would.

Grace herself wasn't sure how she felt. Part of her was exhilarated to be patrolling the streets on her own. Part of her was scared. The police training she'd received in Manchester was perfunctory. Everyone seemed to accept that she already knew what she was doing.

Suddenly on her own in a strange city, Grace wondered if in her zeal to join the WAC and do her bit for the war effort she had exaggerated her role in investigating the horrific crimes that had shaken her little village. If the truth were told, she may have implied that her positions as her father's assistant and, after he left, de facto constable, required more expertise than was actually the case.

If it were up to her she'd be carrying her father's rook rifle as she had at times in Noddweir. But that wasn't allowed.

She tried to put doubts out of her mind. She crossed her arms and hunched her shoulders, attempting to keep warm. A chill drizzle, not quite fog, not quite rain, filled the grey metallic air. She might have been back in Noddweir, standing in the middle of the stone circle on the summit of Guardians Hill. The remains of the temple walls, half hidden by tall grass, were like the smaller, overgrown boulders in the circle. The pair of four-foot or so high altars resembled the larger stones.

The place gave her the same shivery sensation she received from Noddweir's stone circle. The ancient rocks still breathed out the past and caught within their compass, like a wasp in amber, was something unthinkably old and powerful.

Did everyone feel this? The Romans who built the temple must have. Or was it simply her overactive imagination?

As she turned to look around, a cold droplet fell from the brim of her hat and hit the back of her hand, startling her out of her musings. Surely it was only coincidence that her first official investigation should, like her first unofficial one, involve an ancient pagan ruin. She needed to be concentrating on her new job, not daydreaming about the countryside and her old life. By contrast, fogs here were sulfurous, thick and oppressive, not the white, gentle blankets common to the countryside.

She could imagine the fog was smoke from the fires of a Roman encampment on the furthest border of the empire. Here civilization took its stand against the savagery beyond. Even as today the line was drawn here, Britain standing almost alone against Nazi savagery.

For an instant ghostly walls rose around her and she sensed murmurous words she could not understand.

She shook herself free of the illusion. Certainly it was nothing but an illusion. She needed to examine the site of what Baines had described as "the incident."

To her annoyance the site had not been cordoned off, nor had anyone bothered to mark the body's position. More evidence it was considered an accident. She examined the altars. There were carvings on them. A garland, a pitcher, a knife. She could make out a rusty stain on one corner, the victim's blood or simply an innocent discoloration? The city air, she had already seen, blackened everything. She gauged the distance from the nearest foundation. Yes, if the victim had taken a misstep in the dark and stumbled forward she might have hit her head on the stained corner, although it would have taken a very bad piece of luck to fall in exactly the right direction.

She surveyed the dismal scene again. This was not how she had envisioned her first day on the job in Newcastle. How had she pictured it? Striding along crowded streets while heads turned in admiration, staring at her uniform? She'd hardly encountered a soul on the short walk to the temple, and the few pedestrians she had seen were hunched over and muffled up, rushing to escape the miserable cold, seeing nothing but their warm destinations. All carried gas masks. The box holding her own hung from a string draped over her shoulder, a constant reminder that death might fall from the skies at any moment.

The rectangular temple outlined by what remained of its walls wasn't large. About fifteen feet long, Grace estimated. Sweet wrappers lay in the tall grass and under the surrounding hedges. She trudged dutifully around the wet ground, seeing nothing but rubbish, wishing she had a pair of wellingtons. No doubt the spot had already been thoroughly searched.

Wallace was probably right that it was an accident and no one had seen anything. The streetlights had been off. The houses all sat at a distance, windows blocked by the omnipresent blackout curtains.

A rustling in the weeds caught her attention.

It was only a black cat, crossing this tiny piece of wilderness.

A good omen. Black cats meant good luck, just as left-handed swastikas did, according to Grandma.

Grace smiled at the cat, then crossed Chandler Street and started knocking at doors.

•• ● ••

"Do you think Santa will be able to get to us this year?" Six-year-old Veronica Gibson sought comfort from Jim Charles, a boy in his early teens accompanying a group of several children returning home after school. "Will the Luftwobble catch him? It would be awful if he got killed." Her voice wavered.

Short and slight, with a solemn face framed by dark wispy hair chopped off at chin level, Veronica was of an age when reindeer-drawn sleighs bearing presents and airplanes loaded with bombs were both shadowy possibilities moving through the vast misty world beyond the concrete reality of her own neighborhood. She had heard her parents talking about the Luftwobble and Hitler and Nasties when they thought her out of earshot. Their tones terrified her. She could not imagine what would scare adults.

"Santa's clever enough to avoid them Germans," Jim reassured her. "I'll bet he's got a great big machine gun on his sleigh just in case."

Veronica frowned up at the gangly creature beside her. Jim could be unreliable, mean and teasing at times. At other times he was protective of her and other younger children living in the neighborhood. She walked on, thoughtful as always. An invisible sun infused the fog with a sickly yellow light that made everything look flat and dead.

"Made yer list for Santa and chucked it in the fire?" Jim asked.

Veronica nodded. The ashes still flew up the chimney to Santa like previous years, she hoped, but with the Luftwobble up there, could she be sure?

"What did you ask for?"

"A dolly and sweeties and a book," came the reply. "And for me mam—" The little girl broke off and stopped walking. "Look. There's a bobby at the ruins."

A voice from behind them broke in. "That's because someone bashed in some tart's head last night." The boy, around Jim's age, expelled his words in gusts of cigarette smoke rather than the misty exhalations issuing from other mouths. His narrow features were set in a sneer.

Jim showed him a doubled-up fist. "Divn't torment the bairn, Stu."

"You keep yer gob shut, Jim."

Veronica felt tears welling up. "Did…did…the lady….?"

"She got killed, Nica." Stu told her. "Same as you would if somebody smashed you over the head with a big, jagged rock."

Veronica pressed mittened hands to her mouth. The other children had gathered around Stu. He offered them a wicked smile. "It was me what reported her, see. Huns done it."

Jim laughed. "Harraway wi' yer barrer! Who'd be stupid enough to fall for that?"

"Must have been the Huns. They bent her arms and legs so she looked like one of them swastikas they parade about with, the swine."

The children were wide-eyed.

The bobby Veronica had spotted moved off.

"Look. The copper's a girl," Jim said.

"Bloody hell!" Stu tossed his cigarette away. "Like to see some girl stop me in the street and tell me what to do!"

• • ● • •

A few of Grace's knocks were answered, many were not. Those who did answer told her about as much as those who didn't. Grace scribbled in her notebook, mainly to give the impression she was doing her job.

A young woman with a harassed expression and two toddlers clinging to her skirt complained about the lack of moral guidance youngsters had these days. "Hardly any left around here with so many evacuated, but the ones that stayed get up to as much mischief as all the rest put together. What are their parents thinking? Why, the woman at number fifteen caught her next door neighbor's son shoplifting only last week. I wouldn't be surprised if it wasn't some of these wild kids did that poor woman in."

The industrial city and its deafening noise of clock-round war work in factory and shipyard created conditions in which children might be left to their own devices when their mothers were working and their fathers away.

As Grace continued along the street it was always a woman who opened the door, invariably looking her up and down, puzzled and wary. Grace guessed they did not pay her the deference they would have had she been a man, but then, how would she know how city people normally acted?

Questioning her neighbors in Noddweir had been easy. Those who hadn't known her as Constable Baxter's daughter from the time she was a child had grown up with her. In Newcastle she was among strangers. Suspicious strangers. And who could blame them? Her accent set her apart, as did her ruddy complexion. The faces in this gloomy city were all ashen. Or was that her own prejudice showing?

Several doors down, a white-haired woman carrying tins in a string shopping bag arrived at her door as Grace approached. She invited her inside because, as she put it, "I don't want gossip." She had nothing to offer except a fervent wish the Germans would oblige her and the neighbors by turning the ruins into a pit.

"It's a natural place of business for loose women. Nobody can see what's going on over there after dark. Why, only the other day I was telling my friend Ada there'd be trouble sooner or later. A well-placed bomb would solve the problem. I'd be happy to replace a few broken windows. Was the woman one of those…well, you know? Do you think it was a customer killed her? Maybe it was someone from the street. You never know what husbands will get up to."

Everyone had a theory but no one had seen or heard anything. No commotion, no screams in the night, raised voices or running feet. No reason for anyone to put out the light, push aside a blackout curtain, and peer out, as if it were possible to see anything anyway.

But residents were afraid. They did not share the official assumption that the woman had died by accident. "Until the person responsible is found, I'm asking to change to a day shift," one woman told her.

Was it the stress of war that caused everyone in the street to assume the worst, or was it some sort of collective instinct?

By the time Grace finished her circuit the haze and drizzle had given way to pale sunlight, as weak as the third cup of tea from the same leaves. Her damp feet had stopped stinging long before and gone numb. When she spotted a woman whitening her doorstep with a scouring stone, she was reluctant to stop and question her.

The woman gave a start when she became aware of Grace, ceased rubbing with the stone, and scowled upwards.

"Anything to do with that temple, you need to talk to Rutherford at number sixty," she replied to Grace's query. "Old as the hills, he is. Knows all about them ruins. Gives lectures about such things at the church. Them ruins ought to be bulldozed, in my opinion. Magnets for troublemakers, they are."

The woman stood, sniffed, and adjusted the tartan headsquare covering her curlers. Her wet hands were fiery red from the cold. What kind of weather was this for such a task? "Mind, you'll be lucky if you can get him to talk. We hardly see him in the daytime. He creeps out after dark every night. I've moved my wardrobe to block my front room window so I can't see that abomination. The ruins, I mean." Her voice degenerated into a bout of coughing as she wiped her hands on her apron.

"He goes out every night?"

"Aye, hinney. Straight over to them ruins. Only the Almighty knows what he gets up to, or who he meets, or what." She gave another sniff, drawing her apron tighter about her thin frame.

Grace questioned her further and learned nothing more. "And he lives at number sixty, you say?"

"That's right. Six six six would be more appropriate."

"If anything comes back to you, anything strange you saw or heard that night, come round to the police station and let us know."

The woman offered a noncommittal grunt, picked up her bucket and scouring stone, and went indoors. Grace heard her clumping up uncarpeted stairs.

Number sixty turned out to be a ground-floor maisonette, distinguishing itself from the others in the street by the peeling paint on its door and a dirty window. Grace had tried knocking earlier. She plied the knocker vigorously again. Despite her gloves, the cold from the metal knocker flowed into her hand like an electric current. Her fingers were as numb as her toes.

Finally she decided there would be no answer. Presumably Rutherford worked at night, since he went out every evening. He'd be asleep during the day but the racket she'd made should have awakened him. She would have to come back later.

As she turned to go, disappointed and wondering what Baines would say at her failure to find out anything useful, she glimpsed a slight twitch in the still drawn blackout curtain.

Was the elderly Mr. Rutherford deaf or did he want to avoid opening the door to the police?

She remained in front of the door for a short time, in case he was making up his mind but the curtain fell back into place and the door remained closed.

This was her first impression of Newcastle. Much cold, many locked doors.

Chapter Four

"So they've put you on a murder case already, hinney! Good for you. What most of them bluebottles need is a boot in the rear, if y'ask me."

Mavis, Grace's landlady, perched on the end of one of two beds shoe-horned into the room, swinging her legs restlessly as she watched Grace empty her suitcases. Grace had arrived late the night before and the two had barely had a chance to speak.

"No one at the station thinks it was a murder or else I wouldn't be investigating. I'm only an auxiliary."

"Oh, it's a murder. Woman's intuition." Mavis was a petite brunette dressed in drab overalls a size too large. She picked up Grace's peaked uniform hat from the bed and settled it on her cropped hair.

Grace looked up from her suitcases. "Pardon? You'll have to speak slower, Mavis, until I get used to your accent." It wasn't just the accent, she thought. Geordie, the local dialect, resembled a foreign language to her Southern ears.

"Shove your knickers in the top drawer there. Is that why they call them drawers, do you think? Afraid we're a bit short of space here. I'll make some room for your clothes in the wardrobe. You'll get used to living in a place with only two rooms, a scullery, and a netty in the backyard."

"Netty? You mean outdoor privy? I'm already used to those. That's what I grew up with. I'm a country girl."

What she wasn't used to was the cramped layout. The shared bedroom was the first room opening off a short hall leading to the combination kitchen and living room heated by a coal fire in a fireplace fitted with an oven to one side and a well-polished brass fender in front. The kitchen led to a scullery whose claustrophobic space under a slanted ceiling housed a gas cooker. A sink with a cold water tap and wooden draining board stood below the window next to a door opening on to a narrow brick-walled backyard.

"For heaven's sake!" Mavis cried. "What are you doing with that disgusting thing?" She was staring at the charm in Grace's hand.

"It's a keepsake of my grandmother."

"Your grammy was a Nazi?" Mavis' legs in the baggy overalls stopped swinging. She sat rigid, as if Hitler himself had goose-stepped into the room.

"No. It's a charm. Look, the arms are pointed in the opposite direction from the Nazi version. They're anti-clockwise. Left-handed, see?" Grace held the charm out for closer examination but Mavis put her hands up as if to push it away.

"It's nothing to do with the Germans, Mavis," Grace continued. "The swastika has been around for centuries. It's considered a symbol of good luck, long life, and prosperity. The Germans adopted a certain form of it, made it stand for something it was never meant to represent."

"If you say so, but I'm not touching it."

What would Mavis think if Grace told her that the body of the woman found at the temple had been laid out in the form of a left-handed swastika?

She placed the trinket into a drawer. Mavis' reaction was understandable. Not everyone had grown up with a wise woman for a grandmother. Grace clicked the suitcase shut and slid it under the bed. The last thing she needed was to get into an argument with the woman she was going to be living with, possibly for the war's duration.

Grandma had always been a troublemaker and she was still causing trouble.

Mavis surveyed the tiny room bleakly. "Here I am, the best years of me life flying by, ruining me hands working at Vickers. It's good money and I'm helping the war effort but I'm left all alone while me husband fights abroad—not that Ronny wasn't forever fighting at home. Thank heaven we never had any bairns."

Upon arriving the previous evening Grace had noted there were no photos of the absent husband serving in the forces. She wasn't sure how to respond. Luckily Mavis changed the subject.

"What about the rest of your family, Grace? They're still down south?"

"In a way."

"Dead, eh? Sorry. Bloody Germans. I do rattle on. Sorry about your grammy's charm too. Gave me a bit of a start."

"It's the sort of thing gives spies away in novels."

"Is it? I'm not much of a reader myself. Love to dance. I've got a gramophone and practice me steps most nights."

Grace believed her. There were binders of the sort used to store records stacked in the corner. She'd seen others on a kitchen shelf and individual records scattered here and there.

Mavis took off Grace's hat, which was too large for her, and tossed it down. "I don't think I have an outfit to match that."

With her severe haircut, plain face devoid of makeup, and ill-fitting overalls, Mavis didn't look like a woman who gave any thought to fashion or dancing.

"I'm not much of a dancer," Grace admitted. "I can muddle through a waltz or a polka, if you call a fast waltz a polka. Did you go dancing with your visitor last night?" A tall man had briefly exchanged words with Mavis on the door step before departing. "I hope I won't..I mean, I don't want to intrude."

"Hans van der Berg? He's not my fancy man, if that's what you mean. He's angled a bit but I do keep in mind I'm married, unlike some. The neighbors already gossip because I like to go out and have fun. Do we have to waste our lives because we had the bad luck to be young when there's a war on?"

Grace smiled. "If you practice dancing here with Hans, I won't tell anyone."

"I wouldn't want to give him ideas. That reminds me, did I tell you Hans is coming over later?"

• • ● • •

After their evening meal Grace sat with Mavis in the kitchen.

"Was your sergeant pleased with your efforts?"

"Hard to say." Grace frowned. "He was gone by the time I returned. When he met me this morning I got the impression that he felt I was offending him simply by being there, being a woman."

"The men prefer us to stay home. And knit." Mavis indicated the teddy bear she was making, coloured a bright red never seen in nature. "This is for a little girl down the street. Poor bairn won't get much for Christmas as it is and as for the others, Santa needs all the coal he would usually leave for bad lads! I've knitted her mittens and a pixie hood from the same old sweater. Then I've made a paper tooter and one of those twirly things on a string you go cross-eyed looking at. I should have liked to get hold of a bit of coloured chalk."

"That's good of you, Mavis." It pleased Grace to be forming a good impression of this young woman she'd arranged to stay with sight unseen.

"Bairns have no childhood these days. I've also got something different for her. It's a stone with a hole in it. Picked it up at Cullercoats on the coast, years ago. Pretty, isn't it?"

"Grandma told me they're good for protection. You could plait some wool and make her a necklace with it."

"It's a nice idea. She'd like that. Then again, your grammy thought swastikas are lucky! Your family does have strange ideas!"

There was a knock on the front door. Mavis got up to answer it and returned followed by a tall, blond man with deep blue eyes and a thin, tanned face, the man Grace had glimpsed speaking to Mavis the night before. "It's Hans, come to get the old wives gossiping again. This is Grace, Hans, my new lodger."

The visitor gave a half-bow. "Goedenavond, Miss Grace," he said, addressing her in Dutch. "Miss Mavis told me you had arrived when I called last night. I did not think I should come in. You must have been very tired from traveling." Turning to Mavis, he went on, "I have for you a present to honour the season." Delving into a pocket of his shabby pea coat, he brought out a pair of glass Christmas ornaments carefully wrapped in a handkerchief. "I purchased them from a gentleman in a public house."

"Very nice, too, Hans. Thanks. I'll pinch a couple of pine branches from the cemetery—you didn't hear that, Grace!—stick them in a jam jar, and add a bit of tinsel and these ornaments. And very festive they'll look too. Now, get snipping!"

Hans hung his coat over a chair back, sat down at the table, and began cutting strips from sheets of painted newspaper Mavis produced from a cupboard. He gave the impression of being very much at home. Grace deduced that decorative paper chains were to be made.

"Tell us about the adventures of a woman police auxiliary then, Grace," Mavis asked.

"It's not much of an adventure. Knocking on doors in the cold, mostly. How are we going to stick these paper strips together?"

"I've thought of that," Mavis said, going into the scullery.

"It must have been a very bad thing to see that poor dead lady," Hans observed.

Grace reached for a strip of paper at the same moment as Hans laid more on the pile and their hands momentarily met. An accident?

Hans pulled his hand away and smiled.

"No, no." Grace felt flustered. "She had been taken to the morgue by the time I arrived at the station. I've only seen a drawing so far. The odd thing was it looked like her arms and legs were arranged in the shape of a left-handed swastika."

Mavis returned with a basin. "Never mind about that, Grace. Here we are, see? Flour and water paste will hold our paper chain together. Not that Mr. Churchill would approve."

"It is good for people to have a little joy in their lives," Hans replied. "So I shall not tell him!"

Mavis resumed knitting. "Tell Grace how you came to be in England, Hans. It's a good story."

"I was a fisherman. One night I got into my boat and sailed to England—"

"'Got in his boat,' he says!" Mavis put in. "He forgot to tell you he had to dodge sentries, brought other refugees with him, and the Germans sank his boat. Luckily they were near to the coast and got rescued. Well, most of them."

"It was so," Hans admitted. "Now I work as a translator but I am hoping my friend Mavis will help me get work at the Vickers factory down by the river. I wish to strike back more directly at the Germans."

"We do a canny bit of war work down there," Mavis agreed.

Hans nodded vigorously. "Tanks. That is what I want to make. If I could I would gladly drop bombs on the swine." He grasped the scissors and made stabbing motions.

The gesture startled Grace. The man had struck her as mild-mannered.

Mavis patted Hans' arm. "Wouldn't we all like to bomb the Huns? Hans does make fighter planes, though." She showed Grace the silver brooch pinned to her blouse, the crude but recognizable shape of a Spitfire. "He made it from a sixpence."

It reminded Grace of one of her grandmother's many charms. She asked Mavis whether it was such a thing.

"No. It's not a charm. It's to show support for the Brylcreem boys. You know, fighter pilots. Not that we aren't a superstitious lot. There was a girl on this street who got herself into trouble, wouldn't have her baby christened, refused to have it adopted, and then abandoned it and went off. All the old wives said, 'What could you expect from a tart who wouldn't be churched?'"

Grace looked puzzled.

"You're supposed to have yourself blessed first thing after you get home with the baby before you do anything or go anywhere," Mavis explained. "Superstition, see."

By now several piles of newspaper chains adorned the table. Mavis put her knitting needles down and lifted the almost completed teddy bear to her face, examining her work. She scowled. "That poor woman found in the next street. I wonder if she left any bairns behind?"

• • ● • •

The china clock on the mantelpiece maddeningly ticked off each passing minute that Grace was unable to sleep. She gave it a scolding look. The base was inscribed with a breezy declaration— A Present From Blackpool.

Hans had left long since, sent off by Mavis with a peck on the cheek which made Grace wonder again whether she was in their way. Mavis retired but Grace remained in the kitchen. She couldn't turn off her thoughts. She kept imagining the remains of the temple, a shadowed body crumpled before the altars, kept going back over the interviews she'd conducted. She leafed through the newspaper Mavis had left on a chair and found a brief story about the unidentified young woman found there. It was believed to be an accident. Police were investigating. Nothing was mentioned about the body's odd position.

Finally she read a paperback thriller—A Gun For Sale by Graham Greene. Not the best choice, perhaps. Her mother had disapproved of her reading what she termed rubbish. The only books her mother kept in the house were the Bible and *Pilgrim's Progress.*

The clock's relentless ticking sounded loud against a backdrop of rumbling industrial equipment, ships' horns on the Tyne, and a gusty, rising wind rattling a loose drainpipe. And another noise. She glanced at the back window but the blackout curtain was drawn and anyway the backyard would have been a featureless pit.

Probably a rat. She got up and went into the scullery. Biting chill and the odor of fresh washing met her. Mavis' ghostly underthings hung over the cooker. The air in Newcastle was full of smoke. Soot speckled everything, including any washing hung out on lines crisscrossing the back lanes between each street of terraced houses or pegged out in cramped backyards. Before going to bed Mavis had rinsed a few things in the sink and shown Grace what she described as the most advanced method of drying laundry known to womankind, which turned out to be a rack suspended from the ceiling over the cooker, so heat from cooking or baking carried out the task. The contraption was raised and lowered by means of a thin rope looped round a hook in the wall nearby.

"Make sure you anchor it well, mind," she warned. "Otherwise it's liable to fall on your head while you're cooking. Another thing. If you're ever in a hurry to get your knickers dried, stick them under the grill. There's many a nappy been dried that way. Make sure you keep an eye on them so they don't get scorched."

Mavis was surprised when Grace mentioned cooking with wood back home. "One thing about that, no fear of gas escaping if the Luftwaffe pay a call," she had observed. "Who said the old ways are useless?"

The old ways. Returning to the kitchen and picking up her book, Grace thought of her grandmother and her knowledge of charms, herbal remedies, and what she was pleased to call persuasions. The wise woman would surely have enjoyed talking to the study group the woman she had interviewed had mentioned. Such a group would be a likely source of information about the temple, wouldn't they? What god did the temple honour? What rites had been conducted? Was it possible the unknown woman's dying there was not accidental? That her death had to do with the temple in some way beyond it being a place to meet?

Don't be ridiculous, she told herself. Your imagination is running away with you. If Grandma hadn't filled your head up with all her nonsense you'd never have thought of such a thing. Isn't an accidental death bad enough without inventing worse? Besides, you're not supposed to be thinking about police work at this hour.

She lowered the book to her lap and tried to empty her mind.

As she dozed she saw her grandmother. Then her father. Several villagers she had known. Two elderly aunts who had died while she was still a child. All people who had died. She was awake yet unable to control this ghostly slide show. Tick. There was her grandmother. Tick. There was her mother. Was her mother dead, then?

Still half awake, she struggled to add a living person to the display and failed.

What did it mean, this procession of the dead?

Her grandmother smiled at her tiredly, as if to chide her for being so slow.

"Grandma, really!" Grace murmured under the breath. "If you have something to say to me, say it."

A tinny chime announced one in the morning.

Grace came out of her daze. She had better get to bed or else Mavis would find her asleep in the chair when she got up. She yawned and decided to pay a visit to the netty. As she went into the scullery there was a muffled thud and what sounded like a muttered curse from outside.

She stopped cold, heart jumping, hand on the doorknob, head tilted, listening hard. She heard the sound of rapidly receding footsteps.

Grace flung the door open. An indistinct figure hauled itself up over the backyard wall and vanished. Grace went out into the back lane but saw nothing.

She returned to the backyard, shivering in the cutting wind. Using the netty quickly she started back indoors. With eyes now adjusted to the dark, she could better make out the scullery door.

Painted on it was a red swastika.

Chapter Five

"A swastika on the back door?" Wallace shrugged. Grace realized that was his answer to a lot of things. "We can't chase down every kid who plays a prank these days."

Grace had expected her colleague to be more concerned. But then what did she know about him? This Saturday was only her second day on the job. She had reported to Wallace because Sergeant Baines was late arriving. "But surely this sort of thing affects morale, not to mention flouting law and order?"

"You're right, but in this case the only morale it's going to affect is our own. Most likely it was aimed at you, being connected with the police. Quite a few of us have had stones through our windows and rude words scrawled on our doors. Not much comfort, I know, but the best I can offer."

It hadn't occurred to Grace that she might be the target or that her presence could put Mavis in danger. "Too bad mischief-makers can't be shipped off to throw stones through Hitler's windows."

"They will be if the war continues long enough."

The young officer manning the counter clacked away at his typewriter, paying their conversation no attention. Already Grace had become less of an object of curiosity. How would her colleagues react when they found she'd never learned to type?

"What should I do about it? It's upset my landlady."

"Best thing to do is keep your eyes and ears open. Write a report. Mind, the chances are it was a local kid and the neighbors won't say a thing."

"They're all as close-mouthed as the people living near the temple?"

"I'm afraid so. Then again it's likely no one saw anything. The blackout, you know."

Was it always going to come down to that? It was dark and the curtains were drawn. Let's move on to the next case. That and a shrug?

"I'm afraid I didn't find out very much yesterday," Grace began. "Perhaps I wasn't questioning people the right way? Conversations kept drifting away from the topic."

"Nonsense! How do you think you should be questioning them? Ask them where were you, missus, on the night of the murder between the hours of six p.m. and three a.m.?" Wallace laughed. "People won't stand for being interrogated in their own homes or at their favorite pubs. At the station, that's different… especially if they're charged with a crime. But in their own surroundings? They'll clam right up on you."

"You think so?"

"I know so from years of experience. However, you did find out that odd character Rutherford is over at the ruins every night. He could turn out to be very important. He might well have noticed something useful."

"Still, it seems as if I talked myself hoarse for nothing."

"Well, that's the way it works. If you talk to twenty people and find a single useful piece of information, count yourself lucky. Now go back and see if you can winkle out Rutherford."

"Now?" Grace was eager to be back out on the street. A dusty sense of futility hung in the air of this corner shop masquerading as a police station.

"Not right away. First I have another assignment for you. We've been told vandals have been at work in St John's Cemetery too. Talk to the watchman. Not that we can do anything but, as you say, we need to keep up civilian morale, look like we're on the job. Which we are, only not enough of us."

"Could it be related to the vandalism at my lodgings?"

"It's possible, I suppose." From his tone he clearly considered it impossible. He gave her directions. "It will give you a bit of exercise and a chance to see more of the area."

• • ● • •

Grace took one of the station's bicycles. Cars were not used for routine work due to petrol shortages. That disappointed her. Hardly anyone in Noddweir had dreamed of owning a car. One thing Grace had wanted to do when she left the countryside for the city was to learn to drive. Evidently it would have to wait until after the war, like so many other things.

Her thoughts as she pedaled along were decidedly sour. "Exercise and a chance to see more of the area," Wallace had told her. Was that the real reason he'd sent her? Because it wasn't an important enough job for anyone else to waste time on? Was Wallace simply a more polite version of Sergeant Baines, convinced women had no business in the police force?

The day before she was congratulating herself on being assigned to conduct interviews involving a mysterious death. This morning it was clear to her that Wallace had concluded the death was accidental. A prostitute had fallen and cracked her skull in the dark. At worst, one of that class of woman had been assaulted by a client. Criminals preying on criminals would not be a high priority. And at any rate it was the kind of crime where the perpetrator was never caught until, eventually, he happened to be hauled in for something else. If anything came of the case it would have to start with checking missing persons reports to discover the dead woman's identity.

All of which meant that the real reason Wallace had sent her to investigate was to allow her to acclimate herself, to see the locals and be seen by them.

The realization stung her pride.

The watchman's surly reception did nothing to restore it. "About time you got here," he growled.

He was waiting for her beside the cemetery's northern entrance, a dark, forbidding stone archway. He was old, not surprisingly. Much of the country's work was being done these days by old men as well as women. His coat was too big and so were his dentures. With his rough voice and bristly jowls, he was more Charon than Saint Peter.

Grace produced her pencil and notepad.

"Come and see," the watchman said. "Come and see what the little buggers done."

He led her through the archway and down a short, steep drive. The cemetery was huge. Past the open space and its monuments and gravestones she could see over the factories a few blocks distant, then through plumes of smoke across the Tyne to more roofs and beyond rolling hills.

"It's a disgrace, it is," the watchman complained. "It's sacrilege. But what can one man do? I canna be everywhere at once, can I? You'd think there's enough destruction in the world as it is, wouldn't you? But no, the little buggers come in at night and turn over the gravestones of them that's trying to sleep peacefully."

An unassuming monument caught Grace's eye, an engraved pedestal topped by a cross decorated in bas relief with a bird perched over a scroll bearing a Latin motto. Stopping to look more closely she saw what had drawn her attention.

"John Hunter Rutherford," she read the inscription.

"Went to one of his schools when I were a lad," the watchman said. "He was a great one for founding schools, he was."

Remembering the mysterious Mr. Rutherford at number sixty, Grace asked whether his descendants remained in the area.

"That I wouldn't know. They move in different circles than I do, I'm sure."

In the cemetery's dismal atmosphere the bird reminded Grace of a popular fortune-telling rhyme her grandmother often recited to her, based on sighting blackbirds.

> One for sorrow
> Two for mirth
> Three for a wedding
> Four for a birth.

Although some Shropshire versions substituted "death" for "birth," which had puzzled Grace. Did spotting a single carved bird foretell sorrow? That would be a safe bet when war brought new sorrows to Newcastle every day. Did it signal worse sorrows to come, perhaps the long delayed mass bombing everyone in the city expected?

"I don't suppose you know what that means?" Grace said. "I can't read Latin myself."

"Neither can I, but the vicar at St Martha's can. I asked about it when he was here for a funeral. Told me it says 'by neither chance nor fate,' whatever that might mean. Everything's either by chance or fate, isn't it?"

They continued on, passing fallen stones lying half-propped up against their bases, or flat in the wet grass. Most looked as if they had been that way for many years. In places long rows of stones faced each other, leaning this way and that, none of them vertical.

"Look here, Constable. Look what they done."

They had come to a monument topped by an angel. Red covered one wing, ran down the frozen folds of her robes, and spattered the hard, blank-eyed face. Was the red paint—the same color as the swastika on Mavis' door—a coincidence? The maisonette was only a half hour's walk from the cemetery.

"Looks like she was pulled out of a bombed house, don't it?" The watchman grimaced, showing his ill-fitting teeth.

"Did you see or hear anything?" Grace asked hopefully.

"I'm only one man, miss. One old man, alone in the dark, to protect all these graves and report any incendiaries or high-explosive bombs that disturb the peace of the dead. T'ain't time for the graves to give up their dead, though Hitler's lot are having a good go at adding more stones for them needing burial here, curse him." He paused and shook a thin fist at the sky. "I only seen this mess when it got light."

Grace scribbled on her pad. The monument belonged to a man and his wife. An English name. Both had died before the turn of the century. It was unlikely the vandal had anything against them personally. The worst family feuds could last only so long until they eventually died out. Literally.

"Has anything like this happened before? Where the vandals used paint, I mean."

"Usually they tip the stones over, like I was saying. The police need to patrol the cemetery at night. It isn't right. What can I do on me own?"

Grace was sure no one could be spared to protect the residents of a cemetery. She pretended to make another note.

"You'll get after the little buggers, won't you, Constable?"

"I'll file my report with my superior. We'll do what we can."

In other words, nothing.

Grace and the watchman both knew it. Both pretended they didn't.

"What's the world come to? There are times I wish I'd joined all them before the war started." He gestured at the countless graves surrounding them. "They're lucky they never had to see this bloody war. But since I'm still here I have to see it out. Once the Germans are put back in their place I can die happy. Now I need to be getting on with my rounds."

"I can find the way out myself. The police appreciate your efforts," Grace added, but the man was already moving away, muttering to himself.

Policing city streets promised to be frustrating. In Noddweir such incidents were quickly dealt with. Half the village would have been whispering the perpetrators' names before Grace's father received the complaint. No papers were filled out, no arrests made, no trial held. The miscreant would get the sharp side of the constable's tongue. Then he'd get the sharper side of his father's razor strop on his backside.

Grace was feeling the effects of her recent travel and lack of sleep. She looked around. The morning sky was relatively clear. Above the Tyne, barrage balloons protecting the Vickers factory caught the feeble sunlight.

She decided to walk around the cemetery before returning to work. She was already tired of city streets. Here the grass underfoot remained green, and glossy vines climbed over grave stones. One stone was entirely overgrown, a leafy hummock.

She kept a brisk pace, eyes down, occasionally stopping to try to make out inscriptions on the more interesting gravestones, many of them blackened, their writing eroded. Lifting her gaze she was surprised to see a solitary figure standing over a flat grave marker. A man, not a boy who might be intent on mischief. His hands were in his coat pockets, his head bowed down. At the sound of Grace's footstep on the gravel path he looked up and turned, spectacles glinting momentarily.

"Sergeant Baines."

Baines was not in uniform. His eyes were redder than the morning before, his broad forehead an expanse of polished marble. Grace could smell alcohol on him.

Her superior looked at her sheepishly. "I've no doubt you've been told my wife and child were killed in an air raid. I visit them here sometimes."

"No, sir. Nobody said anything."

"Ah, well...now you know...know what everyone else knows...."

Chapter Six

When the knock at the door came early in the afternoon Cyril Rutherford realized he'd spent the day waiting for it. Still, his heart jumped and his hand froze, sending a blob of ink puddling across the complex geometric shape he was copying from a ponderous tome lying open on the mahogany desk.

He gave a soft, strangled moan and grated his teeth together hard enough to send a flash of pain through his jaw. Veins stood out in his thin neck. He crumpled the sheet of paper. His knuckles whitened and his clenched fist trembled before he dropped the ruined work into his wastebasket.

On reconsideration he retrieved the crumpled ball and smoothed it, setting it aside. Certain research notes were best burnt.

Again came the knocking and then a muffled voice. "Mr. Rutherford, the police would like a word with you."

The same woman who had come to the door yesterday? Had she seen him peering out? Luckily he kept the curtains drawn day and night. There was nothing he wished to see outside and no one needed to see in, though busybodies no doubt wanted to have a good look.

Had the room's single gaslight revealed his presence?

He rose, lifting a tabby cat off his lap, and avoided a black cat slinking around his ankles. Rutherford was unnaturally tall and emaciated. Even before the war he had been skeletal. His cats were also skin and bones.

He trod softly in his stockinged feet intending to turn off the light, then decided not to bother. Surely it could not be seen outside?

Another flurry of knocks. "Mr. Rutherford? Are you home? I only need to ask a few questions."

Only a few questions? Did they think he was a fool?

He stood still, heart thudding. The gaslight illuminated a room full of heavy Victorian furniture. It glittered on the collection of oddly shaped crystals on a round table and shone back eerily from three pairs of cats' eyes floating amidst shadowy statuettes atop a long table furnished with massive clawed feet. Another cat thumped down from its perch on the miniature sphinx beside the table.

The knocking did not cease. What right did she have to invade his privacy and ruin his work? A constable! But no better than the miserable brats who tormented him on the street, pointed and laughed or ran screaming in mock terror.

Once—the recollection brought a hot rage to his face—once they had left a dead cat on his doorstep.

At last a moment of silence lengthened into several minutes, while he stood still, listening, barely breathing.

Finally she was gone.

He sat back down at his desk, took out a fresh sheet of paper, rubbed his eyes and stared at the symbol he'd been copying. Then he picked up his pen and started over.

Grace waited quietly on the doorstep of number sixty for several minutes after she finished knocking. She was hoping the elusive Mr. Rutherford would venture a peek around the curtain again. If she caught him out he might relent and speak to her. Finally she turned away. Did the fact that he was so determined to avoid speaking to the police indicate that he had something to hide?

Her chance meeting with Sergeant Baines in the cemetery weighed on her mind. She had excused herself hastily, seeing his embarrassment, but the damage was done. Her presence at the station already irritated him. How would he react when he saw her again? The answer would have to wait for another day, since it was plain her superior was in no shape to come to work today.

She tried to shove the matter out of her thoughts and concentrate on the job at hand, checking the addresses Wallace had handed her when she'd returned to the station. "Ladies of the night shift," he'd called them, adding they were "not working the factory type of shift."

He handed her a photo of the dead woman, taken at the morgue. He also showed her the pictures taken at the temple. The woman's limbs, Grace thought, were indeed in the rough shape of a left-handed swastika.

"You see," Wallace told her, "nothing unusual. She fell awkwardly. Now get along and see if anyone recognises our mysterious friend."

Grace went reluctantly. Dealing with prostitutes was one job the police apparently considered women to be peculiarly suited for, more so even than clerical work. Grace suspected this said something about the male mentality best not dwelt on. However, since the unknown dead woman had possibly been a whore, it meant that Grace was involved in an important part of the investigation so she couldn't complain.

Or so she told herself.

After a few minutes' walk she knocked on a door like all the others she'd seen. Except this one sported a sprig of holly tied with a red ribbon. Rapping on these doors was like unwrapping Christmas presents as a child and hoping one contained a new doll rather than socks and underwear.

The afternoon sunlight was bright but gave little warmth. A plain young woman in a dressing gown answered Grace's knock.

"Yes?" Her dressing gown was a much paler blue than Grace's uniform.

"I should like to have a few words with you. May I come in?"

"Polite." Sarcasm tinged the word but the speaker stepped back to allow Grace to enter.

Grace didn't know what she expected to find in the home of a woman fined a number of times for streetwalking. Red velvet curtains and gilt furniture? In reality the kitchen was almost a mirror image of Mavis'.

"Tea?"

Grace accepted the offer. While she sat and sipped, the young woman smoked.

"Well?"

Grace put down her cup. "It's about the dead woman discovered at the temple ruins."

"Aye?"

"Dark-haired, slightly built, about five-feet-four, mid-twenties. She was wearing a green skirt and overcoat, and a white blouse." Grace held out the photo. "Have you seen her?"

The woman peered at the photo, shuddered, and drew away. "No."

"And the clothes?"

She shook her head silently.

So much for a woman's superior ability to deal with other women, Grace thought as she returned to the station.

It was the same story—or lack thereof—with the other women Grace visited. Not only were they unable to recognise the photo she showed them, none knew of any ladies of the pavement missing from their regular spots. If anything, Grace gathered, there was more competition in certain areas, the source of a bitter complaint about amateurs from one of those to whom she spoke.

"They're not after money so much, though they won't refuse it. They want booze and makeup and clothing coupons. But don't we all?"

Grace was surprised to find one of those amateurs on duty in front of the police station. At least she guessed the girl must be an amateur, to pick that location. There was no need to guess what she was doing there. The clumsy scuffed shoes, the fake nylon seams drawn down the backs of her skinny schoolgirl legs, lips reddened with beetroot juice, eyelashes blackened with burnt cork in the absence of mascara, made her business as clear as if she'd been holding a sign saying "Hello, sailor."

"You'd best move on, miss," Grace told her. Seeing the perky bow of pink ribbon tied atop the girl's head, she felt a pang of pity.

The girl pushed a strand of lank, mousy brown hair away from her eyes. "And if I divn't?"

"Don't talk back to me, young lady. Be glad I'm giving you a chance to avoid trouble."

"Arrest me then, why don't you?"

"I don't intend to arrest you. I can see very well you're not a professional. Is this a sort of lark? Somebody dared you, is that it?"

The girl's lips tightened and she looked as if she was about to stamp her foot. She really was a child. "Arrest me! I'm not moving!"

"Look," Grace said, "I can't arrest you. Go home and wash your face."

"What do you mean you can't arrest me? You're a copper."

"I'm an auxiliary. I'm not empowered to make arrests."

What am I doing? Grace asked herself, arguing with a young girl pretending to be a prostitute about whether or not I can arrest her?

A man in a pinstriped suit went by, a newspaper tucked under his arm.

The girl offered him a gruesome leer. "Sir, sir, may I help you?"

The man gaped at the strange tableau, the importuning streetwalker and the constable, a woman no less. He tipped his hat nervously, and increased his pace.

"I'm going inside, "Grace said. "I'll send a constable to arrest you, if you don't have enough sense to be gone by the time he comes out."

"I'll come in with you," the girl told her.

They were met by Wallace, who grinned at Grace's companion. "Lulu! Back again! That is your moniker, isn't it?"

"Bloody bluebottle," the girl replied, her eyes filling with tears.

"And you know what I'm going to tell you," Wallace continued. "We're not going to charge you. You can do your bit of service like anyone else. Now get along home or we'll have to get your mam come round for you."

The girl's clownish painted lips trembled. She turned to leave. Her attempt to flounce out ended up looking more like an awkward trudge.

"Silly child. Afraid to nick her mother's makeup but imagines she can pass for a tart." Wallace gave a weary chuckle. "Thinks she won't be called up for war service if she has a record of prostitution, you see. Probably hoping she'd find a green new recruit here who'd be taken in and take her in."

"Like me?"

"One with the power to make arrests."

Grace stood on tiptoe and looked over the curtain across the bottom half of the station window. "She's sitting on a doorstep up the street."

"Doubtless working out how she's going to sneak back into her house before her mother sees her."

"I'll go and speak to her. She could come back here and wash her face in the kitchen."

"Better you than me."

"A woman's job, you mean."

Wallace shrugged.

As Grace approached the girl looked up. "Young lady, I want a word with you. What's your name?"

The girl tried a defiant glare. It was no use. She sniveled and blew her nose into a grubby handkerchief. "Lily."

"Where do you live?"

"Down the street."

"Aren't you still at school?"

"Yes, but I'll be leaving soon and I divn't want to work in a factory, miss. Everyone in me class is talking about it. There's only me and me mam, and she's poorly. What would she do if a bomb dropped where I was working? Vickers got hit this spring, you know."

"It could as easily have fallen on your own roof," Grace pointed out. "Don't you realise how dangerous prostitution can be?"

"I heard the services won't take tarts, and respectable women in factories always find out and then they won't work with them or use the same netty or anything, so they can't be sent there. I'm not really a tart, miss, but I thought if I pretended I was…"

"You haven't thought this through," Grace said severely. "Yes, in due course you will be required to do war work. Whatever it is, you might have to leave your mother to go elsewhere to do it. Think of it as an adventure. An opportunity. What gave you this outrageous idea of pretending to be a tart?"

"Well, it was this woman, miss, what used to be our neighbour. She said she done it and it was money for jam and it would keep me out of factories. I didn't want to do it, I only wanted to have a record." The girl started to cry.

Grace strove to keep her anger in check. "A fine thing to tell a young girl. She should have had more decency."

"She was only trying to help. Knew me as a young girl, see. Recognized me when we passed in the town centre one Saturday and took me for a bite to eat. Dressed like a real lady, she was. And when I told her I was scared of being sent away, well…"

"That's as may be. It was wrong of her to put such ideas into your head. I hope your mother doesn't have to hear about this conversation. Mind what I say. She will if you keep trying to get arrested."

Grace watched the girl trot off. It struck Grace that of all the futile things she'd done during her first couple of days on the job, this conversation would turn out to be the most useless.

Chapter Seven

Grace had noticed the church while on duty and before return-ing to her lodgings she visited it. Standing within sight of the Roman ruins, the steeple of the Victorian era building rose grandly toward the heavens, a contrast to Noddweir's Saint Winnoc's with its humble, squat tower.

Sandbags protected the narrow windows of this church, giving the tall building the appearance of a fortress under siege. She went up stone steps worn into a slight depression toward the center by the passage of its congregations over the decades. A handbill pinned to the notice board on the smoke-blackened wall next to the double doors announced a dance at seven Saturday night. Refreshments would be served and a collection made to benefit the Red Cross. A large painted board attached to the far corner of the church pointed to the air raid shelter in the crypt.

She went into the church, stepping into a dim, icy pool of cold. It was evensong. The vicar, rosy-faced and grey-haired, read by candlelight to empty pews.

No, not quite empty. In a back row a shabby man slept, out of the wind, blanketed by a two-week old Chronicle headlined with the Japanese declaration of war. A pair of women huddled in the shadows far apart from each other.

Grace sat in the back, across the aisle from the sleeping man. She tried to imagine she was in Saint Winnoc's, tried to feel the certainty and peace sacred words had once given her.

She had grown up a believer. Her mother had told her about God and, if her mother said there was God, that was good enough for little Grace. She did not question Him any more than she questioned wind or sun or rain or the mysterious power of growth. In Noddweir's small stone church He remained nearby, but where was He in this big cold space? Where was He in city streets where the air itself felt different—not an invisible breath of the eternal perfumed with flowers and growing things or in winter the reassuring smell of earth blanketing the life which drowsed until spring. The gray city was too clearly a product of human endeavour in the material world.

The sleeping man snored and shifted, rustling his newspaper covers. Grace glanced toward him, then to the tiny congregation. For no good reason she had the impression one woman was her grandmother's age, the other the age of Grace's mother when she went away.

She was a child back in Noddweir. She could feel her mother's firm grip on her mittened hand, smell the grayish green herbs piled on the kitchen table at which her grandmother sat.

"Dragging the poor child off to church again, Mae?" Her grandmother waved a pestle in their direction. "You'd do better to leave her with me to learn my persuasions."

"Let's not go through this again, Mother. You know how I feel about those spells and nostrums of yours."

"What's wrong with my persuasions, then? Jesus healed the sick, didn't he?"

"Mother, really!"

Martha pointed the pestle at them. "You're of the blood, Mae. It's in the family. You can run away from it, but you've no business taking the gift from your daughter."

Her mother's grip tightened until Grace's hand hurt. "We're going. We'll both pray for you, won't we, Grace?"

When the service had finished, Grace approached the pulpit. The vicar stepped down, fussing with the papers in his hand, and looked up with obvious surprise.

"Welcome to St Martha's. Peter Elliott." He offered a hand and looked at her quizzically. "Is there anything wrong?"

"Wrong? No. I was surprised. Martha is my grandmother's name. I didn't notice on my way in. What a strange coincidence."

"If you believe in coincidences. And yourself?"

"Oh, sorry. Grace Baxter."

"You're new here, aren't you, Constable Baxter? How may I be of assistance? I hope it's nothing too serious."

In the countryside the local vicar knew everything that went on in the neighborhood. Was it the same in the city?

"Unfortunately, it is rather serious. It's about the woman found dead across the way."

"Yes. Of course. I should have realized that's what you were here about." There was a furtiveness in the way he looked at her, turning his head slightly to the side rather than meeting her gaze straight on.

"I was hoping you might have seen something."

He shook his head. "I live behind the church and retire early. Those of us holding the fort at home have many extra tasks to accomplish and I for one find it more tiring than I once did. Take, for example—" He pointed to a bucket set beside the doorway. "The ladies of St Martha's do the cleaning turn and turn about, all things in their season, and so on. This afternoon scrubbing the floor was my duty. It's hard on my knees. They're afflicted with arthritis, an illness I often think was created in the devil's laboratory."

"Do you have much trouble with crime locally?"

The vicar invited her to take a pew and sat down beside her. They were alone now, except for the sleeping man who occasionally gave a fitful snore amplified in the silence and emptiness.

"Crime? No more than most poor parishes in big cities. Morally speaking, the war has brought many dangers for young people, especially girls posted to war work away from their homes. And then there's the black market. We've also had problems with ladies of easy virtue being a little too obvious at their work. They like to loiter around the ruins."

"We'll do our best to make the ladies keep moving."

"If you could only order that accursed temple to move too! A fine thing to see from the front steps of a church. At least God's house is still standing. There's a lesson to be learned from that if people would open their eyes and see."

"The war tests people's faith."

"Does it test yours? I've found that despite so many off to fight, or evacuated or relocated for various reasons, my congregation is bigger. On Sundays, that is. At evensong I often feel like poor Eddi in the poem."

"And am I the donkey or the ox listening to you now, vicar?"

"Oh, dear, I didn't mean to imply…You know Kipling?"

"The poem was one of my mother's favorites."

"You inherited your faith from your mother?"

"Yes. "

"The war may test it. You must hold fast. I hope you will find comfort here."

When Grace remained silent he gave a slight smile and continued. "St Martha, you know, was the woman who served at the meal for Jesus in Bethany. I'm not thinking of my own service to the community, but of those who live in the surrounding streets, who serve others in their different capacities. Working class and proud of it, and I am proud of them, including those I only see in the street and never in a pew. My church dates from the late nineteenth century and I've conjectured its dedication is an example of subtle Victorian ecclesiastical humour."

Grace saw the vicar shiver. His hands were bone-white with cold. "I'm sorry. You must have been standing in here for a long time"

She stood up quickly. The vicar got up more slowly.

"I would be glad to talk longer but I must open the church hall. It's a meeting of the Benwell Ladies' Benevolent and Social Club tonight. They always have a speaker. Since the war started it's usually a government official. There seems no end of government officials ready to educate us about the war effort."

"I was told that a man named Rutherford lectures at the church. Has he spoken to the ladies? Do you know him?"

"Oh, dear no." The vicar laughed nervously. "I mean 'no' he hasn't lectured to them. But, yes, I do know him. It was another group he used to talk to. They concentrated on mythology and folklore. At first, I mean. But then they moved on to more arcane beliefs. Witchcraft! Seances! When it was brought to my attention I had to turn them out. Those are not fit subjects to be discussed on church property."

"And Mr. Rutherford was involved?"

"Oh, very much so. He used to lead the group but then fell out with them or they fell out with him, I'm not clear which. Is it surprising with everyone's temper on edge with lack of sleep?"

"Do you know anything about Mr. Rutherford?"

A cloud passed over the vicar's affable demeanor. "He keeps to himself. When I've tried to talk to him he's avoided me as if I were Satan himself." Again he gave her a sideways look.

"A strange man with strange interests, it seems," she said.

"We're all created differently. I don't want to give the impression it's all darkness and dread here. We shall celebrate a wedding next week, a cause for joy in these evil times. Speaking of folklore, here's a prime example for you. It's the local custom to toss pennies to children when the wedding party leaves for the church. Not many pennies nowadays, I admit, but a charming gesture nonetheless."

"I can tell you are very fond of your parishioners."

"I am, indeed. I fear certain of my lambs have strayed, and yet I think you'll be impressed how my parishioners help out neighbours in need without being asked. You'll find they have rough tongues and tend to be judgmental, but when misfortune strikes, they're around unasked with kind words, bringing food and offering help in any fashion they can, from loaning baptismal gowns for the new baby to laying out the dead."

The snores from the man sleeping on the pew became a fitful moan. There was the crinkling sound of shifting newspapers.

"Poor soul," Mr. Elliott said. "I've been trying to find a place for him to stay. I don't have the heart to throw him out."

"I must let you go, Mr. Elliott."

"Please, feel free to come and talk to me if you are troubled. Or even if you are not." He stared past her and winked. No. It was his eye glinting in the candlelight.

His glass eye.

That accounted for his odd manner of looking at her.

The vicar had one glass eye and how long had Grace talked to him before noticing?

Chapter Eight

"What's the matter, Grace? You look like you've lost a shilling and found a penny." Mavis was standing on tiptoe to peer at herself in the mirror over the kitchen mantelpiece when Grace arrived home. Still dressed in the green overalls from her factory shift, Mavis tilted a tiny, burgundy-hued hat this way and that on her cropped hair.

"I'd be happy if I'd found a penny's worth of information."

"Chin up. You can't expect to solve all the crimes in the city in two days. How do you like my bonny new hat? Velour. Four shillings, believe it or not!" She spoke to Grace's reflection.

"Very nice." Grace had no idea what was considered fashionable or what a hat should cost in Newcastle.

The gramophone filled the kitchen with crackly crooning from a well-worn record. The singer was asking for another chance. Mavis sang along. She had a high, sweet voice. "Poor bugger never had a chance," she observed as the song ended.

Grace removed her jacket. It radiated cold. "Who?"

"Al Bowlly, the singer. Killed in the Blitz during the spring."

"That's terrible." It made Grace think of Sergeant Baines' family.

"It's the saddest thing, isn't it? Not having another chance."

Grace went to the bedroom and changed. When she returned to the kitchen, Mavis remarked on the book in her hand.

"What's that you're reading?"

When Grace told her Mavis looked puzzled. *"Geordie Night?* Set up here, is it?"

"Oh, no. It's set in Oxford," She held the book up so Mavis could see the cover better. "And it's *Gaudy Night*, not *Geordie Night*. Since you're getting ready to go out I thought I'd settle down and read a bit."

"What kind of book is it?"

"A mystery."

"I'd have thought you had enough mysteries to deal with on the job. I know what will cheer you up. There's a dance at the church hall tonight. Hans wants to go."

"Will Hans mind if I come along with you?"

"He's a dear, but I was hoping you'd take him off my hands tonight. I prefer dance halls by myself. I'm going to one this evening."

"You go to dance halls alone?"

"More exciting than church dances. At the church hall you only meet blokes you already know. Besides, the vicar keeps an eye out for dancing he thinks is improper."

"His good eye, I suppose?"

Mavis laughed. "How do you know about his eye?"

"I stopped at the church after work. What happened to him?"

"Nobody knows. He tells a different story every time. My favourite's the one about how the eye was damaged in a duel when he was a student in Germany. He's fond of making jokes about his sight—talks about turning a blind eye, says it helps him see almost no evil. He should be on the wireless with a turn as the Merry Minister. He's a good sort, but some say he doesn't see half of what goes on."

"Except at the dances."

"Oh, aye. I've kept your dinner hot in the oven. You must be clamming."

Grace looked puzzled.

"You know, hungry. I'll get some tea for us, too."

Mavis vanished into the scullery and emerged with a teapot and cups. Still sporting her new hat, she and Grace sat down at the table. "Fresh-brewed, more or less. Had to reuse the tea leaves, so it's only the ghost of tea."

"It's hot, just what I need." Grace cradled the cup in both hands, warming them.

"There's nothing wrong with having a little fun," Mavis said. "I like to go out and fly me kite. A girl needs a little appreciation now and then. Take your chance while you have it, I say. Two minutes from now a bomb could come crashing straight through the roof."

Grace looked over her cup. "What about your husband?"

"Ronny?" She gave a dismissive wave of her hand. Her fingernails were already painted red. "Anyway, I like to tease a little. I never let the blokes have what they're looking for. I like meeting new people."

"Did you meet Hans at a dance hall?"

"Yes, as a matter of fact. There, you see, you did discover something today."

"I can't see Hans going to dance halls by himself."

"Why not? He's a man."

"Was that how he came to be visiting you?"

"I invited him back here for a cup of tea, didn't I?" She raised her cup and winked. "And that's all he got. That and a kiss. He'll never get nowt but that! Mind you, he's still hopeful, but always so very polite. It makes me laugh."

"Poor Hans." Grace began to eat her dinner.

"If he wants to live in hopes, that's his business. But we've become good friends. So will you go to the dance with him?"

St Martha's church hall was turned out in shabbily festive dress. The Union Jack on the back wall was faded, and the red and green streamers looped from the ceiling had seen happier days. The air reeked of cigarettes and sweat, but music was playing and couples were dancing.

The gramophone occupied one end of a long table placed in front of the flag. On the other end, a starved little tree struggled to hold up its overly large glass ornaments. Peter Elliott stood behind the table.

The vicar looked older to Grace than he had when she'd met him in the dimly lit church. Before long, she realized his hair was no grayer, his gaunt face no more lined, but here he was surrounded mostly by young people, as comfortable working as master of ceremonies as he had been reading psalms.

"Ladies and gents, here's one for the old folk! Any that are here! But first let's shake the dust off the rafters by giving a big hand to our gramophone winder! Now take your partners for a polka!"

Hans continued the vague side-to-side motions he had used for both the waltz and the foxtrot. He was light on his feet, but heavy on Grace's.

"Don't you know the polka, Hans?"

"Polka? No. I apologize for my feet, Miss Grace. They do not speak English."

"What do you call the dance you've been doing? Is it Dutch?"

"I never learned to dance. I pretend I am keeping my balance on deck during rough seas. But does it matter? The point of dancing is holding hands."

When he smiled down at her she felt herself blush. He had caught her thinking that she quite liked holding hands with this tall, fair man with eyes bluer than any sky Newcastle was ever likely to see.

She pulled her gaze away from those blue eyes and concentrated on keeping her feet from under his. Her partner's hands were calloused, like those of the farmers and labourers she recalled in her home village. Like them, his face knew the weather.

Another blond man, shorter than Grace, approached and bowed. He held out his hand and spoke in a foreign language. Hans interpreted. "My countryman wishes a dance."

Grace smiled as she left Hans to dance with her new partner as a contribution to the war effort, and a relief for her feet.

When the record finished she walked over to the vicar. An energetic number which she didn't recognize started. Before she reached him, a matronly woman in a flowered dress stepped in front of her.

"Mr. Elliott," the matron said. "Mr. Elliott, really, do you see what that couple is doing?"

The vicar looked into the melee on the dance floor. The woman was pointing, a hunting dog that had located prey.

"No, you're not looking in the right direction."

"My good eye is. You mean the girl in the red dress and the RAF man?"

"They're dancing far too close for a polka! And, as for the waltz...well...it was sinful!"

The vicar raised his eyebrows. "Yes?"

"They're behaving disgracefully," she whispered.

"Is that so? I fear I did not take dancing at seminary. If they get too rambunctious I will have a quiet word."

"I should think they are already—"

The vicar raised his hand. For a frail man he had a very large hand. "Mrs. Bloom, let us recall how David danced before the ark. We don't want to scare our youth away from the church, do we? Once they are too arthritic to polka they may show up at services."

Mortified, Mrs. Bloom huffed away.

"You've offended her." Grace suppressed laughter.

"Not at all. We are all sinners, and our dance steps are the least of it."

Staring out into the blue haze Grace spotted the girl who had been trying to be arrested as a prostitute. She was dancing with Hans. "I wanted to talk more, Mr. Elliott, but I must rescue a young lady who is about to stray!"

In fact, it was Hans she didn't want to stray. She kept him close the rest of the evening. It was for his own protection, she told herself. The make-believe tart ended up with a merchant navy man. The couple were no longer in the hall by the time the evening ended with a collection for the Red Cross and a rousing rendition of "God Save The King."

Hans took a half-consumed chocolate crisp bar from his pocket, snapped what was left of it in two and offered a piece to Grace, rather as a man might offer a cigarette when lighting one for himself. She refused politely.

He turned red as it dawned on him that a sweet he'd been carrying in his pocket all day was not quite the same thing as a cigarette, "I am sorry, Miss Grace. These are my favorites. I just—"

"It was a kind thought, Hans." She didn't mind his awkwardness. She felt awkward and out-of-place in the city herself.

Soon Hans was accompanying Grace, not around the church hall to the merry strains of a wind-up gramophone, but down the dark back lane of Carter Street.

"Cold enough for frost overnight." Hans paused at the door to Mavis' backyard.

Grace looked up. The sky was clear and starry. "I didn't think you could ever see the stars here."

"It may be tonight is special," Hans said, bending to kiss her.

Chapter Nine

What did the kiss mean? Grace had no time to reflect. The moment she and Hans came in through the scullery a frantic Mavis greeted them. She wore a dressing gown half pulled together over pajamas. "It's a bloody pity the police aren't keeping a better eye on their surroundings! We wouldn't have been burgled!"

"But we're right down the street from the police station," Grace said.

"Didn't stop me back door being redecorated, did it? Now someone's been into me home. They're a dozy lot over there. I suppose they think you living here is protection enough!" Mavis snapped.

"Is anything missing?" Grace asked.

"Nowt so far as I can see, except for one of them crisp bars Hans gave me."

"Any vandalism?"

"No."

Hans pulled out a chair for Mavis and got her to sit. She was shaking, but whether from rage or fear, Grace couldn't tell.

The cold walk back from the church had not driven the warm feelings of the dance from Grace's memory but Mavis' outburst succeeded. Regretfully she assumed her policewoman's role. "What happened, Mavis?"

Hans lit Mavis a cigarette. She took a long drag and tightened her dressing gown around her before speaking. "I'd barely got home. I didn't stay long at the dance hall. I didn't like the crowd. One of them West Indian seamen asked me to dance. Can you believe his nerve? Well, I'd just shut the back door when I heard a noise in the bedroom. A footstep. My heart just about stopped. I didn't move, didn't know what to do. I stood there like I was daft. I didn't hear anything else but I had this feeling there was somebody in there."

"It might have been Grace," Hans suggested.

"That finally occurred to me. I'm not used to having a lodger yet. So I started down the hall to the bedroom, cursing myself for being a fond fool, and then there was this quiet squeak, like a chair being pushed across the floor. I told myself, 'It's only Grace. She'd could be back early, couldn't she?' But when I went into the room, she wasn't there."

"And nobody else?"

"No. I told myself I'd only imagined the sounds. But I couldn't make me believe myself! I put the light on and looked under the bed before I got changed. Couldn't stop shivering so I came out here and stirred the ashes up a bit and threw on a shovel of coal and to hell with the extravagance! That's when the pounding on the front door started. Well..."

Hans' face darkened. "You didn't answer it, did you?"

Mavis took a nervous drag on her cigarette. "As a matter of fact, I did, after my night caller identified himself as an air raid warden. It was Charlie Gibson from down the street. He gave me a bollicking for showing a light. 'Your window's calling the Luftwaffe as loud as one them fat Valkyries at the opera,' says he. Talk about a nerve!"

"I told him it was nonsense and not too politely either. I'm always careful about the blackout curtains. He insisted I went out and looked, and sure enough they was pushed a bit apart, enough to let a bit of light out. Then I realized why it was so cold in here. The window was up a crack. The squeak I heard was the sound of it being closed. Charlie says he'll be on the lookout for people up to no good and advised me to get the sneck fixed as soon as I can."

Anger made Hans' blue eyes look icy. "It's as well you returned when you did. If you'd been here when he broke in or went into your bedroom and surprised him…I will stay tonight in case he comes back. I will sleep in an armchair."

To her consternation, Grace found herself resenting her dance partner's solicitude for Mavis.

Mavis placed her hand on Hans' arm. "No, Hans, really. You're a dear, but we don't want the old wives talking any more than they do already, do we?"

For the second night in a row Grace stayed up after Mavis went to bed. Sooner or later she was bound to collapse from exhaustion, but for the time being she was keyed up from her new job, the dance, and now the break-in.

Also the idea of trying to get to sleep in a tiny room where a semi-stranger was sleeping made her uneasy.

She sat by the dwindling fire, hoping there would be no further incidents. Last night, late, the swastika painter had paid a call. Could it have been same person who had entered the maisonette tonight? Quite possibly it was. Had her presence here triggered harassment, as Wallace suggested?

Tonight she had put aside her mystery. She had had too many mysteries and enough crime investigating for now. Instead she held a Bible. Her mother's Bible. Or rather one of them, the one her mother kept on her dressing table to read privately in her bedroom.

The one she had left behind when she vanished from Grace's life.

Grace had stored it in a box with the few belongings her mother left behind. Later, she had considered throwing them out, but had not been able to bring herself to do so. Packing to leave Noddweir, she took the Bible with her. Now she ran her fingers over its leather cover, softened from years of handling. A speck of remaining gilt flaked off the title. The pages were so thin as to be translucent.

A memory returned. Her mother showing her a Bible. Not this one but with the same insubstantial paper. She told Grace about the Father, the Son, and the Holy Ghost, which to the very young child made no sense at all. The word her mind fixed upon was "ghost." The strange patterns on the pages meant nothing either. But she could see right through the paper, as if it, too, was a ghost.

For a long time afterward her mother's Bible frightened her.

After her mother fled, the volume served as a bitter reminder of her inexplicable desertion. Now Grace could see her mother through the narrow gap where the door to her closed-off memories had been left ajar. Her mother was sitting up in bed reading and making notations by candlelight. The sight had always comforted Grace. Her mother must have been very wise to understand and add her own comments to the ancient words.

She opened the book to where the red ribbon sewn to the spine had been placed years before and saw it marked Chapter Nine in the book of Luke. Verses were scratchily underlined.

"And John answered and said, Master, we saw one casting out devils in thy name, and we forbade him, because he followeth not with us.

"And Jesus said unto him, <u>Forbid him not</u>: for he that is not against us, is for us."

The phrase "Forbid him not" was underlined several times. In the margin her mother, Mae, had neatly written:

Cast out devils. Not invite them in.

What a peculiar comment to write in a Bible! At the bottom of the page was a scrawl in her grandmother's familiar hand.

What is the difference between a persuasion and a miracle if they are for the same ends?

"Oh, Grandma!" The words spilled out, so audibly she hoped she hadn't awakened Mavis.

She turned to the front. Inside the cover her grandmother had written:

To Mae. Read this book if you will but never forget who your mother is, and your grandmother, and all those whose blood flows in your veins.

She leafed through the almost weightless pages. In places she recognized her grandmother's handwriting, all spikes and weirdly shaped letters. Elsewhere her mother's neat writing stood perfectly upright as it marched along the margins. Often mother and daughter had annotated the same page. The ink bled through the pages. obscuring whatever words were on the reverse.

The story of the witch of Endor had inspired Martha enough to run her comments onto the next page. Grace didn't read them all. Quite apart from philosophical observations, the book was filled with the kind of wise woman's lore in which Martha had done her best to interest Grace. Next to the description of Jesus healing a blind man by spitting on the ground and placing the resulting mud over the man's eyes Martha advised:

"If holy saliva for mud not available a poultice of rotten apples will also do."

To which Grace's mother had riposted:

It is not the mud that heals but the belief.

Grace put the Bible down and closed her eyes. So this was what her mother was doing, not peacefully reflecting on the Word as Grace had imagined, but dueling with Martha, the two women ducking and dodging through chapters and verses, firing salvos, searching for cover, seeking the high ground. Had

Martha laid fresh ambushes when her daughter was out? Grace didn't doubt it.

What had possessed her mother? Why hadn't she simply tossed the vandalized book away?

The embers in the grate glowed feebly now. But a few crumpled pages, a good stir with the poker, and Grace could relegate her grandmother's wisdom to the flames.

But, like her mother, she didn't.

The wisdom was part of Grace's heritage.

Chapter Ten

Had Grace slept very long before the sirens woke her?

She had forced herself to go to bed and lay uncomfortably on her back, hearing Mavis' regular breathing. Eyes open, she watched scenes of Noddweir projected onto the smooth, unbroken darkness. Her grandmother, her mother. Then the woman who had died at the Roman temple, whom Grace had not actually seen there. The woman was lying in the middle of the ancient stone circle in Noddweir.

"See who it is," her grandmother urged her.

When in her imagination she approached the awkwardly sprawled body, Grace recognized the face of her mother.

She came awake, heart pounding. Why should she be haunted by a dead woman she didn't know?

What did a single death mean when millions were dying, so many anonymously? Refugees fleeing never to be heard from again. Servicemen unaccounted for, presumed dead. Airplanes and ships lost. Unrecognizable victims of bombings buried in mass graves.

Yet somewhere in the world there must be someone who would want to know what had become of this particular young woman with no name.

Mavis stirred. "Bloody hell!"

Grace reached for her uniform, the first clothes to hand.

Mavis flicked on a torch. She fought her way groggily into her dance hall outfit.

They grabbed their jackets, gas masks, and handbags and ran out.

The sudden cold in the street took Grace's breath away. She trotted through the darkness more quickly than was prudent, hoping not to trip on uneven pavement or slip on a frozen patch. Others were also moving down the street. Murmurs and footsteps, all but invisible. Grace felt swept up in a rushing crowd of phantoms.

The vicar stood at St Martha's side door, he and several boys ready to assist older parishioners down into the crypt which served as a shelter.

Fingers of light swept a starry sky, seeking enemy planes to snag in their deadly rays. A baby cried faintly below.

"Trying to trap a German plane with searchlights always reminds me of trying to catch flies, they're so quick and nimble," the vicar observed to Grace.

"The devil's flies," she replied. "That's what we called them at home."

"Could you wait here with me?" the vicar asked. "It will reassure people knowing we have a policewoman with us."

Grace agreed, unhappily blowing on her hands to warm them. Mavis had already gone inside.

Those seeking shelter streamed past, jackets buttoned wrongly, long dressing gowns showing under heavy coats, more than one pair of feet shod in bedroom slippers. The woman Grace had interrupted whitening her doorstep arrived, still in her tartan headsquare and curlers. She avoided meeting Grace's eyes.

The searchlights continued to dance after the blaring sirens went quiet. There was no sign of enemy planes. No sound of engines or anti-aircraft guns. No tracer bullets stitching across the night sky.

"We get false alarms," the vicar told her. "But you never know. We were hit pretty hard toward the beginning of the month. I hear in London half the population doesn't bother to take shelter any longer, they've grown so accustomed to living through massive bombings. Here, we're still waiting for the worst. One almost wishes it would finally begin and be done with it."

For a few minutes there were no new arrivals. The vicar sent his helpers into the church, went out into the street, looked up and down. "Street's deserted," he said returning to her side.

Grace didn't know how he could see to tell.

"Everyone's under cover safely then," he went on. "We'll join our unexpected guests below, shall we?" He shut the door, offered her his arm, and led her to a stairway. "Oh, yes, the crypt has proved most useful as a shelter. Not its usual line of work, but then what is usual these days?"

The smell of dampness and cold struck up through the stone flagged floor. A single bulb descending from the vaulted ceiling served for illumination.

"Well, vicar, if we get hit we're in the right place!" called out a man with steel grey hair and the worn face of one who had spent his life at hard labor.

"Charlie, there, would rather be caught in the local pub with a pint in one hand and a good hand of cards in the other when he's called to glory," claimed a voice from the shadows.

"Pint of broon's what he calls holy water," added another voice.

"Tut!" the vicar replied. "I'm sure our friend, Constable Baxter, would have something to say about keeping the licensing hours."

The bulb flickered.

"They're here!" a woman cried in panic.

"Now, now, we would have heard the planes," the vicar chided her.

The bulb went out.

There were gasps. A child whimpered. The baby shrieked louder.

"They hit the power station!"

"Bleeding Germans are here, all right!"

"Can't be. We would've heard explosions."

"The floor's shaking!"

"That's your legs, Jack."

One or two of those gathered together turned on their torches. The vicar reached up toward the light fixture, his hand wrapped in a handkerchief. The light came back on.

"Loose bulb," he announced.

A general shuffling about followed the collective murmur of relief as people made themselves as comfortable as they could, draping themselves in blankets and lying down. Someone played a harmonica. Before long the baby stopped crying and went to sleep.

Grace walked around looking for Rutherford. Noticing she was treading on grave markers set in the floor, she shuddered. People had placed mats and rugs on them and were seated or stretched out, apparently unconcerned. A featureless form in a far corner proved to be a couple cuddling, taking advantage of the darkness. Well, it wasn't a crime and none of Grace's business. One man sat rigidly, back to the wall, his face turned straight ahead, obscured by his gas mask. He didn't move as Grace went by. Mavis sat chatting with an unfamiliar young man. Grace didn't find Rutherford and was relieved to see no one from the station either.

"How about a sing-song?" the man named Charlie asked the company at large. He was with a woman who was calmly knitting, and a little girl with a solemn expression.

"Good idea, Mr. Gibson!" the vicar replied. "What do you suggest? I think in the circumstances it isn't likely to be hymns!"

Laughter rippled in the dimness. A man with a baritone voice started singing about a little lad getting fish when the boat came in, and the words were taken up by the others.

The words reminded Grace of former fisherman Hans, and she offered a fervent silent prayer for his safety that night.

"Very good," the vicar said with a smile. "You're all in fine voice tonight, I can see. Since we're entertaining each other, I will be happy to perform a couple of tricks that may amuse you."

Not only children moved to stand in a semi-circle in front of the vicar.

"That's right," he went on. "Magicians always say the quickness of the hand deceives the eye, but since I only have one of them I shall do a couple of tricks where sleight of hand is not needed. First, no doubt someone has a pack of cards with them?"

"Aye, vicar, here y'are. I'm about sick of playing Patience during these raids. I'm not too patient with Patience, you might say." Charlie Gibson handed him a well-thumbed pack of cards.

The vicar nodded his thanks. "In this time of crisis, we are all pulling our weight. Even those naughty knaves volunteered for the duty of defending the king and all the other cards. So the king called a meeting…." He laid the king of clubs on the floor and continued. "The knave of clubs was accepted as a recruit and so was the knave of diamonds, so I shall place them on the king's right hand. But although they also volunteered, the knaves of hearts and spades were rejected, so I must place them on the other side of the king. Can anyone tell me why the king did not accept those two cards for his army?"

Several suggestions were offered and after a few moments the vicar held up his hand. "Very well, I shall tell you. It was because although they were as willing to fight as the other knaves, they were judged medically unfit for service."

"How do you work that one out, vicar?" someone asked in a puzzled voice.

"Because the rejected knaves only have one eye apiece."

Laughter mixed with applause broke out.

The vicar gave a slight bow and began rummaging in his pockets.

"My final trick tonight fittingly involves a cross. As you see, I now have seven coins in my hand. I shall lay them on the floor thus." He arranged the handful as a row of five with one above and one below the middle coin. "Who can move only two coins and make a cross whose arms have the same number of coins?"

The sole adult who attempted the feat soon retired from the attempt.

"The solution is simple, as is so often the case when we are overwhelmed with seemingly insurmountable difficulties," the vicar observed, picking up a coin from each end of the row and placing them carefully on the middle coin. "There it is. A perfect cross with each arm three coins long."

Another round of applause and laughter. A man in the front row of onlookers proposed a game of poker to Charlie. "And let's see if I can win a cross o' cash from you," he said with a grin and a wink.

"Only if you let the vicar play," Charlie riposted.

The vicar shook his head. "I fear I must ask you to refrain. Gambling on church property is something I only need one eye to see and I really cannot permit it."

• • ● • •

As soon as he arrived at the shelter Stu McPherson tried to chat up Mabel Greene. "Where's yer mam, Mabel?"

"At home, in the backyard." She was a little thing, alone, without so much as a blanket to keep her warm.

"Yer family got its own shelter in the backyard, then?"

"Nay. Mam's just afraid of getting buried alive, pinned under bricks and rubble, so she says, shouting for help, bleeding to death or getting gassed by broken mains or dying of thirst before they can dig her out. Or maybe no one will hear her at all. She has nightmares about it and wakes me up screaming in her sleep."

"Me mam's hiding under the stairs. Says there's too many dirty refugees in the shelters. We'd get lops off them."

Mabel hugged herself. "I hope mam doesn't get killed by a bomb."

"Hitler isna looking for yer mam. Howay, why divn't we get out of here? I know a place we can be alone. Yer mam won't expect you back 'til the all clear."

"Harraway with you, Stu! How can you think about such things when bombs might start falling round our ears any second?"

"Makes me think about such things more." He ran his hand down her arm and she slapped it away.

After a while he gave up and wandered off. He was slender. Narrow face, narrow nose, black hair in disarray. He lacked the awkwardness common to teenagers. His movements were as smooth as a snake's.

He hunkered down, leaning back against a stone pillar, snickering to himself at the reaction when the bulb went out. Before he had a chance to steal anything under cover of darkness the light came back on, but the crypt was dimmer than before.

Stu let his gaze run past the huddled shapes. Sheep. As soon as the sirens go, they run where they're told or cower under the stairs. It made him sick. If it were up to him he'd follow his brother, Rob, and go fight the Germans. How could they say he was too young? He had more guts than the lot of them. Give him a gun and put a German in front of him and he'd show them he wasn't too young to pull a trigger.

He stretched his legs across a gravestone set in the floor. He didn't bother trying to read the inscription. Who cared? Dead was dead. No matter who you were it was all the same. You could cower your life away, follow all the rules, kowtow to every toffee-nosed bastard, but you'd still end up underground.

Stu's head didn't move, but his dark eyes flicked this way and that.

An old crow of a woman was perched partway up the stairs. Was she afraid there were ghosts in the crypt or loppy foreign refugees? All the fools were singing but she dozed, handbag at her side.

Stu got up and glided in her direction. No one paid any attention to him. He started up the stairs, gauging the distance to the door at the top. As he passed the woman his hand swooped down.

"Hoy!"

Bloody hell! She was awake!

He leapt up the stairs.

A hand smacked down on his shoulder, unbalancing him. He fell, hitting his knee on a stone step.

A figure loomed over him. A uniformed woman.

It was the policewoman who lived with the tart with the fancy man.

Now old one-eye from the church intervened as the crow reached up and grabbed her bag back. "Little bugger—beg your pardon, vicar," she cawed. "Tried to pinch it, so he did."

"Did not, you old bag!" Stu muttered. He tried to get up, but the policewoman's hand clamped on his shoulder held him down. "I tripped over it on me way out. Coulda broke me neck, her leaving it lying about on the stairs like that."

"You can't intend to go out yet, lad? The all-clear hasn't sounded." The vicar's voice was mild.

"Needs a good braying," screeched the old woman.

Stu ignored her. "Got to go, see? I'm a messenger. I go about on me bike during raids when the phones get cut off. I only waited a while to make sure me mam got here safely."

"We're not having a raid right now and his mam isn't here," his accuser said. "Stealing stuff in the dark's more like what he's up to!"

"But there might be a raid, see, so I left me bike outside, handy in case. If there was a raid, messages wouldn't get through if I didn't show up."

He could see the policewoman looking him up and down, then shone her torch on the boy's worn boots.

"Where did you get that?" she asked. Her voice sounded colder than he'd expected.

"Me boots? Me mam bought them."

"Not your boots, the splash of red paint on them."

Stu's reply was sullen. "Painted me bike red the other day and the bloody brush went and dripped, miss."

Chapter Eleven

The all-clear didn't sound until dawn.

"Thank God that's over," Grace muttered as she strode down Carter Street to the police station. Having spent hours closed up in a crypt, she found the murky air of Newcastle almost refreshing.

Constable Robinson who had hitherto manned the counter in the daytime was on the night shift. When Grace came in, he was leaning wearily against the former shop counter gazing in an abstracted fashion at a sandwich. "You're scheduled for today?"

"No, I got dressed in a rush last night when the sirens went off. Took the first thing to hand."

Robinson gave her an unhappy look. "Until now it's been quiet."

As if on cue hollow thuds sounded above them.

"Relatively quiet," Robinson added as Grace glanced upwards. "Don't fash yourself, Miss Baxter. It's nothing to worry about. We've got a drunk locked in a bedroom who's been trying to demolish the door for a while. We also have a stray dog. He's in the kitchen waiting for his owner to claim him. Quite a quiet night, as I said. But here I am reporting to you. What is it you wanted to say?"

Grace related the thwarted attempt at the theft of a handbag. "There isn't a formal complaint, but when I spoke to Stu he was cocky and belligerent. Not only that, Mavis Arkwright claims someone broke into her flat last night, but didn't take anything."

"What's that to do with Stu?"

"Between you, me, and the lamppost, I'm certain he's responsible for painting the swastika on Mrs. Arkwright's back door. So why couldn't he have broken into her house to scare her further? Of course he has a story to account for the red paint on his boots. Says it's from when he painted his bike."

"Oh, aye? A red bike and a thieving pair of hands? Stu McPherson, without a doubt." He smiled at her surprised look. "He has as they say helped us with our inquiries into incidents of vandalism and petty theft on more than one occasion."

"Is it true he carries messages during air raids?"

"Aye, it is. Not that we've had many raids yet. He's an odd mixture, that lad. His brother was killed overseas not many months ago. Hates Germans, needless to say. The sooner he can join up and starting shooting at them, the better. The way he's going he's liable to kill somebody here first."

"Yes. He struck me as a dangerously angry boy. Best to keep an eye on him."

"Funny how grief takes people different ways. Some want to lash out, others lose heart."

Grace thought of her meeting with Sergeant Baines in the cemetery and nodded silent agreement.

"And then here comes Mavis Arkwright's friend, speaks with an accent." Robinson took a bite of his sandwich and chewed contemplatively. "Stu leapt to the wrong conclusion. I suppose a Dutch accent sounds like German to a kid, and this Hans certainly looks the part."

Grace hoped her cheeks weren't reddening noticeably. She recalled Hans' face as they danced. How handsome he was. It hadn't occurred to her he resembled one of Hitler's Aryan supermen.

"Stu keeps coming in here telling us to arrest the man as a spy," Robinson went on. "Nothing anyone can say will convince him otherwise."

"Why didn't Sergeant Baines send a constable round to grill the boy about the back door business?"

"Stu's hardly the only one around here who's suspicious of foreigners and, more importantly, there was no real evidence he did it, though I admit the red paint is suspicious."

Grace changed the subject. "What about the dead woman? Are we any closer to identifying her?"

"We've put out a request for information on missing persons. But with millions called up, relocated for war work, bombed out, evacuated, killed in raids…well, it can be a long time before it's noticed a person's missing."

The dog in the kitchen gave a sudden loud bark, making Grace jump.

To Grace's chagrin Robinson grinned. "Nerves bad, Miss Baxter? Don't blame you. These raids…" He patted her shoulder.

Now she did flush, but with irritation.

Robinson gave no sign noticing her reaction."Either somebody is trying to break into the station or our furry friend wants to go out for a pee. Well-trained animal, that. If nobody claims him, I think I'll adopt him. Keep an eye on the station for a bit, would you? I'll take him into the back lane. Shouldn't be too long."

The thumping upstairs was renewed as Robinson went into the kitchen. Grace giggled. Did the intoxicated man locked in the bedroom also need to go to the netty? He would have to wait until Robinson returned.

Her hands started shaking. Don't act like a great cauf, she told herself. The old Shropshire terms came naturally to her lips in times of stress. You're getting hysterical. Wouldn't Robinson love to see that? Everybody would know by teatime.

• ● ● ● •

Veronica Gibson watched Grace leave the police station where the nice shop lady used to give her extra sweeties for her pennies. It was funny seeing a girl dressed like a policeman. Veronica thought she would like a uniform like that, then she could go and arrest Mr. Hitler.

Her mam had sent her out to get a breath of fresh air after being huddled in the crypt during the night. She wandered down the street on the lookout for a playmate but nobody else was outside. Before long she came in sight of the place where the lady was killed, according to Stu McPherson.

She had been afraid to go past it after what Stu said and he had called her a scaredy-cat. But she wasn't a baby, she told herself. Besides, she wouldn't be alone at the ruins today. A man stood there, looking down at the two big stones.

She crossed the street.

The man looked old and very tall and thin. When he turned to look at her, his head moved like the canary her mother used to have and his eyes glittered in the same way as the bird's. He held a paper bag in one hand.

"Hello, mister," Veronica said.

"Hello, young lady. Interested in archaeology?"

Since she didn't know what he was talking about she frowned.

"This is a temple made by the Romans when they lived in England," he told her. "A kind of church."

This wasn't a school day and she didn't want to be taking lessons but she had nothing better to do. "Don't look like a church. Where are the walls?"

"They fell down a long, long time ago. Do you go to church?"

"Mam and me don't go to church since the Germans killed her friend's son."

The old man shook his head. "Poor child. What kind of a god lets young people be killed by Germans?"

"Mr. Elliott says God's invisible."

"Well, he's hiding himself, all right. The Romans had different gods, you know. Theirs are a lot older than Mr. Elliott's."

"No one's older than God."

"Other gods are. Would you like me to tell you about them? I have pictures at my house, on gold coins."

Veronica was suddenly wary. The man's face was all bristly and his teeth looked like ruined stones. Was he a bad man? "Mam says I'm not to go with anyone I don't know."

"Very wise, especially in these times. Did you know we're standing near where Hadrian's Wall used to be? He was a Roman ruler. Like the king, you know. He built a wall straight across England. Imagine that."

"No one could build a wall that far," Veronica argued.

"He did, though, almost two thousand years ago."

"Why didn't the Luftwobble fly over it?"

"They didn't have planes in those days."

"Well, then we should've flown over to Germany and bombed them."

The man smiled at her. "Would you like to help get rid of Hitler?"

"Don't be a silly!"

"Not so silly. You and the old gods, working together. You'd be surprised at what you could do."

Veronica didn't like the way he said old gods. The tone of his voice made her shiver. Maybe it hadn't been a good idea to cross the street after all.

Then she recalled Stu's mockery and stood her ground. She looked up at the man solemnly. The paper bag in his hand caught her attention. "What you got in your bag, mister?"

"A present, for my friends at home. Do you want to meet my friends? I live at number sixty."

"What kind of present? A Christmas present?"

"A treat. Something my friends like. Do you want to see?" He extended the bag toward Veronica, holding it by one side so the top fell open.

She took a hesitant step forward and peered in.

And saw a dead rat with a frozen snarl.

Veronica ran home as if the devil was at her heels.

Chapter Twelve

Mavis sat by the fire and looked glumly toward the gramophone. She wished she could replace the sound of Grace's soft snoring with music, but it would be rude to wake her lodger. Would it be rude to tell her she snored?

Having a lodger was inconvenient, especially one who was an auxiliary policewoman. But what choice did Mavis have if she wanted to save up enough to get out of this place? She drummed her fingers on the chair arm. Veronica's Christmas teddy bear was finished and the paper chains all assembled. She needed to do darning but the task didn't appeal to her. She leafed through a copy of *Housewife* Hans had brought over. Home-decorating, wise budgeting, the plight of British women married to enemy aliens. Nothing to do with her own life.

She was too tired to concentrate anyway. She'd fallen into bed and must have been fast asleep by the time Grace arrived back. She hadn't slept well or long, however, thanks to the conversation she'd had in the air raid shelter.

Stan, from work, had sat down beside her. "Mavis. All alone? Where's your man?"

"What are you on about, Stan? Pulling me leg? Ronny's still at sea, far's I know."

"That so? I was sure I saw him coming out of the flicks earlier this week."

"No. It's not possible."

"It was the Crown on Scotswood Road."

"Lots of servicemen on leave take their girlfriends there. You likely saw one of them, not Ronny."

"Don't get het up, Mavis. You're probably right. I must have been mistaken."

The exchange unsettled her. Of course Ronny was still safely out at sea. He would have let her know if he was returning on leave and would have been straight home once he arrived in the city.

More than once during the past year she'd momentarily seen him on the street herself. Even after she realized the man was a stranger, she'd been nervous for the rest of the day. She wanted not to think about her husband. She had put all his photos in the back of the kitchen cupboard and relegated his clothes to a cardboard box behind the table at the rear of the scullery.

She couldn't avoid feeling the gap in the teeth at the back of her mouth when she tried to enjoy a biscuit. Her tongue sought out the gap when she lay in bed in the middle of the night. Sometimes in the day, too. Once she was away from Newcastle, if she had any savings left she'd get her teeth fixed. Another reason she welcomed a lodger bringing in extra money.

In the shelter she started trembling and asked Stan to hold her. Nothing wrong with that.

"You can't let his memory disturb you, Mavis. If he's got that much of a hold on you, he might as well still be here."

"His memory can't knock my teeth out." Might Stan come home with her, for company? But how could he when she had a lodger?

She heard Grace moving around and soon she came into the kitchen.

"Didn't mean to sleep that long. I suppose I was done in."

"Bloody Germans, interfering with everyone's sleep. How're we supposed to stay alert and on the job? Bloody brilliant in its way, got to give the swine that. Tired workers fumble their tasks or have accidents."

"You're right. What we need are posters. 'Lack of sleep sends ships to the deep.'"

"I'm sure the prime minister never gets tired. Did you and Hans get on?"

"He's very nice."

"He's a dear, but."

"But? But what?"

"For a moment Mavis looked as puzzled as Grace. Then she chuckled. "But nothing. It's just how we talk. You must learn some Geordie. You have to admit, though, Hans is a dear."

"A good man to have for a friend, but," Grace riposted.

They had toast and tea. Mavis pressed Grace for details about the dance but she had little to say, which, Mavis deduced, meant she had quite a bit to say that she didn't want to say. Well, that was all right then.

"What was that commotion in the shelter about? I stayed where I was. Didn't want to get in the way."

And hadn't wanted to leave Stan's comradely embrace.

Grace told her about Stu. "I'm sure he's the one who defaced your door."

Suddenly the bite of toast Mavis was swallowing turned into a lump in her throat. She took a gulp of tea. "Vicious little bugger. He's boasted more than once he'd get Hans one day. Like to see him try."

"I gather he hates Germans because his brother was killed in the war, and he thinks Hans is a German."

"He's wrong. No German would set foot in my house. Which reminds me, that missing crisp bar. I found it on the floor behind the chest of drawers."

Grace looked almost disappointed. "After what I heard this morning I was sure Stu was the one involved. So there wasn't a burglary?"

"Oh, someone broke in all right. I never leave the window cracked open. I did air the room out the day before you came." Mavis tried to remember if she had shut the window all the way. It was the kind of habitual action you never remembered. Why would she have failed to do so? "Whoever it was would have no trouble. The sneck doesn't work properly. Ronny never did get around to fixing it, the lazy bugger. Hans offered to see to it, but what if the neighbors saw him at my bedroom window? That would really get the tongues wagging."

Chapter Thirteen

"Fancy another serving, Hans?" Mavis poised a spoon over a serving dish displaying the remains of their evening meal of rabbit stew with dumplings and carrots.

"No, thank you. It was delicious. Shall we not keep the rest for Miss Grace?"

It was Monday. Both Mavis and Grace had returned to work. Mavis put the lid back on the dish. "I've got a helping set aside for her. I don't know why she's so late and it's getting parky out. Now for a bit of pudding!"

"There is a pudding?"

"Aye. Hold on."

Mavis collected plates and serving dish and whisked into the scullery. "It's a favourite of mine. Apple crumble, still warm from the oven. Sorry, hinney, custard's off but the empire won't crumble for lack of it!"

She spooned out crumble. Rain rattled harder against the roof. "It's stotting down like stair rods," she called over her shoulder. "I'll have to lend you me umbrella."

"I hope Miss Grace is not working in the rain."

Mavis put Hans' crumble down on the table harder than necessary. His interest in Grace had begun to annoy Mavis, but why should it? She was very fond of him, but merely in a friendly way.

The kitchen door opened. Turning to greet Grace, Mavis saw instead a tall sandy-haired man in soaked clothing. Her heart froze.

The visitor stamped in. His grin vanished when he spotted Hans. "Who the bloody hell are you?" he demanded in a loud voice.

"Welcome home, Ronny," Mavis' words came out in a strangled whisper.

Hans stood and bowed. "Goedenavond, sir. I am Hans van—"

Mavis' husband reddened with rage. "What the hell are you playing at, Mavis? I come home and find a bloody Hun talking German to me in me own kitchen!"

Mavis stepped between the two men. "Nothing, Ronny, honest. He's a refugee. And he's not German." She moved and spoke automatically. She felt as if she were watching herself in a nightmare.

Ronny sneered. "That's what you say. Look at the bugger! Blue-eyed, tall, blond. I suppose he left his jackboots at home." He leaned forward and prodded Hans' chest with a nicotine-stained finger. "And don't tell me you're a refugee, either."

"I am, for I have come from the Netherlands, sir," Hans replied in a dignified tone.

"And it's crawling with bloody Germans right now! So this is what you get up to behind me back, is it, Mavis? When you wrote you were waiting for a lodger to arrive I expected it would be a woman."

"That's right!" Mavis snapped back. "She's over at the police station right now."

Ronny's face got redder. "Arrested for streetwalking or was it shoplifting? Or flogging stuff on the black market? Perfect company for a slut like you!"

"I think it best I leave," Hans said, addressing Mavis. "Thank you for the meal." Taking his jacket he shrugged it on, bowed silently to Ronny, and departed through the scullery.

"Good riddance to bad rubbish! And don't come back!" Ronny shouted after him. "And now, my lady, a word with you. So you have men to dinner behind me back, do you? The kind of swine who've been trying to sink me ship. The swine I've been on the lookout for, freezing me backside off halfway to the

North Pole. Meanwhile one's in me kitchen at home. And me bedroom as well, no doubt. Isn't that right, Mavis?"

He kicked her chair aside. It hit the fireplace fender with a metallic crash as he caught her arm and pulled her toward him, snatching away the fork she hastily picked up from the table. "No, you don't!"

His familiar smell—alcohol and sweat—enveloped her. Since he'd been gone she'd awakened from this nightmare many times.

He tightened his grasp on her wrist, digging his fingers in the way he always did. "You've forgotten your lessons, dearest. I'll have to teach you all over again."

• • ● • •

Returning from the station Grace's mood was darker than the street. Sergeant Baines had assigned her to take over Robinson's desk duties for the day. There were also files to be arranged. The orders had been passed on to Grace by an apologetic Wallace, Baines remaining absent. Robinson's typing jobs piled up, thanks to Grace's lack of typing skills and the filing went very slowly, indeed. She hoped her incompetence at desk work would be noted.

It was raining hard. She splashed through deep puddles she couldn't see to avoid.

The day was not a total loss. During the afternoon Wallace took her aside. "I've made inquiries and come up with some interesting information on our elusive Mr. Rutherford. You may want to pursue it."

When he told her what it was she'd kicked herself for not thinking of it herself. "But will Sergeant Baines approve?"

Wallace smiled. "I haven't been able to get in touch with him so I guess we'll have to assume he'd want you to continue your interviews."

Though it had been a long day, the prospect of further work not involving a desk energized Grace. She'd grab a bite to eat and then—

Footsteps sounded behind her. Turning, she made out a gleam of light from a shaded torch. She had the impression the torch-bearer was tall.

"Hans!" She took a few steps toward him.

"Sorry, you're not my type!" came the reply from a stranger.

She blushed furiously. "I'm not...I mean, I mistook you for a friend and—"

As he passed, his eyes widened. "Sorry, Constable, I didn't see the uniform."

Who was more embarrassed? She covered the rest of the distance to the maisonette faster than was prudent in the dark. To her surprise the front door was unlocked. Alarmed, she pushed it open.

A tall, sandy-haired man was raising a fist to hit Mavis in the face.

"Stop!" Grace yelled.

The stranger saw the uniform, lowered his fist, and let Mavis go. "You got here fast. I suppose the neighbours complained about the noise? Or did her German friend go running for help? What am I supposed to do, coming home on leave and finding me wife all cozy with her fancy man—?"

"You're lucky I didn't see any violence," Grace interrupted calmly. "I did see a distinct physical threat."

"You women always stick together," Ronny sneered.

"For heaven's sake," Mavis burst out. "This is my lodger. She happens to be with the police."

"Is this place a bloody railway station? At the rate people are coming and going, it may as well be. To think of a copper living in me house! As for you, Mavis—" he pointed at her. "When I get back from the pub, there better be a proper welcome for the homecoming warrior."

"Warrior? Fancy yourself, don't you!"

Ronny took a step toward her, thought better of it, and left, slamming the door behind him.

Chapter Fourteen

Grace removed her jacket, righted the fallen chair, and sat down. "Your nose is bleeding."

Mavis rubbed under her nose and examined her knuckles. "It wasn't Ronny," she replied hastily. "I've had these sudden nosebleeds ever since I was a bairn. Mam was the same. It's easy enough to deal with them."

She took a large key from the kitchen mantelpiece and after a certain amount of contortion dropped it down the back of her blouse. "It'll stop quick now. A good old-fashioned remedy, that is," she said in response to Grace's puzzled look.

"My grandma would be proud of you." Grace couldn't believe that the blood wasn't the result of the proximity of Ronny's fist to Mavis' nose but she didn't say so. "What do you intend to do to remedy this old-fashioned situation when your husband comes back?"

Mavis stared at her. "And they say Northerners are blunt." She dabbed at her nose. "Not but what it's a good question. We could retire early and push the beds against the door. He can sleep on the kitchen floor tonight and lump it."

Grace observed she would be happy to move out while Ronny was on leave.

"Don't bother being tactful," Mavis replied. "I'd best lock him out. Wouldn't be the first time. He can go and stay with one of his low-life friends."

"As your husband, surely he has the right to be here? So I don't see how—"

Mavis laughed and pulled the bottom of her blouse from the waistband of her skirt. She caught the falling key and returned it to the mantelpiece. "See, the blood's clotted already. What really upset him was Hans was here and here I am all done up like a dog's dinner when I didn't expect him—Ronny, I mean. Surprised he didn't shout I was keeping Hans' pajamas warm in the oven. That's one of his favourite accusations." She paused while tucking her blouse back in place. "What if I got the landlord to change the rent book so it only has my name on it?"

"That would be worth looking into as a last resort if things don't improve, I suppose. But if you still want to be married—"

"I don't. I've thought about moving away and not letting on where I went. Then when I got wherever it was I'd give out I was widowed. I wish I was! It's a terrible thing to say, but the Germans could do me a real favor." She sighed. "I suppose in your work you have to get used to dealing with family rows. I don't know how you could stand it, Grace. Special training, I suppose?"

The abrupt change of subject made it obvious Mavis preferred not to say more about relations between Ronny and herself, and indeed, looked sorry she had blurted out as much as she had. Grace gave a rueful smile. "You might say I started my training early. Dad, he was a bit free with his fists after a couple of pints himself. It was no wonder my mother up and went."

It wasn't a thing she normally spoke about but under the circumstances…

"And she left you behind? What kind of mother does that? Did you ever hear anything from her?"

"Not a word since the day she walked out."

"Well, good for your mam. For walking out, that is."

• • ● • •

Having given Mavis strict orders not to let anyone in until she returned, Grace went out into the rain and searched the local pubs for Ronny.

She had intended to follow up on what Wallace had discovered about Rutherford, but now Rutherford would have to wait.

There were a great many pubs and the closest she came to locating Ronny was at the Dying Swan whose sign featured a crudely painted fowl of indeterminate species, beak upthrust in what appeared to be its dying gasp.

Emerging into the bar from the temporary lobby erected around the pub door to prevent light spilling into the street, she was greeted by the smell of spilt beer, the click of dominoes, the shouts of darts players arguing over scores mingling with loud conversations at scattered tables. Pale faces turned toward her and the noise level dropped a little.

"Come to arrest us for being too noisy, bonny lass?" a man called out. "I'll be happy to step outside with you!"

"Not your turn to be arrested yet!" Grace riposted with a smile as she approached the bar.

"Going to buy us all a pint, then?" the same voice responded.

"For that, it is your turn!" she replied over her shoulder.

A roar of laughter greeted the sally.

In reply to her inquiry the barmaid told her she'd seen Ronny there earlier but he'd been ejected by the landlord.

"It was because Ronny started kicking up a terrible racket," she went on, polishing a glass with a tea towel. "Loud and obnoxious, you know how people can get when they have too much. And the language! I used to live in Liverpool and the lads there got nothing on Ronny when he gets going, I can tell you. No one was pleased to see him walk in here. The sooner he goes back to sea, the better. Sefton over in the corner playing dominoes was talking to him, maybe he knows where he's gone. In trouble again, is he?"

"Not yet," Grace replied grimly and beckoned over the man pointed out to her, an older man wearing a flat cap, his heavy coat open to show a neat black waistcoat bisected by a gold watch chain. He brought his pint with him, setting it down on the bar.

"That's right, lass," he said in reply to her question. "We was cracking on a bit. Ronny's an old marrer of mine." He took a swallow of beer. "I met him the other day by accident and we caught up on all the news."

"What day was this?" Grace asked, wondering how long Ronny had been back.

"Two days past, maybe."

"And what about tonight?"

Sefton admired himself in the gilt-edged mirror behind the bar as he continued. "He come in tonight in a rare bate. Asked if I'd heard owt about his wife carrying on. So, being an old marrer, like I said, I thought I should tip him the wink. See, me wife told me a while ago there's been gossip about Ronny's wife and this fellow who's always hanging round their place."

"He's a Dutch refugee."

"That's what me wife says he claims to be. Aye, she's a rare one for gossip, is the wife. Told me she heard about it standing in the queue at the butchers. Not surprising, is it? There's nowt to do when you're waiting to be served except talk about other people. And of course she knew I've known him donkey's years. Should have kept me mouth shut when he asked me. Then he started yelling he'd swing yet for his wife and her fancy man. Wouldn't shut up so the landlord threw him out. You canna blame the man, really. Got his licence to think about."

The rain was threatening to turn to sleet when Grace emerged from the pub. She decided she'd best return to the maisonette. She was afraid Mavis would let Ronny back in despite her instructions.

•   •   ●   •   •

Cyril Rutherford could hear the sleet ticking against the temple's twin altars as he studied the vague black silhouettes of houses across the street. No sliver of light betrayed a curtain pulled ever so slightly to one side. What could anyone see, anyway? His torch was switched off.

From where he stood, the altars were faintly visible in the otherwise featureless dark despite any apparent source of light. It pleased him to imagine they were radiating ghostly power.

The exposed skin of his face was numb, his cold hands clumsy blocks. He felt as ancient as the temple, felt as if he were turning to stone.

Stone lasted so much longer than flesh and blood. But stones could feel nothing. Stones had no hearts.

It would be a relief in these times to have no heart.

His gaze left the featureless houses and moved down to the ground at the base of the altars, to the lumpy shadow there that he knew to be a corpse.

Chapter Fifteen

Sergeant Joe Baines sat and stared at the telephone on the kitchen table as if it were an unexplored bomb. A monstrous headache pounded on the inside of his skull. He took his glasses off, rubbed his eyes, and looked at the telephone again. It was blurrier but no less frightening.

Hell! Now he'd have to call Chief Inspector Harris at headquarters. This corpse couldn't be passed off as an accident. Inspectors became involved when it came to murder. The last thing he wanted, them sticking their noses in. Necessary, however.

At least he didn't have to take a bus to bloody headquarters, or so he hoped. The last time he'd been there was when he was put in command of this sub-station. The Central Police Station was housed in a great grey monolith at the corner of Pilgrim and Market streets. With its upper story windows set back between rows of columns, it struck Baines as a cross between a fortress and a Greek temple. Although what attackers was the station built to repel? The populace of Newcastle? Its foyer was decorated with columns that would not have looked out of place in Egypt.

To Baines the architecture reflected the attitudes of the higher-ups ensconced within, confused and out of touch with the realities of crime and the city they served. In his experience communications from headquarters always meant interference and trouble.

He got up and found the whiskey bottle concealed amid cleaning supplies beneath the erstwhile kitchen's sink. He took a slug, returned to the phone, and made the call.

Harris did not interrupt as Baines outlined the situation. A long silence issued from within the Central Police Station.

Finally Harris' querulous voice came down the line. "Yes, yes, I can see you need an inspector. You've got no one but constables there. But who doesn't need an inspector? I'm being squeezed here. From above. And all sides for that matter. All these regulations. The more laws Parliament give people to break, the more crime we have. And two more inspectors left us for the forces a week ago."

The whining voice was a dental drill boring into Baines' aching head. He held the receiver further from his ear. When he'd joined the force he'd worked in the same station with Harris, then still a year from his rise in the ranks. "I know it's a bloody nuisance, sir. But I can't handle a murder investigation with no one but constables. Well, I could, but when I was found out my head would be on a pike."

The prospect of being separated from his throbbing head was not unattractive to Baines. He glanced toward the cupboard under the sink. He didn't think the phone cord was long enough to reach that far.

"How are you handling it so far?" Harris wanted to know.

"I've assigned a constable to interview the neighbors. Wallace. He's familiar with people in the area."

"Arthur?"

"You know him, sir?"

"We started out together. A good man."

"Back then, I suppose he was, if you say so, sir."

The voice from the Central Police Station suddenly sounded less shrill. "Wallace was an inspector before he retired. He can handle a simple murder investigation."

Baines couldn't believe his luck. "But, sir, if it's discovered that—"

"Oh, never mind. If the higher-ups don't like it, I'll take the blame. It would be most helpful to me if I didn't need to detail anyone to deal with this right now."

Most helpful to me too, Baines thought. "Very good, sir. If that's what you want I'll inform Constable Wallace. He'll probably enjoy having a case he can get his teeth into."

"I'm sure he will. Report progress directly to me. Give Wallace my regards, will you?"

Baines put down the phone, leaned back in his chair, and closed his eyes. He'd had a lucky break.

He recollected telling his wife, Freda, about his visit to headquarters at dinner. She was naturally excited at him being put in charge of a station, even if it was a small one with only a handful of constables. She laughed when he described the sculpted gryphons high up on the facade of the police headquarters in town.

"Gryphons? Never noticed them before. Next time I go by I'll take a closer look."

"What's a giffon?" His daughter Maggie was surrounding her peas with a wall of mashed potato. He'd had no idea she was listening.

"It's a lion with the head and wings of an eagle," he explained. The little girl scowled. "Oh, that's silly."

"No, it isn't," her brother Joey piped up. "Those monsters can fly after bad men, catch them in their big claws, and carry them straight off to jail. And they can fight the Luftwaffe. I'd like to see a Junkers JU 88 tangle with a flying monster."

Joey had his planes memorized as well as his alphabet.

At the memory, Baines put his head down on the table and cried.

• ● ● ● •

"It would appear, Miss Baxter, that while you were chasing Ronald Arkwright someone else caught up with him."

Grace had finished explaining to Sergeant Baines how she had searched the pubs for Ronny. Between that and the air raid the night before, she'd overslept. She admitted it was inexcusable to be late the third day on the job. She'd expected a bollicking but instead Baines simply listened wearily to the speech she'd rehearsed on her way to the station.

"Someone else caught up to him. He was murdered last night."

"Good God!"

"A coalman making early deliveries reported the body. Must have happened during the night. In the same bloody place where our mystery woman was found. Done in with a knock on the head. Oh, and laid out in the shape of a bloody swastika. No doubt about it this time." His eyes sat at the bottoms of two bomb craters. He apparently hadn't been sleeping much either. "We're keeping this swastika business quiet as we can. We don't want the public getting the idea there's a crazed Nazi sympathizer living locally. It would mean panic, attacks on businesses with German names, all sorts of civil unrest."

"I understand. No photos from the crime scene yet?"

"No. There's a sketch, though." He took it from the folder on the table and handed it to her.

Grace examined it. "It's definitely the left-handed version, sir, the same as the first one."

"Was it?" Baines took the report back, scowled, and adjusted his eyeglasses. "Constable Wallace thinks it's a coincidence, that both bodies just happened to fall that way. He's out interviewing the people on Chandler Street and we've dispatched a constable to Vickers to notify Mrs. Arkwright. Queer situation, you lodging with the wife of a murder victim. Fetch me a cup of tea, would you? Get yourself one as well," he added.

Grace did as she was told. She couldn't very well refuse to get tea for herself.

The way Baines sagged in his chair he looked as if he were carrying the whole weight of Ronny's corpse on his shoulders. He put the cup to his face and inhaled its steam as if to revive himself before taking a sip. "In a way it's handy having an office in a kitchen. Well, that's all we know so far, although you have a head start on the investigation given you know a bit about Ronny's movements last night."

"Does that mean—?"

"That I am assigning you to assist Constable Wallace? Yes. He was insistent about it and I was happy to take his advice."

"Thank you, sir."

"Don't thank me. Thank Hitler. Every able-bodied man in Newcastle is off to fight him. We're left to keep the peace with the halt, the lame, and the blind."

Did Baines mean even a woman is better than a blind man? Grace hadn't seen any officers who were halt, lame, or blind. Then again she had the impression they were avoiding her. At least Wallace was friendly.

"But don't get the impression I've changed my mind about women in the force," Baines continued. "It's a dangerous job. These days it's dangerous for women and children in their own homes, never mind women trying to police the streets."

Recognizing the reference to Baine's loss of his family in a bombing raid, Grace took a slow sip to avoid having to reply.

Baines swirled the liquid in his cup, stared into it, and spoke to Grace without looking at her. "I regret our unfortunate encounter in the cemetery. I was not at my best."

"Sir—"

"It must have made a bad impression on a country girl."

Grace stopped herself from telling him she'd known worse drunks in Noddweir.

"Let's say nothing more about it," he went on. "The war has affected all of us and we must all carry on regardless. Now explain why you went looking for Ronny after he stormed off. I would have thought it more prudent to stay to protect Mrs. Arkwright if he returned."

"I hoped to scare him enough to make him avoid any more confrontations. I thought it would be helpful to Mavis."

Baines gave her a bleak smile. "You couldn't have scared off a bloke like him. He has a history with us, you know."

"I hoped my uniform would put him on notice we had our eye on him."

"Although you were off duty? Never mind," he told her before she could reply. "What about the wife's friend, the Dutchman?"

"Hans van der Berg?"

"You say Ronny suspected him of having an affair with Mrs. Arkwright? Was he?"

"I don't think so."

"He might have been?"

"I couldn't say. Mavis and I only met a day or so ago. I'm not sure what to make of her situation yet."

"Most murders are crimes of passion. You don't need to belong to the force to realize that. The majority involve family members, husbands, and wives."

"Your thought is Mavis went out to look for Ronny after I left?"

"Can you say for certain she didn't?"

"No, sir. But what about the first death? Dead from a head wound, found in the same place, the body arranged identically. Surely the similarities suggest a connection?"

"For that matter how do we know the mystery woman didn't have a connection to the Arkwrights?" Baines set his cup down. "Another thought. Perhaps the gossip is right and the Dutchman really is Mrs. Arkwright's lover. There's possibilities there."

Grace felt her face getting hot. "I can't imagine him killing Ronny, sir."

"You already think you know him better than you know the woman you're lodging with?"

Grace didn't like the way Baines raised his eyebrows.

"I was only thinking how people can be prejudiced against refugees."

"No doubt. Our job, however, is to find criminals, not to fight prejudice, real or imagined. Write down what you learned last night for Wallace to read when he comes in. We have a list of local aliens. Robinson will find out where the Dutchman is living and where he works, then you can go and talk to him."

Chapter Sixteen

It struck Grace as peculiar that Sergeant Baines was sending her out to interview a man who was likely to later in the day visit the place where she was staying. Why not let her talk to him then? It was odder still he had assigned her to speak with Hans at all, a man she knew, however slightly. Shouldn't the job have gone to Constable Wallace?

Most likely it meant Sergeant Baines did not take Hans seriously as a suspect. He had made it clear he did not take Grace seriously as a member of the police force. The task was a good way to keep her busy and out from underfoot.

Which did not answer the main question preoccupying her as she bicycled toward the refugee shelter where Hans worked. How did you officially interview a man whose kiss you remembered so vividly?

It was a problem she did not have to deal with. Hans had not arrived that morning, she was informed. It had never happened before. Maybe he was ill. He wasn't in trouble with the police, was he?

Grace said no, he was a witness, to put his supervisor's mind to rest. She was a well fed woman with a clipped accent Grace didn't recognize, dressed far too well for the dingy offices where she worked.

"He seems such a nice man, and we do screen these people, but."

A visit from the police had instantly convinced the woman that the nice man was, in fact, a nefarious spy or saboteur, and nothing Grace said shook her conviction.

Was Hans going to have trouble at work now? That concern was overridden by a more pressing worry. Why wasn't Hans at the shelter? Had his encounter with Ronny upset him enough to make him miss work? Another possibility refused to be shoved aside. Had Ronny gone out looking for Hans? And had the predator found the prey?

Grace coasted down the steep hill toward the Tyne, squeezing the brakes all the way. Lost in foggy conjectures, she found herself too suddenly at the T-junction at the bottom of the hill. She clamped on the brakes as hard as she could and the bicycle slewed sideways and came to a halt at the edge of Scotswood Road as a huge lorry rumbled past.

She wasn't surprised to find Hans' lodgings located on a run-down street near the river, not far from the Dying Swan pub she'd visited during her futile search for Ronny Arkwright. What she didn't expect was the dance hall occupying the ground floor of the corner building. The Palais de Paree looked the sort of establishment that had never seen better days.

Music escaped into the chilly air to mix with the muffled roar of machinery from the works across the road. Who would want to dance at this time of day? There was a door beside the dance hall entrance. Beyond a steep stairway led to the second floor flat Hans had listed as his residence. The narrow window in the stairwell was partially obscured by a crude wooden cut-out of the Eiffel Tower.

Grace stood in front of Hans' door, feeling uncomfortable. The sound of music from below reminded her of the dance at the church. She knocked.

Her summons was greeted by a series of heavy thumps inside the flat. The door opened. The man who spoke to her in what she recognized as a Dutch accent was not Hans. He was short and powerfully built with a crutch under one arm, the other arm in a sling. He answered her questions in a gruff voice. He shared the flat with Hans and his name was Joop Pieck.

Joop was shorter and stockier than Hans, his dark hair cropped to little more than a shadow. He thumped across the room with his crutch, sat at the table, and invited Grace to take the other chair. Fish boiled in a pot on a cooker in the corner.

"Hans is in trouble?" Joop echoed the supervisor at the refugee center.

"No. I just need to speak with him. Do you know where he is?"

"Nee. Nee. He did not come back last night."

Grace felt a pang of alarm. "Is that unusual?"

"Ja. Not like Hans. He is a clock. Hans is in trouble," Joop frowned. "You are police. He is in trouble."

"No," she said, but her heart, beating too fast, was saying yes, yes, yes. "Do you have any reason to suspect he might be in trouble?" she forced herself to ask.

Joop shrugged. "We are foreigners. We are in trouble here always."

"Does Hans ever drink? Is there a pub he likes?"

"Nee. He spends time with a lady friend, that is all. Friend he says. Only a friend."

"And he always returns in the evening?"

"Ja."

To her chagrin, Grace realized she was relieved knowing Hans wasn't in the habit of spending nights with Mavis or anywhere except his own flat. But it made his disappearance—already she was thinking in terms of a disappearance—all the more alarming.

She stared across the table at Joop, trying to read his features. His face resembled weathered wood. His tone of voice revealed nothing beyond the struggle to put his thoughts into English.

"I worry about Hans," Joop said. "I am afraid he makes trouble for himself."

"How?"

Joop frowned. He appeared to be trying to find suitable words and failed. He tapped his head. "Wrong, here. Since we sank. He is angry sometimes. Other times scared. He wakes at night, shouting. He sees things in his sleep. Bad things. What could he do when he is bad in the head?"

"Is that why he is not working for the merchant navy?"

"Ja. He is afraid of boats now. Afraid of the water." Joop sounded as if he couldn't believe such a thing was possible.

Grace asked him to describe what had happened. It had nothing to do with the investigation but she couldn't help herself. She wanted to know. Joop appeared almost eager to tell his story as best he could. He confirmed they had fled the Netherlands, seeking refuge in England. As they approached the coast a Luftwaffe patrol spotted them.

"The planes came at us with a bad noise. Bad. Screaming. Then bombs. All around. Hitting the water. At first they miss us. We are all on deck, cursing the mof. We are only fishermen. Save your bombs. Damn mof."

Joop's lips tightened and his features clenched in anger as he spat out the Dutch term for the hated Hun. Was it at the memory or his inability to communicate it adequately? "More planes. More bombs. Closer this time. Water falling over us."

His hands made swooping motions over the table. "Then boom! We are hit! And again! Suddenly I am lying on the deck. Fire and smoke is everywhere. I get up and look for Hans. My foot hits something. An arm. No body. Only an arm.

"Through the smoke I see water. The ship tips sideways. The water is almost to the deck. Black water. And there is Hans, sitting down. His eyes. Such eyes. Bad. Dead.

"Hans, he is not a good swimmer.

"Planes come back. I cannot see through the smoke. I hear them screaming down. They shoot at us. Why?

"'Hans,' I say, 'you cannot stay here.' He will not go into the water.

"'Hans, another boat will save us,' I say. He does not say yes. He does not say no. He does not move or look at me. He is looking at the black water with his dead eyes.

"I take his arm and pull." Joop made an appropriate motion with his good arm, hitting the crutch leaning against the table.

It crashed to the floor, startling both him and Grace. He was silent for a moment. The boiling fish filled the air with a strong miasma. Below, Glenn Miller was playing.

"Then we are in the cold water," he resumed. "The planes scream. Bullets hit the water around us. How long? Forever? They go away. I help Hans swim. I think we will drown. We keep going. It is getting dark. Suddenly a shout. A boat has appeared.

"When we get to land, Hans can speak again. The dead look is not in his eyes. Not gone. Now it is in his head."

"Didn't I answer enough questions this morning?" Mavis let Wallace into the maisonette and showed him into the kitchen.

Wallace took off his helmet and set it on the table. He unslung his gas mask, hung the box over the back of the chair, and opened his notebook. "I realize I'm inconveniencing you, Mrs. Arkwright, but in the circumstances…"

"That's as may be, but the last I saw of Ronny was his fist in front of me face. You canna expect me to be bubbling about him now, can you?"

Brightly colored paper chains hung from the ceiling and looped up from the mantelpiece. On a side table two pine branches in a jam jar bent under the weight of tinsel and a big glass ornament apiece.

"I'm here to get information, not to tell you how you should feel." Wallace had been called to break up fights between the Arkwrights, so he and Mavis knew each other. His official visit was an uncomfortable situation for them both. "Constable Baxter told me she observed Ronny threatening you when she arrived home last night. I gather he then left."

"Yes. But I could have handled him if she had not been here."

"But you hadn't before Constable Baxter arrived?"

Wallace doubted any little brunette could have handled Ronny on her own. Mavis certainly hadn't succeeded very well in the past.

"What did you do after Constable Baxter left?"

"I sat down and had a good cry."

"And after you sat and cried what did you do?"

She gave him a grim smile. "Why I got up, went to bed, had a few more tears. Then I went to sleep."

"You didn't leave the house after Ronny left?"

Mavis shook her head.

Wallace persevered. "You like going out? You like the dances?"

Mavis looked surprised."What does that have to do with anything?"

"The neighbors wouldn't think it odd if you left the house at night."

"Oh, they notice everything. Tongues wag, all right." The kettle whistled. Mavis had been preparing tea. She brought cups to the table and sat down across from Wallace.

"I meant they might not notice on any particular night, it being a common occurrence."

"Been listening to gossip, have you? If you're suggesting I followed Ronny—"

"So you didn't go out after he left?"

"Actually, I did, to use the netty. Is that against the law now?"

Wallace ignored the remark. "And Mr. van der Berg, the Dutchman…" He paused and sipped his tea. It was part of the ritual when a constable came calling. "The neighbours, as you say, talk and since they see this man who visits often and then your husband turns up dead the very night he arrives on leave, well, certain questions must be asked and—"

"Hans wouldn't hurt anyone!" Mavis interrupted angrily "Hans and I aren't having an affair, if that's what you are thinking. Grace can tell you that."

Wallace made another note and pondered a moment, tapping his teeth with his pencil.

Mavis struggled to control her temper. "I think I'll have a tab," she said and offered one to Wallace before lighting her own.

He refused.

Mavis took a long drag and tapped the ashes into her saucer.

Wallace asked her what Hans did and she described his work with refugees.

"Why isn't he with the merchant navy? I understand he was a fisherman?"

"He's never told me why he does that particular work and, though we are friends, it never occurred to me to ask. Mind, living in a strange country as he does, it must be nice for him to hear his native language."

"Did he bring you those oranges as a friend?" He indicated the fruit in a bowl beside the makeshift Christmas tree. "Haven't seen oranges in the shops myself. Nice Christmas present, oranges."

"He's not involved in the black market, if that's what you're hinting at."

"No? That would put him in a minority. It isn't polite to ask where a gift came from, is it? Still, a foreigner…"

Mavis had looked Wallace straight in the eye the whole time he'd been questioning her. She is a tough little thing, he thought. But then she'd have to be to have survived marriage to Ronny. He persisted. "Ronny didn't let you know he was coming home on leave?"

"No."

"According to the report of an investigating constable, a witness claims to have seen Ronny in the city a few days ago."

"Oh? Last night was the first I knew he was back."

"Any idea where he might have been before coming home?"

"I don't know and I don't care." She abruptly stubbed out her cigarette, almost knocking over her empty cup.

Wallace could see her cheeks reddening. "We both know Ronny was a swine, Mrs. Arkwright," he said gently. "But even swine are entitled to justice."

Chapter Seventeen

In the deepening twilight, Rutherford carefully closed the door to his maisonette and looked up and down Chandler Street to make sure he wasn't observed. He made a shushing sound at the cat that bounded onto the front step to brush his ankles and gently nudged it away with his foot before crossing the street.

Darkness was pooling in the open space around the remains of the temple. Rutherford bent and pushed aside a patch of thick grass growing against part of the ancient foundation. He smiled with satisfaction seeing the trap hidden there had been sprung.

Straightening up, he tried to suppress a cough. Coming out into the cold always set it off. He wiped watering eyes. The cold affected them badly too. He would have preferred to stay indoors, but it was necessary for him to do what was expected of him. He must be careful not to draw unwanted attention to himself.

He looked at the altars. As the remains of sunset drained from the sky, they resembled pale gravestones.

In his imagination Rutherford could still see the corpse lying in front of an altar. Had the police he observed as he peered from his window noticed the body's positioning? Did they understand what it signified?

There was evil at work in the world. Evil that needed to be dealt with in its own way. The body made that clear, didn't it? Yet who would understand? Even those he had considered his friends, who should have assisted in his efforts, had shuddered and turned away from doing what must be done.

Rutherford felt a prickling along the back of his neck. It was more than the chilly breeze. Power lingered here where offerings had called to the old gods who abandoned their temple centuries ago. He looked to the sky but the night was overcast. No stars showed. The city might as well have been buried in a cavern beneath the earth.

Muttering a scrap of Latin, Rutherford forced himself to continue on his way. He didn't want to be late.

The darkness embraced him. He felt, as he always did when he was out at night, as if he wore a cloak of invisibility, protecting him from prying eyes. But tonight his skin continued to tingle and he felt something had followed him from the temple.

When he stopped to check a trap where a brick was missing at the side of a step, the follower caught up with him. Or so it seemed. He sensed a presence, yet risking a surreptitious glance over his shoulder, saw nothing stood behind him.

He didn't dare to stop again. Whatever it was kept pace. He could sense it at his back, could feel the gap between it and himself, could feel a skeletal finger poised an inch above his shoulder, ready to touch it.

It was too dark now for him to go more quickly without risking falling over an unseen object or walking into a lamppost. Moving to the centre of the street, he resolved not to turn around again.

After a journey that seemed much longer than usual, Rutherford arrived at his destination. Before going inside, he put his hand in his coat pocket and fingered an Egyptian ankh, over which he had uttered certain protective charms.

By the time he reached the flat roof of the building he sensed he was, finally, alone. Up here the wind was stronger. His eyes teared up until he could barely see the structure at the roof's edge, an oversized oil drum with a conical top, a door at the back, and slits at eye-level.

Rutherford entered the contraption. It was claustrophobic, a metal coffin. He didn't like it, but he had to do what was necessary. Out of the wind he was suddenly flushed from exertion.

Through the slits he could see the Tyne, lined by Vickers' works on this side of the river, and Gateshead on the opposite shore. Or rather he could see them in his mind's eye where he knew them to be. Between the cloudy sky and the blackout he might have been staring into the Stygian depths of Hell.

There was a ringing knock at his metal door.

• ● ● ● •

Agnes Cooper undid her tartan headsquare, laid it on the corner table, and lit a candle in front of a plaster Jesus. Only a stub remained and the shadows cast upwards by the flame made the Son of God's beatific face faintly monstrous, as when children hold a torch under their chins to scare one another in the dark.

Agnes knelt to pray. Her knees hurt from kneeling before her doorstep, scrubbing away the cloven hoofprints that were there every morning. Often, in the night's darkest hours, she was awakened by the scraping of those cloven hooves on the steps downstairs, the scratching of claws at the door. That no one else noticed the prints did not surprise her.

Each day, as soon as the sun was up and it was safe to go outside, she cleaned away the traces of those nocturnal visits. The harder she plied her stone the harder he squeezed her heart in his talons. Although she implored the Lord for protection, her chest continued to hurt.

She rose and gingerly moved her left shoulder, trying to work the pain out. Had Satan got inside? Surely not.

From the moment it was built near the Roman wall, the vile temple had served as a gateway between Earth and Hell. Strange she had not realized that when she moved into this home as a young woman. Perhaps it was because the evil had strengthened over the years, as the evil abroad in the world had strengthened until it was now a howling black cloud ready to swallow all of God's creation.

Though a wardrobe blocked most of the window looking toward the temple, she was able to peer out when frightened by noises. Many times she had watched the fiend Rutherford cross to the shrine at sunset, no doubt waiting to commune in the dark with whatever demons were there. And she also saw shadows dancing around him, following him when he left.

There were always shadows in the street where they shouldn't be. And voices whispering unintelligibly in infernal tongues. They got into her head. At times she felt she was about to grasp what they were babbling. But she feared if she did, she would certainly go mad.

Now Rutherford and his demons had begun to make blood sacrifices to whatever pagan deity the Romans had worshiped there.

She had found certain evidence of sacrilege being performed in the ruins—a thing so blasphemous she barely dared think about it.

Hands shaking, she had wrapped what she found by an altar in thick brown paper and hidden it in her chest of drawers. She knew she must tell the vicar. But she was afraid. If she alerted him, would his prayers be powerful enough to protect her?

A guard at the civil defense centre at the Benwell Waterworks directed Grace to the stairs to the roof. Constable Wallace had had the sense to check the records and discovered why the man was always out at night.

He served as a fire watcher.

Grace rapped at the door to Rutherford's metal roost again. The windy darkness all around was unnerving, the infinite deep in the hour before the world's creation.

Finally the door squeaked open. In the light from her torch Grace saw a pale, unhealthily thin man with the stooped shoulders of a scholar. His metal helmet was too big for him. Grace wasn't sure what she had expected, but certainly not this beaten-down old man.

"Mr. Rutherford? Cyril Rutherford? Constable Baxter. I need to have a word with you."

Rutherford stepped out onto the roof with obvious reluctance, eyes downcast, as if he expected to be whipped. "That was you following me?"

"No."

He appeared distressed by her denial.

"Have you been followed, Mr. Rutherford?"

"No. It must have been my imagination."

"I'm sorry to have missed you at your home earlier. It's quiet right now. While it is, could you answer a few questions?"

A coughing spasm rattled in his lungs on a deep baying note. "Right now? On the roof in the dark?"

"If you would. It took me long enough to find you! Now about the woman found dead in the—"

"Don't ken owt about that," he cut in, but his voice quavered.

"Is that why you've been avoiding me? Because you know nothing? Usually it's the other way around. You saw nothing? Heard nothing? You live right across the street from those ruins and you're always out and about after dark. Surely you—"

"I'm a fire watcher. I must be out of a night. People will gossip about owt, as if nobody else went out at night." Another bout of coughing gripped him.

"You sound terrible." The poor man looked so frail, and if the neighbors were inventing malicious tales about him, he might be justified in hiding indoors and avoiding callers. Being a recluse wasn't a crime. "I suppose these damp nights make that cough worse?"

"Coming in from the cold or going out into it will set me off."

Grace had begun to feel sorry for the man. "Horehound tea's what you want. My grandmother swore by it for colds and coughs. Works a treat, it does."

"Your grandmother had herbal knowledge?" Rutherford sounded surprised. "I have a great interest in such remedies. The concoctions wise women made are as effective as anything chemists offer."

His interest in the subject had immediately overruled his evident fear of her, Grace noted.

"Here, Rutherford, stop blathering to the bonny lass!" The voice was that of a man emerging on the roof with a bucket, carrying it over to where Grace and Rutherford were standing.

"Take no notice of him, miss. Always talking nonsense about cures for this and that, and dancing about under the moon. He was carrying on the other night as how his rheumatics were playing up again. Pity his herbs don't help them, isn't it?"

Grace glared at the intruder, annoyed at being interrupted as she was starting to gain Rutherford's trust.

The short, round fellow took it for a questioning look. "Bringing up buckets of sand to put out any incendiaries, see? Got more below, like."

"You don't know what you're talking about, you fool," Rutherford snapped.

The short man looked bewildered. "You plan on putting out them incendiaries with spells?"

"That's not what I meant," Rutherford managed before starting to cough again.

"Dancing under the moon?" Grace asked.

The other answered for Rutherford, who was now loudly sucking a cough sweet, happy enough to resort to a chemist's offerings, despite his professed interest in more effective herbal remedies. "We got to cracking on about bombers' moons the other night. Cyril here reckoned the moon had seen many strange sights and let on he tried to organise a nocturnal event, as he put it—" he leered at Grace "—but the people in his study group were so outraged at the idea they kicked him out of it. Isn't that right, Cyril? Serves the old goat right, begging your pardon, miss. Dancing under the moon in the altogether in this weather, I ask you. Bats in the belfry…" He tapped his forehead significantly and left the roof.

Rutherford looked sideways at Grace and lowered his voice. "I was extremely disappointed to find out the Tyneside Scientific and Literary Circle had only academic interest in what we studied. Oh, they were quite happy to talk about Roman curse tablets or the worship of Hecate, but would they take an opportunity to use certain knowledge to perform a service for their country? Ha!"

Grace realised the circle must have been the group Mr. Elliott had mentioned to her during their conversation in the church. "They refused?"

Rutherford nodded. "Now, you'd think they'd leap at the chance to help the war effort, wouldn't you? But no, every time I suggested we go up on the moors to raise a cone of power and direct its full force toward breaking that swine Hitler, what did they do? Said as soon as they lit a bonfire an air raid warden would appear from nowhere and tell them to put that light out! As if any would be out there in the middle of the night. Or else the weather was too cold or wet or windy, and anyway they were too old to dance sky-clad. And then they voted me out of me own group!"

"Cone of power?"

"Aye. You wouldn't have read about it in the papers but there was one last year down south for a similar purpose."

"How do you know about it if it wasn't in the papers?"

"Don't forget the abdication crisis not so long ago. All over the country bairns were singing about a certain American divorcée stealing the king instead of the real words to "Hark, The Herald Angels Sing." They never got that from any paper! But it's a wonderful demonstration how fast and far word of mouth travels, and that's how I heard about last year's attempt to mess up Hitler's plans. I thought it was well worth trying again, since desperate measures are needed for desperate times."

"True enough. I'm surprised the group didn't agree."

"They were afraid. They confine their efforts now to séances. No doubt there is knowledge to be gained by contacting the spiritual realm, but in times like these what is needed is action."

"I should say so. Where does this group meet?"

Rutherford's expression changed. His lips tightened. "They'll have nowt good to say about me. I'm saying nowt else." He stepped back into his shelter and clanged the door shut.

Chapter Eighteen

"You don't think Rutherford has anything to do with the murders do you, Wallace?" Baines removed his eyeglasses, set them on the kitchen table in the middle of assorted stacks of papers, rubbed his eyes, and stared wearily up at the stained ceiling.

He looked unhealthy, drawn and pallid. At least he'd arrived at the police station on time.

"No, sir. The old man's belfry's full of bats, if you ask me, but our Miss Baxter has him pegged as a person of interest."

"Miss Baxter." Baines let the name out in a long sigh and squeezed his eyes shut. "A country girl. Brought up with too much rustic wisdom, I gather. Talked to Constable Harmon at Craven Arms before she arrived. He spoke highly of her abilities. Apparently her grandmother fancied herself a witch and Noddweir was in thrall to an old stone circle on the hill looking down on it. Superstitious lot, villagers."

"It's true Rutherford does seem to take an unholy interest in the ruins."

"Better her wasting time on the fool than you, Wallace. What interests me more is this business about Ronny being back in the city for a while before he showed up at home. Do you think it's true?"

"It sounds possible. I'm going to put out feelers. Possibly a… shall we say prewar business rival…wasn't thrilled to see Ronny back, or maybe Ronny wasn't thrilled to find out someone had moved in on his business while he was away."

"Moved in on his business? Not his wife?"

"I won't neglect that angle either, sir. And what about our mysterious young lady? Any identification yet? Anything helpful in the missing persons reports?"

"Nothing so far."

"They're taking their bloody time getting the information to us. They need to get moving. Half the people I talk to round here are scared out of their wits. It's bad enough there's a madman in Berlin ready to rain bombs on us, now they're convinced there's a madman lurking in the streets of Benwell. They're afraid to go out after dark. Afraid for themselves, afraid for their families."

Baines groped around the untidy tabletop, spilling forms onto the floor until he found his eyeglasses and put them on. He blinked as he looked at Wallace, as if trying to clear his vision. "Well, there's a war on, you know. It makes everyone anxious to begin with."

Yes, Wallace reflected as he left Baines' office. There's a war on. And that's become an excuse for anything and everything.

• • ● • •

The streets of Benwell felt colder than ever as Grace went door-to-door asking if anyone had seen Hans lingering in the area on the night of Ronny's murder. Not surprisingly, no one had, but they invariably wanted to know if he was suspected of being the murderer who had already claimed two victims and, if not, why wasn't she helping find the culprit?

Grace had to admit to herself she was relieved as one person after another denied seeing Hans. It was not a very professional attitude. It was exactly what Sergeant Baines would have expected of her, she thought grimly.

Baines had shown a total lack of interest in Grace's conversation with Cyril Rutherford. He was focused instead on Hans, now judged to have fled. Running away was a sign of guilt, Baines insisted. Or fear, Grace countered. If, indeed, there was not a perfectly simple and innocent explanation for Hans not returning to his flat.

When Baines told her to interview the local residents it felt more like a dismissal than an assignment, a way to get her out of his office and away from his police station. After all, the higher-ups might force a woman constable on him, but they couldn't stop him merely going through the motions of working with her.

Grace was certain Rutherford was withholding information relating to the murders. She couldn't say why she felt that way, or why the temple made her feel uneasy. The only place in Noddweir that felt anything like the ruins was the ancient stone circle on the hill overlooking the village. As a child she once confessed the Guardian Stones, as they were called, frightened her. "You have too much imagination, Grace," her mother admonished her. From then on, for a long time, she believed the sensation the stones gave her was only her imagination.

Now she experienced the same feeling from the scanty remains where the bodies had been found. She shivered. It was as if she had been touched by an icy draught originating deep in the darkness beneath her rational mind, from a door cracked open in a subbasement of her soul. And beyond the door lay what?

Did others feel that too? Or was it something only perceived by a woman with the blood of generations of wise women flowing through her veins?

Grace rapped at the McPhersons' door. A dumpy woman in down-at-heel slippers and a dirty pinny peered out. She was, as her first words revealed, not a happy woman.

"For heaven's sake come in quick and stop letting the heat out!" She stepped back to allow Grace to enter, banging the door shut behind her. "Stu!" she shouted as they went down the hall. "What you been up to now, you little bugger?"

The boy sat at an oil-cloth-covered kitchen table reading the local paper. His mother disappeared into the scullery and clattered pans about. Another demonstration of bad temper, Grace thought, noticing there were no signs of Christmas decorations, however poorly made, in this home. A photo propped up on the mantelpiece showed two men in uniform which, going by the looks Stu shared with the younger, she deduced to be the boy's father and brother.

"Going to ask you a few questions, Stu—"

Mrs. McPherson looked in. "Take a chair, miss. Can't offer you any tea, we're down to our last couple of ounces. Stu, stand up when you're talking to your elders. Do you want the constable to think you was dragged up in the gutter? Kids!"

Stu stood, slouching, his expression sullen.

"We are hoping you can help us with our inquiries—" Grace began.

"We are hoping you can help us." The boy mimicked her soft Shropshire accent in a high voice.

Grace flushed. "You're not doing yourself any good, young man. Just answer the questions. Now, are you out in the blackout a great deal?"

"Nowt wrong wi' that. I go and visit me marrers most nights. We play cards. Won five bob the other night. And when there's air raids on, I do me bit, taking messages about. Not like them what do nowt but complain. Me brother—" he pointed to the photo "—he done his bit and what did it get him?"

Stu's mother emerged from the scullery. "He was a good lad, Constable, was our Robbie. Still got the telegram."

Grace was beginning to feel uncomfortable. "I'm sorry for your loss, Mrs. McPherson, but you must understand I have to ask these questions. I'll be as quick as I can." She pressed on, aware of his mother sobbing quietly behind her. "So you are out most nights. Did you see anything suspicious the night Ronny Arkwright was killed?"

The boy sneered at her. "Yes, I did. Mam, will you stop that carrying on? It's getting on me nerves!"

His mother stepped round Grace and dealt the boy a sharp slap. "Don't talk to me like that!"

Stu rubbed his reddening cheek and looked at Grace. "I seen that square-head hanging about that night, him what's pretending to be Dutch." He stabbed a stubby forefinger at her.

"Why aren't you coppers going after him? It's obvious to me. He knocked off Ronny so he could move in with Mavis!"

Grace realized she was letting the interview get out of hand. Before she could correct its course, the boy continued, his voice growing shriller. "If you bluebottles done yer job proper, he would swing for it! I'd be happy to string him up meself if I could catch him, make him pay for me brother as well!"

He was shouting now. His mother shouted louder. "Be quiet, Stu, and go to your room!"

As the boy shuffled away down the hall, Mrs. McPherson turned toward Grace. Confirming she had seen nothing on the night in question either, she continued, "There's been a lot of talk about the Dutchman. I don't know what to think. Some say this, some say that. If you ask me, you should be looking into Ronny's past. I always thought he'd wind up in jail. After he joined up, there was a lot fewer burglaries round here, for a start. He'd steal money off a blind man if he got a chance, and he done much worse than that before the war. Then there was that big fight he had with Charlie Gibson. Charlie got the worst of it that time."

"That time? You mean Charlie might have caught him in the blackout and gone a bit too far?"

"Charlie has a very bad temper and he had a long history with Ronny, miss. I'm saying nowt else. Just telling you, talk to Charlie."

Wallace arranged to arrive at the Whistling Chicken shortly after it opened early in the afternoon. The pub called itself the Dying Swan, but its sign's badly rendered bird, intended to represent a swan performing its fabled death song, reminded locals of a more prosaic fowl. The building occupied a corner at the bottom of a precipitous street leading down to Scotswood Road. Factory buildings ran in an unbroken stained brick wall along the opposite side of the road. The air was filled with a smoky haze from chimneys and the clanging of shunting trains.

Entering the pub he spotted his man immediately. He was sitting at a table in the back of the room, flat cap pulled down. His coat was open to show off his black waistcoat with its gold watch chain, just as he had worn it for years.

Wallace sat down across from him. The man showed no more surprise than a stump. "Sefton. Keeping office hours again? I heard you retired."

"I could say the same for you, Wallace. Always thought old coppers was glad to put their sore flat feet up."

"War called me back, Sefton. What's your excuse?"

"Same as you. War. Just doing me bit."

"You weren't called up to do your bit by sitting in a pub, Sefton. Don't try to tell me the authorities are expecting the invasion to start at the Whistling Chicken."

Sefton's gaze darted across Wallace's uniform. "You was an inspector in the old days."

"Before I retired, yes." Wallace got up and bought a couple of pints. He knew Sefton habitually drank Newcastle Brown to show his civic mindedness.

Sefton peered out from under the bill of his cap. "It's not like I'm carrying a gas pipe anymore. I'm too old for violence. It's strictly business now. I saw opportunities I couldn't pass up as a patriotic Geordie."

"The black market, you mean."

"Keeping up me countrymen's spirits. What could be more patriotic? A few extra ounces of tea, chocolates, these things makes all the difference when it comes to morale. Hunting for that little extra takes people's minds off bombs and finding so much as a cup of sugar—well, there's a major victory to celebrate even if Hitler's still occupying Europe. Between you and me, last week I found batteries for a lassie's torch. Shops was all out. Said she'd tried ten different places. Now she's walking the streets safely at night. Who knows what I saved her from? And you try to tell me I'm not a patriot!"

"Is that what Ronny Arkwright wanted to talk to you about? The black market?"

"Ronny Arkwright. Isn't he on the convoys?"

Wallace ignored the question. "You told Constable Baxter he was back a few days ago."

"Yes, now you remind me. A bonny lass. I did just that." He tapped a finger on his cap. "Getting forgetful. Old age, you know. Seemed to me the constabulary would want to be informed about a troublemaker like Ronny being back."

A trio of men arrived. Their greasy overalls identified them as factory workers. They stood at the bar and talked loudly. "Bloody Germans are nothing but rats," said one. "They need to be exterminated, the whole lot them," added another as the publican chuckled.

Sefton leaned over confidentially toward Wallace. "Look, Wallace, I've always been straight with you, haven't I? I know nowt about Ronny's doings. He just wanted to find out what his old marrers was up to."

He screwed up his face into a bad imitation of sorrow and continued. "Do you think I like spending my golden years having to scrounge about for a living? You know how it was in the old days. I had to leave school early to help support my mam and dad. If I'd had the chance for a proper education I'd be a respected businessman now. A pillar of our great city." He raised his glass in an ironic salute and drained the last of his ale.

"That's all very well, Sefton, but as fate would have it, not so long ago you had a conversation with a former petty criminal who promptly turned up dead."

"Aye, strange, that," the other remarked callously. "Mind, there's a new bunch of lads growing up fast who'll be carrying on Ronny's proud tradition of petty theft and fighting and setting fire to anything that'll burn, and likely worse."

Wallace fetched two more pints.

"Got anyone in mind?" He paused. "But you're right. We're only now getting a look at the first form of those rising lads. Stu McPherson, for example. He's already been in trouble and still in school."

"A bad one. Impatient. Wants to solve everything with a knife."

"It's what the world's coming to."

"Bloody shame, ain't it?"

"Depressing. Maybe I could do with some of those morale-raising chocolates you mentioned."

"All out." Sefton reached inside his coat, brought out a ration book, and slid it across the table. "Will this do?"

Wallace scooped it up. "Things are tight, Sefton. You say business is good?"

Sefton tugged on the brim of his cap as if he was trying to pull it down and hide under it. "Forget it! Last time we done a deal you double-crossed me."

"I had no choice. I was set up. You know that."

Sefton considered the statement for a while. "Aye. How did we end up knee-deep in this line of work?"

"We?"

"If it weren't for blokes like me, coppers wouldn't be able to make a living. What else could you do?"

"Take up pest control." Wallace stood. "We'll talk again. In the meantime, ask around. Find out what you can about Ronny's doings since he got back."

Chapter Nineteen

On the way to visit the Gibsons, Grace considered Stu's statement he had seen Hans hanging about, as he put it, on the night of Ronny's murder. Since Hans was Mavis' regular visitor, his presence was nothing out of the ordinary, even if a boy like Stu, with a well-known axe to grind over his brother's death, could be believed.

She would have to think it over later. Now she must talk to the Gibsons.

Once again she plied a door knocker in hopes of locating useful information. She supposed it was an acquired skill. In Noddweir, where people left their houses unlocked, she would simply push the door open a crack and call out.

This time she stood on the well-scrubbed step at the far end of Carter Street from Mavis' home. By contrast to those cramped living quarters, the Gibsons lived in an upstairs maisonette, meaning they had the luxury of a couple of extra rooms and an attic.

What had Mrs. McPherson meant when she advised Grace to interview Charlie Gibson? "He had a long history with Ronny," she had said but refused to say anything further, merely pointing out where the Gibsons lived as Grace departed.

The door opened and a grey-haired man Grace recognised from the air raid shelter peered out.

"Mr. Gibson?"

"That's right. Police, is it? More scandal for the old wives to gossip about. Stop freezing your backside on the doorstep and come upstairs."

She realized he was younger than she had taken him to be the first time she saw him. Mid-forties at most but prematurely grey. Grace followed him up a staircase fitted with a narrow strip of coarse carpeting and into the kitchen where a woman introduced as his wife sat at a table placing gifts into bags sewn from scraps of material. Two honeycomb tissue paper ornaments—one a scarlet bell and the other its twin but bright green—hung from the ceiling light, adding a meagre festive air to the noticeably chilly room.

"Well, Joan, seems we've been favoured with a police visit," Charlie informed her. He pointed Grace to an armchair at one side of the fireplace. He didn't sit but picked up a poker and stirred the dying flames in the grate. He appeared agitated, prodding the coals so awkwardly he spilled ashes out onto the hearth.

His wife didn't bother to look up from her work. She was the woman Grace had seen with Charlie in the church crypt. "Me old man been fighting again, has he, miss? I keep telling the stupid bugger to control his temper. It's caused us enough trouble as it is, and it don't give a good example to the bairn."

"It's not about your husband, Mrs. Gibson."

"Bloody right, it ain't!" he said loudly, shaking the poker.

"Charlie," his wife scolded, "put that down and don't start yelling or you'll wake Veronica up and she's just gone off."

Charlie reddened. He shook the poker again but it fell out of his hand and clattered at his feet.

"Children are always too excited to get to sleep on Christmas Eve," Grace smiled, hoping to alleviate the tension.

Joan finally looked up. "Got bairns of your own, then?"

Grace admitted she did not, adding she was not married. To her surprise, Joan's mouth tightened and she turned back to the parcels she was creating. "These are little bits and pieces for Veronica," she explained. "We have a dolly's pram Charlie bought off one of his friends, nicely repainted and hidden in our wardrobe. And sitting in it right now is a dolly I got. Clothes and everything. Saved up for ages to get it too. The bairn will be thrilled."

"Never mind about that," Charlie said. "The police don't call unless they think you're sitting in something and I don't mean a pram. So what's the story, Constable?"

Grace opened up her notebook. "I'm here about Ronny Arkwright. We're interviewing everyone in the street. What can you tell me about him, Mr. Gibson?"

"By God, I could tell you a lot about that swine—"

"Charlie!" his wife said in a warning tone.

He ignored her and plunged on, red-faced with anger. "No, Joan, would you rather the constable heard gossip and half of it lies? Well, miss, Ronny and I have known each other a long time. In the old days we was marrers. Before the war we done business together."

Grace looked up from making notes. "What kind of business, sir?"

"This and that. Bit of painting, collecting scrap to sell, repairing stuff, moving furniture, that sort of thing. Made good money too, but he was ever one for the tarts. Spent all his money on them. I kept telling him to save it while he had it but he took no notice. You canna do a thing with these young lads. Then he got engaged to Mavis down the street. God knows what she saw in him. She's a canny lass."

"Who likes to go dancing when her husband is away," sniffed Joan from the table.

"Well, he's away permanently and she can dance all she likes now. Where was I? Oh yes, telling the constable here about before the war. I done that stuff in me spare time, since I worked at the Elswick pit then. Ronny never seemed to be working that hard but he always had a well-stuffed wallet. Claimed he was lucky at cards. It's true he always won when we played. He got pinched by the police more than once but like many a lass before her, Mavis thought she could reform him once they married. She's had a sad time of it—"

"You're rambling, Charlie," his wife broke in. Turning toward Grace, she continued. "The point is, not long after Ronny and

Mavis got married we found out Phyllis—our daughter—well, she had his bun in the oven. She was only fifteen at the time."

"She said they used to carry on in the cemetery," Charlie added in disgust.

"Then Veronica is your granddaughter?" Grace asked.

"Aye. But we've raised her to think we're her mam and dad."

"But surely her mother—"

"Phyllis had the bairn in her bedroom here, miss. A week later she stole the few coins I had in me purse, left Veronica behind and buggered off," Joan cut in. "No idea where she's gone and don't want to know either."

Grace wondered if Phyllis was the girl Mavis had mentioned.

"Aye," Charlie said. "We've always done wor best for Veronica but now I can't work like I could and things is tight, and that's Ronny's fault as well."

His voice had begun to rise and Grace noticed his large hands had knotted into fists. "After Veronica was born, I went round and confronted the swine, asked him what he was going to do for her. He laughed in my face! Me, his bairn's grandfather! And the next thing I knew he took me unawares and knocked me down! So there was a fair old fight but he didn't fight fair. Got hold of me arm and deliberately broke it."

He held up his right arm. It looked withered and the forearm was at an odd angle to the elbow.

Joan began to cry. "For God's sake, Charlie, you'll wake Veronica!"

"I see, Mr. Gibson—" Grace began.

"No, you don't," Charlie was now shouting. "Bloody doctor messed up, so me arm don't work proper no more. No strength left in it, can't straighten it. I had to leave the pit. Did you expect me to be another Tommy on the bridge, shivering in the wind and holding out me hand for charity? I got me pride. I want work. Now I have to spend me nights walking about telling fools to put their lights out and me days picking up odd jobs as best I can."

A thoughtful Grace left soon afterward. It seemed there was quite a bit Mavis had not told her about Ronny, but was that surprising? They'd met only a few days before and what she had heard tonight was not the kind of thing a wife would talk about to a comparative stranger. But it certainly provided food for thought. Charlie did not appear to have realised his own words made him a suspect in the death of a man he so obviously hated.

From what seemed a great distance came the sound of singing. Christmas carols. The sound drifted in and out of her hearing as the cold breeze shifted, ebbed, and rose again. A church service? Carolers making the rounds?

When she dreamed of leaving Noddweir she never imagined spending her first Christmas Eve away from home questioning people about a murder. Then again, her childhood Christmas Eves were better forgotten. If her father chose to stay home and drink, or go to the pub and return drunk, it always ended the same way.

A chorus of "Deck the Halls" came ever so faintly to her ears. It made her think of the poor decorations in the home she had left. She could not tell from which direction the music came. Perhaps it was filtering down from Heaven.

• ● ● ● •

Charlie Gibson stamped around the room in a fury. "You've got a mouth as big as Tynemouth, Joan! Why tell the police wor private business?"

"You said as much as me, Charlie. Everyone knows about Ronny and Veronica," his wife shouted back. "Nobody knows where Phyllis is to check anything we say. So long as we stick to that, what can they do? She's got your temper, Charlie, and plenty to be angry about with Ronny. He always had money but never gave us a penny for Veronica and what worries me is—"

A door opened and their sleepy granddaughter appeared in yellow pajamas, rubbing her eyes. "The noise woke me up, mam," she complained. "Will you come and tell me a story if I go to bed nicely so I can be asleep when Santa comes?"

Chapter Twenty

When Grace returned to her lodgings she discovered two disassembled beds leaned against a wall in the kitchen. Mattresses and bedclothes were piled up in a corner with Grace's suitcases perched on top.

Mavis stood on a chair pulling down paper chains and singing along with the gramophone. Dance music, not carols.

Grace frowned. "What's that?"

"It's Joe Loss and his band. You never heard "In the Mood"? Noddy wherever really must be Noddy nowhere."

Grace said nothing. She thought the musical selection entirely inappropriate.

Mavis looked over her shoulder at Grace and flung the last handful of decorations on the floor. "He's back, Grace. You just missed his arrival. They stuck him in the bedroom. Give us a hand to turn the mirror round, would you?"

Grace dragged a chair over to the mantelpiece and helped Mavis with the task. "When's the funeral?"

"Boxing Day. The vicar's been round already. He suggested taking the decorations down as this is, as he put it, a house of mourning," Mavis chuckled. "Little does he know!"

"But the mirror…?"

"Nowt to do with him. It's what you always do when there's a death in the house. I've heard it's to stop the deceased's soul from getting trapped in it. Quite gives you the shivers, don't it?

Imagine me going to comb me hair and seeing Ronny looking at me out the mirror! You have to do what's thought right, and what's thought right is turning mirrors to the wall. Oh, and stopping the clock as well."

She hopped down and looked around. "What about me tree? I'll have to hide that. Damn the man—"

Grace looked askance at her but said nothing.

"Oh, well, he'll be gone soon," Mavis went on. "Good job I've got something black to wear. Where were you detecting tonight then?"

Grace indicated she had just come from the Gibsons, noting Mavis tightened her lips at her mention of the name.

However, Mavis merely remarked she intended to take Veronica's gifts round to their house the following day. "Any news of Hans?"

"No sign. Nobody knows where he's gone."

"Whatever could have happened to him?"

Grace hesitated, then plunged into what she knew would be a sore topic. "It's been suggested he was involved in Ronny's death."

As expected, Mavis flared up. "Bloody rubbish! I suppose I'm suspected of hiding Hans in me cupboard here? At least Ronny being in the bedroom makes sure Hans and me aren't!"

"I don't think Hans could be involved either, but I'm not in charge of the investigation." Grace quickly changed the subject. "Charlie Gibson mentioned the fight he had with Ronny."

"Aye, it was a nasty bit of bad luck for Charlie. I suppose he told you about Veronica?"

"Yes, he did. It's kind of you to take an interest in the girl."

"It is, isn't it? She's no blood relation to me. I felt sorry for her having a bastard like Ronny for a father. She'll find out soon enough Charlie's not her real father, if she hasn't already."

"I think the Gibsons are having trouble making ends meet with Charlie being out of regular work. He talked about a tommy begging on the bridge."

Mavis laughed. "You've got it wrong, hinney. It's not a tommy on the bridge, it's Tommy on the bridge. He was a right character, was Tommy. Had the reputation of being the worse swearer on Tyneside and he had a lot of competition! Born almost blind in the old days and couldn't work, so took to begging. He would stand on the boundary between Newcastle and Gateshead, halfway over the swing bridge. He was a cunning bugger. If he saw a Newcastle bluebottle coming to arrest him, he'd hop over to the Gateshead side and vice versa."

Grace asked why policemen from both forces had not arranged to arrive at the same time.

"Well, they couldn't cut him in half, could they? So he got away with it. Half the city turned out for his funeral. A few will do the same for Ronny, if only to gawk and gossip."

Grace was silent. Poor Tommy with one foot in one place and the other in another. It reminded her uncomfortably of her grandmother's occasional references to heaven and hell and the world in between, the latter being a place where appearances were not always what they seemed.

"There's a veil between us and them two unseen places," her grandmother had said. "You can shake it a bit if you have the wisdom, the knowledge of what to do, but you better not shake it too hard. You never know what might come out from behind it."

Grace recalled Rutherford's disgust with his study group and its séances. The reclusive eccentric scholar and the irascible old wise woman would have enjoyed chatting. Or, at any rate, arguing.

Grace thought about the two bodies recently discovered. There was still no missing persons report to link to the anonymous woman. Could there be a connection between the deaths and the place they were found? In the case of the woman it was possible she had been plying her profession, but on the other hand Ronny was known to have been engaged in illegal activities before the war. Had one or both fallen afoul of an attacker hiding in the shadows? Was the arrangement of the limbs significant rather than mere accident? Was the display meant to frighten away a supernatural evil or merely to frighten another human being? An implied threat?

Grace was convinced Mavis could give her details about Ronny's pre-war career and possibly information, providing a valuable starting place to begin investigating his death. But this wasn't the time to question her.

Mavis poked her arm. "Wakey wakey! I've asked you twice to give me a hand with these mattresses. We'll have to put them on the floor for now. What a Christmas this is turning out to be!"

Chapter Twenty-one

Mavis clicked off the wireless when the King's speech ended. "God bless his majesty for telling us to be thankful we've been delivered from past dangers. Ironic, isn't it? Pity Ronny couldn't have waited a few days to be murdered instead of spoiling Christmas Day. Well, it's the last one he'll spoil."

Grace couldn't hide her dismay at Mavis' callousness.

"Oh, go on, Grace." Mavis gestured around the kitchen. "Look at it. Mirror turned to the wall, the clock stopped, and me poor little Christmas tree hidden in the coalhouse and all wor nice decorations taken down. Don't want to scandalise the old wives, do we? They gossip enough as it is. Black doesn't suit me either."

Mavis wore a plain black dress, although it struck Grace as too short for mourning attire. "I don't know how you can talk like that with Ronny still in the house."

Mavis scowled in the direction of the bedroom. "Aye, back in the house and just what I wanted to find under my tree. Did you sleep well last night? I didn't get a wink. That's Ronny, still bloody interfering and causing trouble even after he's dead. Never mind, we'll have tea a bit early. And since we've no silly hats from crackers, I made some the other day specially for the festive season."

She produced a pair of hats made of newspaper, perched one on her head at a jaunty angle, and went into the scullery to start the kettle boiling.

The cloying scent of lilies filled the air. Ronny's closed coffin sat across a pair of trestles in the bedroom, surrounded by flowers. The house smelled more like Easter than Christmas.

Grace's hat was shaped like a boat. It reminded her of Hans. Where had he gone? Had someone dragged him down a dark alley and beaten him so badly he was unable to get home? Or worse?

Would he be the next person found in the temple ruins?

Or had he experienced one of those episodes his roommate had talked about and got himself into trouble?

Surely he couldn't have run off? He wasn't a murderer.

Mavis returned. "Mind, tomorrow's tea will be better. Mrs. Gibson promised to come in and help me get it ready while the funeral's going on."

"You're not attending it?"

"Women don't do that around here, Grace. Got to stay home and get something ready to eat after the funeral. I've already had extra food brought round by the neighbours. You're eating a wee bit of it now."

Grace took another bite of her fried luncheon meat and recalled the vicar's comments concerning the kindness of his congregation. "Shouldn't this be kept for tomorrow?"

"Don't expect too many to visit. Most of Ronny's marrers are in the forces and he never had that many to begin with. Or at least none that would dare show their faces in a decent household. Eat up. I know it's not turkey and stuffing, but—"

She was interrupted by a brisk knocking on the front door. "Damn! Hide your hat!"

Grace recognised the caller as the man she had conversed with at the pub and mentally dubbed Mr. Gold Chain. When he spotted Grace he stopped in his tracks and looked at her in confusion and perhaps a hint of fear.

"Don't worry," Grace told him. "I'm not here in my official capacity. This is where I live."

He took off his flat cap revealing sparse slicked-down grey hair. "Give me a start, you did. Bloke never wants to find a copper waiting for him."

"Blokes like you don't, Sefton." Mavis all but carved his heart out with her glare. "Sandwich? No? Cup of tea then?"

"Nay, lass. Only called to pay me respects and to ask if there was owt I could do for you. Me and Ronny, we went back a long way."

"Right nice of you." Mavis' voice was cold. "Nowt springs to mind."

"Ronny and me had business interests. If he left anything undone…any loose ends…undelivered merchandise let's say…?"

"I'll keep it in mind, Sefton."

"Aye, do that. Owt I can do, let me know."

Mavis showed him to the bedroom and waited outside. Grace imagined him standing in front of the coffin, holding his cap. Thinking what?

After Sefton left, Mavis looked ready to spit. "Him and Ronny went back a long way, all right. Too bloody long!"

"What does he do?"

"Something he wouldn't want you to know about. Ronny never told me much about their dealings. The gall of it, showing up today. Wanted a private talk in case I was in on any of Ronny's schemes!"

The visit had soured the mood and Mavis made no attempt to bring out the newspaper hats again. She lapsed into an uncharacteristic silence.

Then there was another knock.

The two callers came into the kitchen in a frigid gust scented by lilies, a tiny old woman in black, face shadowed behind a veil, accompanied by a big-boned woman, younger, also dressed in black.

The elderly woman hobbled over to Mavis with the aid of a walking stick, and gave her a hug. "Oh, my poor dear. How awful for you. We're terribly late, aren't we? I forgot what street you are on. I said it was…" She paused and half turned toward her companion. "What did I tell you?"

"Chandler Street," said the other woman.

"Thank you for your trouble," Mavis told her. She took the elderly woman's arm and led her out of the kitchen. "He's in the bedroom."

Mavis stared after the trio but resisted the urge to follow them. They stayed with Ronny's coffin a long time, then emerged into the hallway and she heard the old woman again. "Such a good boy. What would I have done without him after me old man ran away? But then I always raised him to be a good boy and to be a good husband. Sometimes I worried, but he was a good husband, wasn't he?"

"Yes. Very good."

Then came the sound of the front door opening and closing, a brief gust of perfumed cold, and Mavis walked into the kitchen, eyes narrowed, lips tight.

Grace stared at her in astonishment.

"I know what you're thinking, Grace! But what do you expect me to say? The poor woman isn't old as she looks. She started going soft in the head years ago. She's Ronny's mam."

• • ● • •

It took a cigarette to calm Mavis' nerves. "Ronny came from a good family. Good, until his father ran off. Ironic, isn't it? His mam's being taken care of by relatives."

"Will she be at the funeral?"

"No. Her niece, the woman who brought her, told me she wouldn't be up to it. She said if Mrs. Arkwright ever asks about the funeral, she'll tell her she was there. Kindest thing to do, really. The poor old dear won't remember one way or another."

Mavis asked Grace if she would like to accompany her to the Gibsons. "I'm going to take Nica her presents before we get any more visitors."

"I don't know, Mavis. I haven't anything to give her, and I don't like to go empty-handed,"

"Oh, aye. Let me think. Why don't you give her the mittens or the pixie hood?"

"But you knitted those for her yourself. It wouldn't feel right."

"I know, you can give her my Spitfire brooch."

Grace protested it was a gift from Hans, but Mavis waved her protests away. "I can get another one. Wrap it up and we'll be off."

Carter Street felt bleak and cheerless, a feeling exacerbated by the knowledge that it was Christmas, a time for joy.

Mrs. Gibson invited them to come in from the cold cheerily enough. Looking up past her, Grace could see Veronica peering round the corner of the landing. "Come to check to see if we have a black market turkey and brought your marrer with you as a witness, have you?" Mrs. Gibson asked Mavis with a smile.

"We'll keep your secret if you'll slip us enough for sandwiches," Mavis replied.

"Come in then, and I'll see you get some! Nica, visitors for you!"

The little girl led them into the kitchen and pointed proudly at a doll's pram sitting by the fireplace. "See? Santa brought that! But I don't know how he got it down the chimley. Do you?"

Mavis smiled. "It's secret. And here are some little things there wasn't room for in your stocking."

Veronica exclaimed most enthusiastically over her teddy bear and tucked it into the pram beside a cross-eyed dolly.

"She'll appreciate the hood and mittens when she's out in the cold," her grandmother remarked softly.

Then Grace handed over the hastily wrapped brooch. When the little girl struggled to attach the silver aeroplane to her jumper, Grace pinned it on securely for her.

"By, but it's lovely," Veronica smiled broadly, inclining her head to see it. Turning to her grandmother she asked, "Will there be any more presents? Is auntie going to come today, too? She brings ever such nice things."

Mrs. Gibson changed the subject hastily. "Where's your manners, Nica? You never said thank you to these ladies."

• • ● • •

"Children are told Christmas night is magical," Rutherford informed his cats. "But, of course, as magical animals you already know that."

A tabby sitting under the table mewed.

"Ah, you think I have forgotten my friends? Of course not." He opened a drawer and removed a box. Cats swarmed to him from shadowed corners or jumped down from perches around the room. One or two latecomers hastily pattered down the hallway when he called "Puss, puss, pussy!" in a high-pitched voice.

Opening the box, he distributed several rat carcasses to the waiting cats. "Ah, you know the call to come and eat a treat, and I hope you appreciate how many times I get my fingers pinched by traps hidden in nooks and crannies," he said, sitting down at his desk and taking up a scribbled piece of paper. "But then," he addressed the nearest feline, "cats are not only magical but know more than they ever reveal. Except to their friends. To think you were all gods long ago and now nasty boys try to catch you to torment you in back lanes. But the temple knows. There's always a nice fat rat caught in one of my traps there."

He smiled to himself and turned his attention to the paper he held. "My feline friends, according to my calculations, the time is almost ripe to erect a cone of power, yet fools refuse to contemplate the notion. Still, we must do what we can. Perhaps I could persuade the older children...but would that work? They probably wouldn't agree to take their clothes off and that's vital. And how to get them up on the moor at night to begin with?"

He rubbed his eyes. "Always problems. But first let us work out the ritual." He commenced writing, consulting books now and then. The shadowy room's quiet was disturbed only by the crunching of cat jaws, the rustle of paper, and their owner's occasional distracted comments.

"If I can get enough to agree, enough to make a circle...but how to hide the fire?...we'd have to avoid air raid wardens and other nosy parkers...now, the incantation..."

There was a brisk knock on the front door and before he could react singers struck up a spirited "God Rest Ye Merry Gentlemen."

She rifled through the gaudy paste jewelry in her dressing table's drawer until she found a cigarette packet. It was empty.

"Bloody hell, Joe! You said you'd bring me more tabs. Bloody awful Christmas this has turned out to be."

Joe Baines sat up in bed and laid a tentative hand on her arm. "I'm sorry but—"

"Sorry! You're always sorry, Joe. Sorry's the word for you!" She didn't bother to move away from his hand, letting his fingers lie against her skin as if she didn't feel them, as if they were of no consequence.

"I know I haven't been at my best today."

She tossed the empty cigarette packet back into the drawer. "No? Really? I'm not sure I can recall what your best is like anymore. Here it is Christmas and if your face got any longer you'd be sweeping the floor with your chin."

Baines squeezed her arm in supplication. She offered as much response as a statue, so he took his hand away. "I didn't mean to...well, I never thought I'd react like this, but it's the first Christmas, you see. My first Christmas alone."

She jerked around and glared in the dim lamplight. "Alone? What am I, then? A piece of bloody furniture?"

"I didn't mean...I meant without...without..." The words wouldn't come out.

"We both wanted your wife out of the way, didn't we?"

"But not the children. And I didn't want their mother dead."

"That's not what you said before. How many times did we sit right here in this bed with you moaning about how she made your life a misery? How you'd do anything to be rid of the bitch?"

"Talk. Just talk. I didn't know how it would be..."

She apparently had a sudden change of heart, because she leaned over and put her arms around his sagging shoulders. "Don't feel guilty, Joe. It's not your fault the bloody Germans dropped a bomb on your house."

"No," he said, his voice a faint echo. "It wasn't my fault a bomb hit the house."

Chapter Twenty-two

On Boxing Day, the day of the funeral, Carter Street residents came calling. They came not so much to pay their respects to Ronny, Grace thought, as to show their support for Mavis. Grace was stiff from sleeping on a mattress on the kitchen floor for a second night but she did her best to keep the teapot filled.

Mrs. Gibson arrived first, bringing newspaper screws of tea and sugar as gifts for Mavis "for to help out wi' the funeral tea, hinney." Removal of her coat revealed she was swathed in a green pinafore over a shabby black dress. "Shame about Ronny, hinney," she said perfunctorily. "Give us your bread knife and I'll start making sandwiches." She slapped a loaf on the round wooden breadboard, took the saw-toothed knife, and started cutting thin slices from the loaf. "Don't expect many, do you?"

Mavis shrugged. "Not really. Charlie, what about him?"

"Aye, he intends to be at the funeral, sorry to say."

Grace was surprised to see Lily, the aspiring prostitute, arrive with her mother, who looked frail but had a powerful voice.

"Sorry about Ronny," the woman began. "Me daughter here the same. Who's going to follow the coffin, then? No men about the house to do it, are there?"

"They're all hiding in me backyard, Mrs. Dixon," Mavis said.

"Wouldn't surprise me a bit," came the reply.

Lily, considerably cleaned up and looking younger without her homemade makeup, dared send a few sulky glances in Grace's direction as Mavis showed the two visitors to the bedroom.

More local residents arrived. Grace recognised a number, having interviewed them. Conversations filled the kitchen. She had trouble enough deciphering the local dialect while concentrating on a single speaker. Listening to the mingled voices she might as well have been sitting in the middle of a marketplace in Istanbul—although there she might have caught the conversation of an expatriate or two.

Sefton showed up again, closely followed by Charlie Gibson. Mrs. Gibson looked up from arranging sandwiches on a plate and frowned.

"Rotten cold weather to be standing about in a cemetery," Sefton observed, warming his hands at the fire.

"Oh, Ronny's toasty enough," Charlie replied.

"Charlie, you know this is not the..." his wife began.

"Does it look to you as if the widow is upset?" he replied. "Not that I blame you, Mavis. I've nae doubt you're glad to be shot of him. As for me, I reckon he got what he deserved." His face reddened. "I just wish it was me what gave it him, the swine."

"His marrers would say different," Sefton put in.

Charlie swung round. "What marrers were these, then? A bunch of thieves and worse." He was shouting.

Sefton matched his volume in defense of Ronny and the two started arguing.

There was a muffled thudding. Grace entertained the sudden thought the departed had risen from his coffin to warn them they were disturbing his rest, but then realised a neighbour was banging on the party wall to indicate they could hear the shouting and were not pleased about it.

Evidently the neighbours on the other side did not bother with a warning since, as the argument between the two men became more heated, Wallace arrived.

"Howay, lads, this is too much noise. Let's have some respect for the dead," he said.

"I was just saying Ronny got what he deserved, and—" Charlie snapped at him.

"There's them who reckon you was the person who gave it to him," an exasperated Wallace interrupted. "And others who hint you spend most of your air raid duty hours in the pub. Easy enough to slip out on the pretence of needing to use the netty, but go down the back lane somewhere else instead. Things go on in the blackout the light of day would blush at. My advice is to watch your step, Charlie, and gan canny. We all know you had an axe to grind with Ronny."

"Better to be lounging in a pub with the entire street on fire than visiting tarts!" Sefton gave Wallace a wink.

"Why, you—" Charlie shouted, grabbing the other man by his lapels.

"If I have to I'll arrest you, Charlie," Wallace said. "Have some sense, man. It'll be a hard enough day for Mavis as it is. Go outside and cool off a bit. It's almost time."

As the men left, Wallace turned toward Mavis. "I'll go with them to make sure no riots break out. Don't want the vicar to be upset."

Mavis thanked him. "And come back for the tea, won't you? We'll have it ready by then."

Mrs. Gibson sat down and started to cry. Had Wallace really had to air his suspicions of Charlie for everyone in the room to hear?

Wallace joined the party which followed Ronny to St. John's Cemetery. Surrounded by monuments and gravestones, the handful of men—they could hardly be termed mourners—stood shivering in a cutting wind off the river. Two others stood at a distance behind them, flat-capped and patient, waiting to shovel earth back into the trench into which Ronny's coffin had been lowered. Here and there dingy seagulls pecked forlornly at the grass. A thin drizzle fell from a grey sky.

A man who said he was the cemetery watchman stopped Wallace and asked for news about the matter of the vandalised statue.

"You'll have to come round the station and talk to Constable Baxter about that."

"I will, but women in the force, what good is that, I ask you?" The watchman pinched out his cigarette and lodged the stub behind his ear.

"Aye, that may be so," remarked a member of the party, "but you got to admit they're red hot workers when they get down to it."

A gust of wind stirred dead flowers on a grave next to Ronny's.

Wallace scanned those gathered at the grave. It's your funeral when you find out who your friends are, he thought. Or your survivors found out. By the look of it Ronny didn't have many, unless those living elsewhere couldn't be bothered to come out into the cold to see him off.

Was Charlie Gibson there to make sure the man who should have been his son-in-law and given Veronica a name was buried with a final bitter, unspoken curse?

Sefton's presence was not too surprising. They'd been marrers in the old days and it was only right he should show that much respect to Ronny, even if his departed friend had been a well-known swine.

Mr. Elliott read the funeral service, shoulders hunched, hair ruffled in the wind. Earlier at St Martha's Church he had reminded his scanty congregation that they had all entered the world empty-handed and would leave it in the same state.

Was that true? Ronny had left with a mystery in his pocket, and the cleverest pickpocket could not get hold of it.

He glanced at two men who stood on the other side of the grave. Their faces were familiar. Both were involved in Ronny's illegal activities before the war. He had attended the funeral in the hope such acquaintances would appear.

Now the minister declared that man did not have long to live, cut down flower-like, fleeing like a shadow.

Wallace found himself wondering at the local custom frowning on women attending funerals. Perhaps its roots were in Victorian ideas of protecting frail womanhood? Then there came the more practical notion: if everyone went to the funeral who would prepare the funeral tea awaiting mourners afterward?

He could just do with a nice hot cup of tea. He studied the two men across from him. Both looked like retired dockworkers. They were the Anderson brothers, now well into their seventies, with records as long as the funeral service seemed to be taking.

The oldest was Mike, whom Wallace had lately been told by Baines was involved in blackmail but unlikely to be prosecuted since the victim refused to press charges. The younger brother, Matthew, was notorious as the more violent of the pair. He had recently served time for severely coshing a Salvation Army lass, a crime that so disgusted the area the force had had several anonymous tips within days of the assault.

The blackout indeed covered a multitude of sins. Had the brothers seen something useful to the current dual investigations?

And now finally came the end of the service, a couple of handfuls of earth thrown into the grave, and Wallace was free to quickly step around its foot to address the men starting away.

"One moment, you two. I want a word."

Chapter Twenty-three

The men who had attended Ronny's funeral returned to Mavis' kitchen. Cleaning the dirt off their soles on the scraper in the niche by the front door, they came into the kitchen slapping their hands together, and clustered near the fire before starting on the sandwiches and eggless sponge cake laid out on mismatched plates on the table. Quantities of weak tea were drunk. Things were said that are always said on such occasions and sound shallow and meaningless except at the very moment of grief, when they strike to the heart. Before long everyone left. The men held their hats, anxious to leave, while the women hugged Mavis and offered useless but well-intentioned advice.

Mavis took a deep breath when the final visitors were gone. "Thank heaven that's over. I need a breath of air." She went out into the backyard.

Grace, who was tired herself, sat down at the table. She closed her eyes for a moment and when she opened them, there stood Hans, unshaven and dressed in crumpled clothing.

"Look what the cat dragged in," Mavis said, coming in behind him. "Where you been, Hans? Helping Santa out, was it?"

Hans laughed loudly and then pantomimed covering his mouth, as she continued. "You didn't have to come to the backyard. There's a front door. Scared me out of me wits suddenly seeing you."

"Sorry, Miss Mavis. I didn't want to disturb your guests."

"Oh well, at least you've turned up again like a bad penny. Grab a chair and tell us all about it."

"I am happy you are not angry with me."

"We were worried sick about you, Hans," put in Grace. Mavis appeared to have a remarkably cavalier attitude to her missing friend's abrupt return. Her husband had just been buried. Anything else must feel trivial for the time being. But Grace saw how she bit her lip and gave Hans a sideways glance as he settled into a chair.

"I hope you are not angry with me either, Miss Grace. I would never want to worry you." He briefly put his hand over hers where it rested beside her plate.

Her attempt at a smile failed miserably. She was duty bound to report Hans' return, meaning he would be brought to the station to assist the police with their inquiries, as official announcements would have it.

Hans guessed what she was thinking. "I shall go to the station shortly, but first I wanted to assure my two good friends here I am not floating facedown in the river or locked in a police cell somewhere."

"Doesn't mean either might not still happen," Mavis pointed out. "What did you have to go and do a bunk for? Talk about suspicious behaviour, me husband found dead and me so-called fancy man disappearing. No doubt that fond fool Baines suspects us both."

So Mavis did grasp the situation after all, Grace thought. "She's right, Hans. Why did you run away?" Simply to see his reaction, she probably should have asked if it was because he had killed Ronny, but she couldn't bring herself to do it.

Hans admitted it did not look good. "But you see, I am a foreigner and always suspected. In such situations regrettable mistakes are made, and I did not wish to be found hanging from a lamppost. I stayed at a hostel. It was for those who have lost their homes. They were very kind and gave me a meal.

"It was foolish of me," Hans went on. "Naturally, I will be suspected in the circumstances."

"What about suspects not called Hans?" Mavis asked Grace.

"Could be a person from Ronny's past, a private grudge. His death might be payback for something that happened before the war. Sorry, Mavis, but you did ask."

"For that I would pick Charlie Gibson," Mavis replied. "What if he caught Ronny in the blackout and decided to administer a little private justice for being so crippled he couldn't work at his old job? Not to mention for Nica. She's not been long at school. Everyone knows her story and kids can be cruel."

Grace considered the idea. "The Gibsons obviously love her, and Charlie has a quick temper, saw that myself."

"Charlie may not have the strength he once had, but a cosh can do a lot of damage in the right hands," Mavis pointed out.

"Do you think there's a link between the two deaths?" Hans put in. "The way the arms and legs were arranged, and both of them found at the same place?"

"Do we have to dwell on it? There's more darkness than light these days, what with bombs and factory smoke hanging over these streets." Mavis added, "How about if I play something on me gramophone?"

She had a whole binder full of Glenn Miller records. Before long Grace began to feel she was back in the church hall with Hans.

"Let's dance!" Mavis said.

Hans looked nervously from Mavis to Grace.

Mavis grabbed a chair and started whirling around the room with it. "Me chair's me usual partner. A bit stiff in the legs, but he never steps on me toes."

Hans stood and with a slight bow offered Grace his hand.

They moved carefully around the limited floor space, managing to avoid the furniture.

Hans put his face close to hers. "How could I have stayed away from you, Miss Grace? If I may be so bold, may I ask to escort you to the cinema?

• • ● • •

"Can you believe it, Jim? The Hun's back." Stu gestured toward Mavis' window. An occasional faint squeal of music leaked into the street. "If he knew what was good for him he'd have stayed away."

By chance Jim had run into Stu on Carter Street. "What you hanging around out here for, Stu?"

"Couldn't take no more at home. Mam's been beside herself. We sat down yesterday to eat and all of a sudden she says 'Robbie's here. He's come to spend Christmas with us. Can't you feel him, Stu?' Then she starts bubbling."

"Could you feel him, then?"

"Bloody hell, no!"

Stu didn't ask why Jim was out. Jim's old man was someone who'd as soon beat his son as look at him after he'd had a few, and since he was off work today he'd doubtless had more than a few.

Stu took out his knife. "Maybe I ought to give Rob a Christmas present and put this in the Hun's back? What d'ya think?"

A tinny snatch of song made its way outside, something about love.

Jim dug his hands into his jacket pockets. "Let's walk. It's too cold to be standing around."

They set off, going nowhere in particular, just keeping ahead of the chill.

"Put yer knife away, Stu. What if a copper come along? You need to stop all this talk about killing people. Even if Hans is a German, he's not the German who killed Rob."

Stu reluctantly pocketed his knife. Looking at the shiny blade, rubbing his finger carefully along its razor edge, made him feel better, made him believe there would be justice some day.

The two boys walked on in silence, close enough friends they didn't need to talk. Turning the corner, they came to the temple.

Jim leaned against an altar. "Don't it seem strange how you go out to walk around and always end up at these ruins? Like they were some kind of magnet?"

"You're daft."

"Well, we're here, ain't we?"

"Where else would we be in Benwell? There's nothing. You only notice when you get here because you've arrived somewhere."

Jim shook his head. "Yer a deep one, Stu. Either that or a fool."

"Maybe, but I ain't standing where them dead bodies was laid out. The tart's arms and legs was bent just like a swastika. I seen them."

Jim shrugged. "And you was telling me I was daft for thinking there's something queer about this place."

"I'm not talking about some old stones, I'm talking about dead bodies." Stu paced around the foundations. "It was the Hun killed Ronny," he said suddenly. "He's carrying on with Ronny's wife, isn't he? Another reason he should be dead. One of these days, he's going to pay, and everyone helping him is going to help foot the bill."

"What? You mean like Ronny's wife? What would Ronny think of that?"

"Ronny's dead. He ain't thinking nothing."

"And that copper staying with her? You wouldn't kill a copper?"

"Wouldn't I? I'd do anything to beat the Huns."

"Anything? Are you sure?"

"What yer getting at?"

Jim nodded in the direction of Rutherford's maisonette. "Old geezer there used to give these talks at the church hall. Friend of me mam's went. Reckoned he was always going on about ancient knowledge. Reckoned he could stop the Nazis with some magical rubbish, only nobody would help him do it."

"Don't surprise me none. He's soft in the head."

"That's what everyone says. Rutherford reckoned if they'd only give him a hand with what he called a cone of power, it would do the job. Said it'd get this god the Romans worshipped right where we're standing to help defeat Hitler. Me mam's friend rattled on and on about it, but said she wasn't about to dance naked around a bonfire."

"Ah, yer pulling me leg, Jim."

"I'm not. Swear to God."

Stu looked at him. "What god?"

"Whatever one you like." Jim pushed himself away from the altar. "I'm gannen eeyem. Dad'll be out of it by now."

Stu took a last look around before they left. He had never noticed before but the altar against which Jim had been leaning had a knife carved on one side.

Parting from Jim, he continued home, thinking about the carving. They didn't mess about, them Romans. No doubt when the temple still stood, sacrifices were many. After the building's remains were hidden by darkness, would shadows detach themselves from the altar and move around within its confines? He cast an uneasy look back as he reached the corner of Carter Street.

Rutherford's idea was daft, Stu told himself on his way home and again when he had sneaked in past his mother and locked himself in his room. Daft.

And he was daft for not dismissing it out of hand.

But Rob was rotting in his grave and he could hear his mother sobbing in the kitchen.

In the light of day religion was obviously rubbish, a superstition left over from the past. But at times, in the darkness of his room without any distractions from the temporarily invisible workaday world, Stu could almost believe in God.

Even if He hadn't answered his prayers to avenge Rob.

Maybe the Roman god was more powerful. The ruins of his temple remained after thousands of years. The Romans had conquered the whole world, or so he'd learned at school. They must have had real gods. Strong, fighting gods. Roman gods hadn't advised their followers to turn the other cheek, had they?

What they wanted was sacrifices on altars decorated with carvings of a knife. The idea appealed to him. If the old god wanted blood, if the god existed, was still alive somewhere, wouldn't he want such offerings to resume?

That black cat that hung about the ruins would be a good start. Certainly worth thinking about. It might take some doing, though, since he'd tried to catch it before and now it raced off as soon as it saw him. Thinking of the cat reminded him of

Rutherford's mangy herd of flea-bitten pets. Might have better luck nabbing one of them.

His thoughts swung from Rutherford's cats to the cone of power business Jim had mentioned.

And yet…what if? What if there were the smallest chance of it working?

Stu was resigned to hanging for killing one Hun.

Would he dare make a fool out of himself to stop the Nazis completely?

Chapter Twenty-four

It snowed the day after Boxing Day, too late for Christmas when snow might have been appreciated. There was enough for Grace to leave footprints on the pavement on her way to the police station. She admired how the streets and rooftops were for once a clean white. The sky remained the dirty grey of despair.

The station was cold. Wallace was typing two-fingered on an ancient sit-up-and-beg typewriter, scowling near-sightedly at the form he was labouring to fill in. He looked up when the tinkle of the bell on the shop door announced Grace's arrival. "Thank goodness you're here. I can't make out half of Baines' scrawl. Why can't he type his reports up instead of expecting us to do it?"

"Probably thinks it's women's work."

Wallace grinned. "Now you mention it…"

"I never learned to type," Grace informed him firmly.

Wallace's eyebrows went up. Before he could say anything Grace asked if he'd noticed anything useful at the funeral.

"Apart from Sefton, a couple of Ronny's old acquaintances attended it and by acquaintances I mean accomplices. I'm wondering how they would have known to be there to pay their respects if he hadn't let them know he was back."

"In which case might Ronny have been making plans with them?"

"Either that or getting ready to resume any business they'd been up to before he went into the forces. Of course they knew nothing, as usual."

Grace went into the kitchen and brought back two steaming cups of tea. If Wallace had to do the typing at least she could fetch him tea. "Sefton came to see Mavis," she said. "He was trying to find out if Ronny had left any unfinished business she might know about. She said no. The conversation wasn't friendly."

Wallace cradled his cup in his hands. "Warms me poor, abused typing fingers nice, this does."

Grace ignored the hint. "What does Sergeant Baines think about it all?"

"He doesn't seem all that interested."

Two constables arrived, tracking snow into the room, and greeting Wallace while ignoring Grace.

"Don't mind them." Wallace remarked. "They're bashful. The Dutchman's story of how he got here appears to be correct, so far as it can be checked with the refugee people. Seeing as Holland is under Nazi control right now, we can't find out anything from there. He may have had a criminal record. No way of knowing."

Grace suppressed a wince at hearing Hans described as "the Dutchman." She told Wallace about Hans' return, where he had gone, and his reasons for flight.

"Running away certainly makes him look suspicious. On the other hand, with a bit of time a person can calm down and think up a plausible story."

"He'll be coming to the station to be interviewed." She also hoped he wouldn't say anything incriminating. He was not, after all, a native English-speaker. She made a mental note to check the Arkwright file for his statement in due course.

"What about Charlie Gibson?" she asked. "Just between us, he'd be my first pick as a suspect. There was that scene at Mavis' house while Ronny's body was still there."

"Charlie has a legitimate grievance."

"His daughter, Phyllis, has a grievance as well."

Wallace laughed. "If that's what you call a bairn in Shropshire! A grievance! I'm not surprised she took up with Ronny. A right pair they were. She was a little devil, always in and out of trouble. She came close to knifing one of the lasses in her class for going out with a boyfriend of hers, did Phyllis. All three of them fourteen at the time!"

Grace wasn't sure why but the image of the temple came into her mind and with it a conjecture. "Suppose she met Ronny somewhere during those missing days, and for some reason they arranged to meet again at night? Too far-fetched?"

"I don't know, but I'm glad she's not our problem."

"Her mother told me Phyllis stole money from her after Nica was born and left the baby behind. She said she doesn't know where Phyllis went."

"Went to work as a tart, of course. What else would a girl like her do?"

Grace thought about her visit to the Gibsons and how delighted Nica had been with her presents. What a shame it was for a girl to have such wretched excuses for parents. "Does Phyllis come back to visit her daughter? Nica asked her grandmother whether her auntie was going to bring presents. Do you think...?"

"That auntie might really be mam? Happens all the time. Could be worth looking into."

"What about that misguided child who's trying to pass herself off as a prostitute? She told me an old neighbor put the idea into her head."

"It would be the sort of thing Phyllis would do." He called over a constable who was filling out reports at a table by the shelves. "Briggs, you've dealt with Lulu."

The young man smiled in amusement. "Yes, sir, I have at that."

"Any idea who convinced her to try to get herself arrested?"

"No, sir."

"Have you seen her with any tarts?"

Briggs shook his head.

"Do you know Phyllis Gibson, Constable Briggs?" Grace asked.

Briggs looked from Grace to Wallace.

"Answer the lady," Wallace said. "She won't bite. Furthermore, she's here to stay, whatever Sergeant Baines might have told you."

"Yes, sir. Um, no, miss. Never heard of this Phyllis." He looked nervously back at Wallace. "Should I know her?"

"You haven't been with us long enough, Briggs. If you were here when Phyllis lived in the street you wouldn't forget her. Any unfamiliar ladies of our fair pavements been around in the past week or so? You check on the ruins regularly."

"The tarts—excuse me, miss—have abandoned that as a meeting spot. I wonder why?"

"Aye. Well, the locals were always complaining we couldn't keep the ladies away. I hope they're happy now!"

The doorbell announced a new arrival.

Wallace stood up. "Constable Robinson. Just the man I want to see." He slapped the carriage return lever hard. "I've been helping you out with these forms, but now you can take over yourself. Tapping them keys will warm you up!"

Chapter Twenty-five

Lily's mother was not happy to have a constable call. "I suppose this is what you're here about!" To Grace's surprise she showed her a magazine. Tales of Wonder. The cover showed panicked crowds fleeing a futuristic city over which loomed a bright green cloud.

"I don't imagine it's illegal, Mrs. Dixon. What is the problem?"

"Look what it says on the cover. 'The Menace From Space.' What sort of rubbish is that for a child to read? As if we wasn't menaced enough by them Huns, let alone green clouds from space." Mrs. Dixon was every bit as loud as she'd been when she'd visited Mavis the day of the funeral.

"I understand, but—"

"She stole it, didn't she? And somebody saw her do it. She don't have money for such things."

"That's not why I'm here. I want to speak with Lily, but not about stealing."

Mrs. Dixon stopped waving the magazine about. "Well, that's a relief." She glowered at the cover. "Me daughter lets her imagination run wild, she does. It's going to get her into trouble."

Grace thought it a distinct possibility. "Children all have overactive imaginations. She'll grow out of it."

Mrs. Dixon tossed the magazine down on the kitchen table and brushed her hands together as if to clean off any toxins from the green cloud. "I done my best, with me husband off to the war. She needs a strong hand, Lily does. All this nonsense about her trying to get herself arrested. The neighbours made sure I knew about that. Now I'm ashamed to show me face in the street."

"I've spoken to her about it. I don't think you need to worry about it anymore, Mrs. Dixon. She's not that kind of girl." Grace hoped she sounded reassuring. Really, she had no idea what kind of girl Lily was.

When Grace confronted her she was a sulky kind of girl. She sat slumped on the edge of her bed. "You going to take me down to the station? I'll go peaceable."

"I'm only here to talk to you, Lily."

"Got nothing to say."

Grace decided to take the blunt approach. "The old neighbor who told you prostitution was money for jam. That was Phyllis Gibson, wasn't it?"

Lily straightened up, alarmed. "You won't get me to say nothing bad about Phyllis. She's me friend."

"All I want to know is when did Phyllis put these ideas into your head?"

"Summer." The girl's voice trembled.

"Do you see her often?"

"No."

"But you've seen her more than once?"

"I shouldn't have said nothing." She screwed her face up in defiance.

"When was the last time? You must tell me, Lily, it's important."

Lily shrugged. "Seen her down the street one night last week."

Grace had decided to interview Lily before confronting the Gibsons. It appeared Phyllis had visited her parents recently. They had lied about not seeing her or knowing the whereabouts of their granddaughter's "auntie."

She could see how Phyllis, no doubt well turned out and confident, would appeal to a child living under straitened conditions in Benwell.

"You shouldn't pay attention to what Phyllis says, Lily. One last question. Your mother thinks you stole a magazine. Did you?"

Lily scowled and remained silent.

"It looked quite interesting. I read detective novels myself."

Lily gave Grace a curious look. "You won't tell, will you? They're me dad's. I found a box of them in the back of their wardrobe."

• ● ● ● •

"Off to your room now, and mind you shut the door." Veronica's grandmother shushed the little girl away with her hands, the same voice and gestures she had once used to shoo Molly, their cat, off the kitchen table.

Veronica went slowly to her room and closed the door until it clicked, shutting her off from whatever was going to happen that she wasn't supposed to know about. Molly had gone away a long time ago. Veronica's father had explained that because of Mr. Hitler there wasn't enough food for pets so Molly had to go to a new place. It was mean of Mr. Hitler to take food from dogs and cats, Veronica thought. He must be a very bad man.

She sat on her bed with her red knitted teddy bear. The Spitfire brooch looked nice on Teddy. She had made sure to pin the brooch through his pretend fur and not his skin. As soon as she heard the police lady's voice in the hall she had rushed into the kitchen to show her how well Teddy looked wearing the brooch.

The brooch made her think of aeroplanes. On those days when the sky was clear and blue, the planes, flashing in the sunlight, looked the same size as the brooch. Veronica knew they were actually big and only looked little because they were a long, long way up. But she liked imagining they were really were small, like the brooch, tiny little things buzzing around. You could jump up and grab one if you were quick enough.

If you caught one from the Luftwobble you could throw it on the ground and stamp on it.

She straightened Teddy's brooch and held him at arm's length to admire the effect.

Low voices came from beyond the door.

"Why are you bothering us again?" her mother was saying. Then she said about something or other being "on the loose" and "two already. I'm not sending Veronica to school alone until he's caught."

The voices grew louder. She heard her auntie's name. Phyllis.

Putting Teddy on the bed and putting a finger to her lips to tell him to stay quiet, she crept over to the door and put her ear against its cool wood.

"It weren't me," her father was saying, making Veronica wonder if her father had been bad. Was that why the police lady was here? She couldn't imagine her father being naughty, let alone naughty enough to make the police come round.

Before she could speculate further, she heard them talking about somebody called Ronny. She didn't know who Ronny was but whenever she heard his name her parents voices became raised.

"Come over and threatened us a few days back, he did," her mother was saying. "We feared for wor lives. We had no choice but tell him where she lives."

"But you didn't tell me." The police lady sounded like Veronica's teacher when she was annoyed. "Are you afraid Phyllis was involved? Is that why you lied to me?"

Her father laughed, but it was a funny sort of laugh, not like when he was laughing at something funny. "Ronny don't get his, he'll cut your throat likely as not."

"I'd advise you to be careful in your dealings with the police from now on, Mr. Gibson. You have an ugly history with Ronny."

"I defend me family from a criminal and it's me under suspicion, is that it?"

Veronica didn't know what suspicion meant but it didn't sound like anything you would want to be under. The voices grew quieter. The last words she clearly heard were those of the police lady asking for her father to write down Auntie Phyllis' address.

Well, even Veronica knew that Phyllis lived in Goat's Head.

Chapter Twenty-six

Peter Elliott met the doctor on the landing.

"She's in no danger, Mr. Elliott," the doctor told him. "No sign of a heart attack, but she thinks that's what it was. Convinced she's dying. I'm going to check her again tomorrow."

Elliott loosened his scarf to show his clerical collar and continued up the stairs, rubbing his hands together to warm them. From above came the burbling of women's hushed voices. A half dozen women turned their heads expectantly as he entered the front room.

A woman rushed over and grasped him by the hand. He recognized her as a parishioner but couldn't recall her name. "We're so glad you're here, vicar. Poor Agnes has been crying out for you. Well, not you personally, but for a man of God. Those were her exact words, 'A man of God. I must see a man of God.'"

Elliott muttered reassurance so automatically he was hardly aware of speaking. He was surprised to see a wardrobe blocking the window, making the room oppressively gloomy. It was a peculiar room for a wardrobe and an even more peculiar spot.

"I found her sitting on her doorstep," the woman continued. "Looked dazed she did, so I helped her upstairs."

"It's to do with that temple across the street," another woman said. "Worship of idols is going on there. It's bringing God's vengeance down on us."

Elliott rather doubted God was interested in retaliating for idol worship by making an aging woman ill.

The women had clustered round him, like so many pigeons around a man with a bag full of bread crumbs, burbling and bobbing.

"It's not God done it to her," another put in. "It's the demons been called up by them blasphemous goings-on."

"Blood sacrifices in front of them altars and the bodies laid out like swastikas," someone else chimed in. "Blasphemy is what it is, vicar."

"Where is Mrs. Cooper?" Elliott asked, not certain what the women expected from him.

"Miss Cooper," corrected the woman, who continued, annoyingly, to grasp his hand. "Miss Cooper is lying down."

"Take me to her, if you would, Mrs. Walker," Elliott said, relieved to have remembered his parishioner's name.

Agnes Cooper was, in fact, propped up in her bed. Under hair full of curlers her face was the color of a gravestone.

Elliot sat on a chair pulled up beside the bed. "Miss Cooper, I am Mr. Elliott, from St Martha's. I was asked to visit you. The doctor tells me you are in no danger. Illness troubles our souls. Would you like to pray?"

"Not yet, vicar. I need to tell you things first. They are after me, you know. Any moment now…"

The woman's voice sounded so weak and rasping it made Elliott wonder if the doctor's prognosis had been too optimistic. "You're perfectly safe here in your own room, Miss Cooper."

"Not from the things that are about. When I was scrubbing Satan's prints off my doorstep today I could feel eyes staring at me back. Fiery eyes, from the direction of them ruins. Then it felt like a hand reached right into me chest and squeezed me heart in its claws. It's because someone is sacrificing to pagan gods over there."

"There are no pagan gods. There is only one God. Anyone who thinks he is worshiping such gods is deluded and worshiping demons."

"Demons is bad enough, vicar. Demons is bad enough."

Before Elliott could decide what to answer, Agnes gestured toward the chest of drawers littered with religious statuettes, arrayed next to the glass housing false teeth at night. "It's in the top drawer," she whispered.

Elliott got up and pulled open the drawer. Inside was a piece of folded brown paper.

"Look inside that," Agnes said. "I wrapped it up when I found it by over there."

Elliott carefully undid the paper. He stared at the contents, then at Miss Cooper.

"It's a holy wafer isn't it, vicar? Someone up to no good stole it. It was Cyril Rutherford, I'm sure of it. He's always out there at nights. Anyone will tell you."

It did look like the remains of a wafer. Elliott lifted it to his face. Did the crumbs smell faintly sweet or was that his hopeful imagination? "It's only the wafer part of a chocolate bar, Miss Cooper. Someone must have dropped it."

"It isn't, vicar. It's a holy wafer."

"I assure you we are very careful with the host. Anything left over is consumed immediately."

"That Rutherford's a sly one. He was on church grounds for them meetings."

"We don't reserve any of the host at St Martha's. There would be no way for anyone to steal any, if that's what you're thinking."

Elliott felt he was being watched. Turning, he saw the women had clustered by the doorway, still resembling hungry pigeons.

"She's telling the truth," one said. "Rutherford's always studied evil things. This war suits him well.'

"Aye," Mrs. Walker chimed in. "Evil's loose in the world, running at the heels of Hitler. It's come alive again in places where it was sleeping for centuries."

Elliott thought evil was more likely to descend on Newcastle from the sky in the form of German bombs than crawl out of what remained of the temple on Chandler Street in the guise of an ancient god.

"We need it destroyed," Mrs. Walker said. "Can't you do that ceremony over there, vicar?"

"I would need special permission, Mrs. Walker. Exorcisms are rare."

Elliott had spent his career dealing with evil as it affected people or was exhibited in people's actions. He believed implicitly that Satan walked the Earth but he had never considered confronting Satan personally.

It was necessary to calm the women before hysteria swept the street. He did his best to reassure them and left.

• • ● • •

Before evensong Elliott made his way around the empty pews of his church, checking as always to see if any of the homeless were sheltering inside. At first he supposed he would be alone for his prayers. Then he heard a noise, a faint keening.

He glanced around. He couldn't tell what direction it was coming from. It was a sound of pain. Of a soul in agony. Suffering so intense that the utterance it gave rise to was inhuman.

He shivered. What if Miss Cooper was right about demons? He immediately chided himself. Still, he felt his heart speed up and his breathing quicken.

Elliott moved toward the front of the pews. The sound grew louder.

Was someone badly hurt? The cries were shrill yet terribly weak. Eerie.

They came from the altar. Was that blood running down its front?

The awful squealing continued as he approached.

There, soaked with blood, squirming spasmodically and crying, nailed to the altar, was a rat.

• • ● • •

By the time Grace left St Martha's church the sun had set. The cold streets felt warmer than the church interior. The vicar had been amazingly composed, considering the nasty surprise he'd had. He was greatly upset that the church had been violated, less outraged than sorrowful. The rat's suffering pained him.

The rodent was dead when Grace arrived but after sending for the police Elliott had gone back to the altar and waited, forced to listen for what felt like a long time to the creature's final agonies.

"I thought I shouldn't interfere with the evidence," he told Grace. "And I didn't want anyone else to move it, either. Mind you, I have no compunction about setting out rat traps, but it's not the same, is it?"

Children playing a vicious prank, he had guessed. And Grace agreed.

"I shall have to notify the church authorities of this desecration so appropriate measures can be taken. Until then services can be held in the church hall," he continued. "We're being pulled apart by hatred and hysteria. I just came from visiting Miss—well, never mind her name—a local resident who showed me the remains of what she insisted was a holy wafer. Found it at the ruins, she said. It was nothing but a bit of a sweet. People are in such a state between the war and these murders closer to home they get upset about anything."

Outside the church Grace flicked on her torch and walked around one side of the building.

A coating of frozen snow crunched under her feet. Shining the light toward the ground she could make out bicycle tracks. No doubt the culprit had lurked, hoping to see the reaction of the congregation, not realizing how poorly attended these services were. As it happened his effort had only been witnessed by the vicar.

Elliott had asked Grace to be discreet with her inquiries. He didn't want people gossiping about sacrilege in the church, especially after recent events.

Grace followed the bicycle track out into the road, where it met almost bare asphalt and vanished.

She couldn't help suspecting Stu McPherson. It was unfair to the boy, of course.

She told herself to put her work away for now.

This evening Hans was taking her to the cinema.

• ● ● ● •

Hans held Grace's hand as they made their way up the narrow aisle, having allowed the bulk of the crowd to leave ahead of them. One or two patrons were still in the auditorium and followed the pair into the lobby where shaded torches were switched on and pointed downwards as their owners emerged into the blacked-out street.

Each time the lobby doors opened, a cold wind gusted in as if to welcome them back to the real world after an hour or two spent sitting in shabby plush seats in a cavern lit only by discreet wall lights and the shifting illumination of black and white images.

Grace had had a difficult time concentrating on the film, constantly aware of Hans' hand on hers and afraid to glance at him too often. When she did steal a swift look she was disappointed to see his attention engaged by what was happening on the screen.

As if he had heard her thoughts he suddenly spoke as he buttoned up his coat. "Would you have thought such a charming old lady had secrets, Miss Grace?" he said, referring to the film they had just seen.

"A good question!" she replied. "Did you like that hint she really had been on the train? You know, the empty tea packet?"

"It was very clever. So very English, too. I am sorry I do not know all the words of your national anthem to sing with everyone at the end. It is an embarrassment to me."

"Don't worry about that—" Grace began as they reached the outer door. She was interrupted by a loud bang.

Hans yanked her roughly back from the door and dragged her toward the staircase leading to the circle. An usherette attempted to stop him. It must have seemed as if Hans was attacking Grace.

"Quick! Take cover!" he cried. "Planes are firing at us! Bombs will be next!" His voice shook. He released Grace and fastened his hands on the usherette's arms.

The frightened girl shouted for the manager as Grace attempted to reassure Hans. "It's only a car backfiring, nothing to worry about!"

Grace realized this was one the episodes Hans' friend Joop had told her about. Hans must think he was back on the fishing boat, under attack by German planes.

She managed to pry Hans' hand from the terrified usherette's arm. He was looking around wildly.

A portly man, evidently the official summoned, appeared at the top of the staircase. The usherette yelled. "Call the police! This man hurt me arm!"

Grace tried to restrain Hans but he shook her off. The manager ran downstairs and got hold of him. Hans struggled, crying out in Dutch.

Finally between the manager and Grace they succeeded in restraining Hans. The dead look in his eyes departed. He collapsed on to the bottom step and put his head in his hands.

Grace was trembling. "He's a refugee with bad memories, sir," she told the manager. "Got in a panic and didn't mean any harm. I'll get him home."

She had expected the manager to be angry. "Poor devil! The terrible things some of them must have gone through. You and your friend come into me office and he can sit down for a bit to calm down, like." He turned to address Hans. "Bombed, were you? Sorry to hear it. Those bloody Huns. This way, then."

Chapter Twenty-seven

Next day Grace and Wallace caught a Scotswood Road tram to the Central Station, the city's great railway hub. They intended to question Phyllis Gibson, the mother of Ronny's daughter, at the address Grace had obtained from the Gibsons.

They then boarded a Gateshead tram at the monument to George Stephenson, not far from the Central Station's portico.

"Local lad, Stephenson was," Wallace had remarked as they waited, sheltering from a light rain under Grace's umbrella. "Me favourite's always been that one." He had pointed to a larger-than-life statue of a miner lounging at one corner of the steps at the foot of the monument. "Me grandad was a pitman and used to crack on he was the model for it. Grandma would say she could well believe it, given how much time he spent lying on our front room sofa."

The tram crossed the Tyne to the Gateshead side on a bridge Wallace called the High Level, which struck Grace as odd because it consisted of two levels. A train emerged from the upper part as their tram approached the lower. Running trains on what was essentially the ceiling of a pedestrian and traffic bridge struck Grace as a precarious arrangement.

Glimpsed through the tram's rain-pocked windows, the city and the river presented the appearance of an impressionistic painting, albeit a monochromatic one.

Wallace tapped on the glass. "That baby bridge between us

and next one is the Swing Bridge, where Tommy stood outside the long arms of the law."

Grace recalled Charlie Gibson's complaint that he didn't want his injured arm to turn him into another "Tommy on the bridge." She said, "I heard about that. And the bridge beyond it is the Tyne Bridge. When I was coming up to the city on the train a whole crowd of servicemen rushed to the corridor windows on that side as we approached the river. The man standing next to me told me that was the name of the big green bridge and he was always glad to see it."

"Aye, Geordies love it. Symbol of home, you see. If we'd walked over this bridge we'd get a good view of the quay and all. Some afternoon when you're off work, you should go down there and explore the alleys running off it. What we call chares. Steep, narrow, lots of stairs, the kind of place visitors think must be full of Victorian romance but all they find is bad smells and worse language, and lucky to get away without a knock on the head if they're stupid enough to go into them at night. But there's a canny little museum in one you should see. Devoted to the Great War. The lass that runs it, her man was killed in the war, and she never married. Keeps it up as a tribute to him and all the dead."

He settled back in his seat and continued. "Speaking of the dead, now and then some poor soul bent on doing himself in jumps off one of the bridges. Favourite one's the Tyne Bridge. Sometimes they miss the river and hit the quay. On the other hand, if they fall into the river and are still alive when the River Police fish 'em out, they're rushed to hospital and introduced to a stomach pump. Not pleasant, to say the least."

"Do the authorities ever have cases where they accidentally fell or were pushed?"

"It would be hard in either case, since they'd have to climb over the railings."

Grace craned her head around for a last view of the river as the tram left the bridge behind. "I'll have to come back some day and take it all in." She changed the subject back to the business at hand. "I expect you'll be doing the talking when we get to Phyllis' flat?"

"No, that'll be your job. The woman's touch and all that." Wallace lapsed into silence for the rest of the journey.

• • ● • •

Phyllis Gibson may have served as a role model to Lily but she didn't resemble one to Grace. Slight and nondescript, she wore a short-sleeved dress patterned with splotchy red flowers. Her dull brown hair was in curlers and there was a scrubbing brush in her hand. She didn't appear to be surprised by their visit.

"Well, well, well, it's Constable Wallace and his girlfriend," she observed. "Can't arrest me, got no authority in Gateshead, do you? How's the street doing? Come in out the wet and give me a hand scrubbing me scanties. And wipe yer boots!"

The nails on the fingers grasping the brush were long, their polish chipped. Makeup carelessly applied to the tired face only partially hid the bruise around one eye.

"I suppose you got the address off me parents."

"We're not here to discuss your parents," Wallace said.

"So what is you want, seeing as you can't arrest me for anything? Pardon me if I don't ask you to sit down. I have to get ready to go out soon. The woman I share the place with scarpered, and to pay the rent on me own means longer working hours."

"We've come for a friendly chat, Phyllis," Wallace told her. "I'm only here to escort my colleague safely through the wilds of Coatsworth Road."

"And have an easy afternoon off work while you're at it," Phyllis riposted. "Well, start chatting."

"Go ahead, Grace."

Grace hesitated, then squared her shoulders and began. "About the recent deaths in Benwell. No doubt you've read about them. I'm sorry to have to ask about the latest incident, but we understand—"

"You mean that swine Ronny? I don't call that an incident. I call it good riddance. I don't have much to say about him and none of it is good. He got what he deserved. You'll hear the same story from anyone what knew him. That fond fool Mavis needed her head examined, marrying him."

It was sad, Grace thought, that Phyllis would speak of the father of her child in such words. But in certain circumstances love could turn bitter, as it manifestly had in Mavis' marriage. No wonder Mavis had expressed relief she had had no children.

"We'll take Ronny's swinishness for granted," Wallace intervened. "What we want to know is when did you last see him?"

Phyllis glared at him. "Not for years. Never gave a penny to help raise the bairn."

"You haven't seen him recently?"

"Of course not. Why do you think I moved to Gateshead without leaving me address? To make sure he could never find me. Told me parents not to give it out. You want me opinion? I think it was Ronny did in that woman nobody knows. Maybe she refused him. He was that kind of man. Thwart him, give him lip, he'd bash your face in as soon as look at you."

"Your black eye...that's not Ronny's doing?" Grace asked.

Phyllis' laugh was sharp, short, and bitter. "You think Ronny would've stopped at one eye, miss? I'm in a dangerous line of work, you know." She glanced at Wallace. "More dangerous than police work."

Grace wasn't sure why Wallace imagined she should be successful talking to Phyllis simply because she was the same sex. What did she know about how city people lived? In Noddweir women didn't resort to prostitution. If they were desperate and unscrupulous they got pregnant and earned wedding rings. "When did you find out Ronny was back?" Grace asked.

"When I read in the paper that he was dead. If you find who did it give him a medal."

After her visitors left Phyllis sat in an armchair and stared out the front window. She could feel her face hot with anger. She lit a cigarette, stubbed it out violently, jumped up, threw on an overcoat, and went out into the cold.

There was a phone in the back of the pub at the end of the street. The barman gave her an inquiring look, seeing her in the place at this time in the afternoon. She ignored him and made her call. The phone rang only once before it was picked up.

"They've been," she said. There were only a few patrons, talking quietly, so she had to keep her voice down. "No, I didn't tell them anything they didn't already know, I don't think. That Wallace's a sly one. Why did you let them talk to me in the first place?"

The voice on the other end of the line made excuses. Regular police procedure had to be followed. It would seem suspicious, otherwise.

"Why? Who are they to question your orders?"

Her face felt hotter than ever. She was going to need a drink when she got off the phone. "Look, Joe. With Mona gone, I need a few quid to make next week's rent. Of course you could always make an honest woman out of me."

She closed her eyes and let the tinny voice drone in her ear, the monotonous buzz of a fly. A buzz she'd heard before.

"I know you don't have a permanent place to stay right now. But why haven't you found anything yet? Don't you want to, Joe?"

Things were better when his wife was alive. He'd arrive at Phyllis' door crushed by his job and a wife who never stopped criticizing. The wife—her name was forbidden between them—considered him a bumbler. She told him he could never do anything right. Phyllis had sympathized and taken him to bed.

Now she was beginning to wonder if the wife had been right.

"How long have we been together? I've done everything you've asked. I stopped seeing clients in Benwell. I let Mona take over for me on your side of the river. And did I ever ask you to leave your wife, Joe? You know I never did. But now she's gone...."

Then someone was coming into the office and Sergeant Baines had to go, or so he said. The phone clicked down.

Chapter Twenty-eight

Dark clouds gathered as Grace paced around the temple foundation. A bitter swirling wind found its way into the neck of her jacket. She pulled her collar up and put her chin down. Her interview with Phyllis had been a failure. She had learned nothing useful. Wallace remained silent on the way back to Benwell. Had he pointed out all the landmarks worth noting on the way to Gateshead or had Grace disappointed him, her only ally?

On returning she was drawn to visit the ruins by the sudden conviction that she had overlooked a vital clue. Was it intuition that drew her or something stronger, the mysterious knowledge her grandmother claimed she carried in her blood? Was the temple's lingering influence calling to Grace's wise woman's blood?

She hadn't mentioned her intention to Wallace. She knew what he'd say. Why shouldn't she feel drawn to the temple? It was the site of the murders she was investigating.

Whatever the reason for her coming here, it was a quieter place to think than her lodgings, with Mavis singing along with the gramophone and talking twenty to the dozen about her plans for the future. The city sounds, while not so familiar as the sounds of the countryside, had become familiar enough to recede into the background.

What would a Roman soldier, arriving at the temple with an offering, have made of the noise from factory and river, the blare of sirens, the whistles of shunting trains? Probably he would have drawn his sword, convinced the place was under attack by demons.

She stepped into what had been the temple's interior. As she did so the wind died down. Or was it blocked by invisible walls? It had to be her imagination but it felt warmer. Gazing at the nearest altar, her thoughts turned to the two bodies found there.

She turned her head to stare across the street to Rutherford's window. Was he peering back at her through a crack between the frame and the blackout curtains?

Rutherford was interested in strange topics and, more importantly, had apparently adopted the ruins as his own. This suggested when he was at home he kept a close eye on them. Admittedly when on duty during the night this was not possible, but before and after could he, without realising it, have seen something that seemed unimportant but might provide a signpost to point her and Wallace in the right direction?

The irony of hoping this might be so, given the war had brought about the removal or painting over of signposts in case of invasion, did not escape her.

Surely Grace had not been summoned to the temple to gain such an obvious insight, one that could easily have occurred to her while listening to a duet between Mavis and Al Bowlly. No, she was certain there was something here to aid her.

She scanned brown weeds, then prowled back and forth, pushed aside a drift of rubbish with her toe. Sweet wrappers, scraps of newspaper, a piece of broken glass. Finally, feeling foolish, she gave up the search.

The moment she stepped back outside the remains of the wall the icy wind resumed fingering her neck. Shuddering, she pulled at her collar and her fingers brushed the two chains she wore. One held a cross, the other her grandmother Martha's charm. She had decided to wear the latter after finding the colloquies between Martha and Grace's mother, Mae, in the Bible she'd brought from Noddweir.

She smiled. So there was something here at the temple that might help her after all. She was wearing it.

• ● ● ● •

"I must be off on my fire watching duty shortly." Rutherford ushered Grace into his front room. He had in fact already donned his jacket. Cats perched here and there, purring in asthmatic bursts. Several pairs of eyes gleamed from dark corners. "If you suppose you're going to take me off guard again, you are mistaken. I have nothing to say to you."

Grace scooped a striped cat from an armchair, saw the upholstery was covered with cat fur, but sat down anyway.

"I was curious. It occurred to me you could probably tell me a lot about the temple."

Here to earn Rutherford's confidence, Grace had guessed rightly he wouldn't be able to resist showing off his knowledge.

"I don't have much time. Briefly, it was built near a fort on the Roman wall. It wasn't meant for mass worship. Individuals came to it to make personal offerings. That's why it is so small. The inscription on one of the altars shows it was dedicated by Tineius Longus as a thank offering for a promotion."

"You read Latin, then?"

"No one can seek wisdom without knowing Latin. I have learned however that universities are not where true wisdom is to be found. What you must understand is that the temple was dedicated to Antenociticus, a local god. The old gods may not care much about Benwell with the Romans so long gone, but Antenociticus will protect his own territory."

"Yes, I know about that sort of thing." Grace took off the chain holding her grandmother's charm and handed it to Rutherford. "I expect you'll be interested in this."

She thought his eyes widened noticeably when he saw the trinket. Although he quickly controlled his expression, his hand trembled.

"Where did you obtain this?"

"It's a family heirloom. My grandmother was a village wise woman, and her mother before her, and so on back for many generations."

That her own mother had broken that tradition she did not reveal.

"A wise woman?"

"Yes. She made herbal cures and worked what she called persuasions. That's how I knew horehound tea would be good for your cough. You see, I really have an interest in these old remedies and beliefs. They're in my blood."

Rutherford pulled out his desk chair and sat down abruptly. "Persuasions, too, you say?" He sounded thoughtful. "Do you know anything about how to work them?"

Grace did not reply for a moment, trying to compose a suitable reply without lying about her lack of knowledge. Fortunately Rutherford rescued her from the dilemma.

"Of course you are quite right to say nothing," he said with a smile. "Such efforts are frowned upon these days, as I am all too aware. On the other hand you must have inherited at least some of your grandmother's skills. As you say, it's in your blood. Can't escape it. Why else would you, an officer of the law, have brought that charm to show me? Did you feel anything tugging at you when you were over at the temple?"

"Yes. Whatever it was that called me there did so in order to tell me to show it to you."

"The old gods speak in subtle ways. If we are not alert we can miss their message." Rutherford handed the trinket back. "A particularly potent charm in these dark days, miss. Since the Nazi have stolen this ancient symbol and perverted it, a swastika facing in the opposite direction from theirs should be particularly efficacious against them, especially if used correctly, coupled to the higher powers. But it's a dangerous thing to carry around in war time. People will inevitably misunderstand."

Rutherford strode around the cluttered room in obvious agitation. His sudden movements frightened one or two smaller cats, who hid behind the sphinx.

"There's a great deal of interest in such esoteric matters at present. In spiritualism, for instance," he continued. "It's not surprising when you consider the toll the war is taking and people wanting to know if their loved ones are happy now they have passed through the veil, or whether their missing relatives are alive or not."

Why had he suddenly veered off into spiritualism? "It's frowned on by the authorities, of course."

"There's always the chance of being charged with creating a public mischief or more likely obtaining money by false pretenses. You do not frown on spiritualism yourself?"

"Certainly not. I was brought up to respect such knowledge."

"Would you like an introduction to the Tyneside Scientific and Literary Circle? They have shown me the door but Mrs. Llewellyn, the woman now running the group, is a good friend. She was the only member who voted to keep me in after the recent unpleasantness. I can give you a note to her. As it happens, they're holding a séance tomorrow night. A strictly private meeting, you understand. I have a strong sense that with your background you'd be most welcome."

So that was why Rutherford had introduced the subject of spiritualism. The vicar had mentioned it had become one of his former group's interests.

"I'd be grateful for an introduction. Where will this séance be held?"

"At Mrs. Llewellyn's house in Jesmond. I'll give you the address."

Hurrying along Chandler Street, Grace turned down the narrow back lane of Carter Street. It had been almost too easy gaining Rutherford's confidence. Then again how many in Newcastle could display a left-handed swastika charm and hold forth on herbal remedies? Perhaps her grandmother's trinket wasn't magical, yet it might as well have been. Or was her grandmother assisting Grace's law enforcement efforts?

For a moment, drawn in by her own charade, Grace wondered whether she might learn anything about the deaths at the temple during a séance. The spirits of murder victims would have good reason to want to communicate with the mortal plain.

"Don't be silly, Grace," she muttered to herself. "Don't forget, you're only pretending to believe in this nonsense."

"Are you sure?" came her grandmother's whispered reply.

Although nothing more than a memory of her grandmother's voice, the whisper's effect was so startling that Grace almost ran into the figure at the backyard door of her lodgings.

A woman with an elaborate hairstyle and thick tweed coat. It took Grace a moment to recognise Mavis.

"Grace! I didn't expect to meet you lurking in the back lane."

"Life is full of surprises. I wouldn't have known you at a distance with that hair."

Mavis looked uncomfortable. "It's a wig. Bought it second-hand. Wait till we get inside and I'll tell you about tonight."

"Oh, no, Mavis. I can guess. You've been out dancing again and Ronny hardly buried."

• ● ● ● •

Rutherford danced around the room with an armful of cats, singing away to the effect he had caught a witch loud enough to drown out their outraged meows.

"Yes, my pretties," he told them as he deposited them on the floor, "I'll be welcomed back into the group once they realise the young woman I sent them has great powers! Then it'll be easy to take charge again and move forward with arranging me ceremony. And best of all her presence will make it more effective than owt any of us can do ourselves. But now let us see if I have caught some treats with which you may celebrate."

Putting on his jacket he went outside to check the rat traps at the temple.

The first trap had, indeed, attracted a victim.

Tentatively he placed a finger on the fur. "Still warm," he muttered. "My cats will like that."

Kneeling on the frozen ground he gingerly pulled the trap from the hole in the foundation. It was the largest and most powerful trap you could purchase. Newcastle rats were big. The trap would break your fingers as easily as a rat's spine. He found a stone and smashed the rat's skull. The rodent had seemed comatose but there was no use risking its bite.

Humming happily, he slipped the rat into his jacket pocket, reset and replaced the trap, and got back to his feet.

And realised two teenaged boys had appeared behind him.

"Mr. Rutherford."

Such boys rarely spoke to him and they never addressed him as "Mr. Rutherford." And these two stood directly between him and his home.

"What do you want with me?"

One of the boys stepped forward. He had a narrow, mean face. Rutherford had seen him occasionally. What was his name again? Stu something.

"I...I don't have any money."

"We don't want money."

What then? Rutherford remembered the two corpses found not far from where he stood. He started to shake.

Stu took another step toward him. "We want to hear about yer cone of power, Mr. Rutherford. Maybe we can help."

Chapter Twenty-nine

Wallace had donned a well-worn three-piece suit of a vintage indicated by the generous turn-ups on the trousers, a sartorial touch that rumour had it would soon be banned under regulations intended to conserve material and labour for the war effort. He might be dressed too formally for a visit to the Duke's Arms, but wearing his uniform would guarantee tight lips all around.

The pair he wanted to talk to, the Anderson brothers, occupied their usual corner, backs to the wall, keeping an eye on the door and sipping drinks, silent and watchful, looking like elderly rats.

Which is exactly what they were, Wallace thought. Hitler might replace the king as the country's new landlord, but the rats in the cellar would continue with their thieving and fighting as if nothing had changed.

He bought a pint and sat down beside them, amending his previous thought. They were large, brawny rats despite being on the wrong side of seventy. They both looked as if they'd spent their lives at hard physical labor. In reality the only labor they'd done was beating people up.

"Going to get us bad reputations if our marrers come in and see us boozing with a copper," Matthew complained. "People'll think you was treating us in return for information, Wallace."

"Information is always gratefully received by poor coppers on the beat," Wallace returned.

"Poor, he says," sneered Mike. "Nobody greasing your palm to turn a blind eye to little indiscretions like in the old days?"

Wallace leveled a cold stare at him. "Little indiscretions like blackmail or bashing defenceless lasses on the head?"

For a few moments the trio drank in what might have passed for companionable silence. Finally Wallace put down his glass and wiped his mouth. "Charlie Gibson been in here tonight?"

The brothers exchanged glances. "Not while we've been here."

"Surprised, since it's his favourite pub."

"Good God!" Matthew gasped in mock horror. "The copper on the beat really does know all about them living on the streets they patrol. But you won't see him here at night. He's an air raid warden, you know. He'll be on duty as soon as it's dark."

"Aye, maybe so. But an air raid warden is entitled to pop in for a quick drink when it's quiet."

Mike looked surprised, pushed back his cap, and scratched his head. "Is this man joking or not?" he asked his younger sibling.

Wallace persisted. "Ronny went on a pub crawl the night he was killed. Did he come in here that night?"

"How do you know we were here that night?" Matthew asked. "Are we supposed to keep a record of every bugger's comings and goings and send it to the station weekly?"

"You're here every night, regular as clockwork." Wallace swallowed the last of his pint. "I'm surprised the landlord serves you, the number of times you've been arrested for fighting here. You think I don't remember?"

"That was in the old days, before you was retired," Mike said. "Since then me brother and me, we've reformed."

Matthew made a fist. "And lucky for you we don't think with these anymore."

"Heard you haven't changed," Wallace said.

Matthew put a big hand on Wallace's shoulder in what an observer might have mistaken for a friendly gesture. "If we ain't changed our ways, why are you still sitting up instead of lying on the floor bleeding?"

Mike gave his brother a warning look and the big hand left Wallace's shoulder.

"Have you two talked to Sefton lately?"

Mike frowned. "We don't work with Sefton no more."

"Sounds like you boys do nothing anymore but sit in the corner here and drink."

"That's right," Matthew growled. "We ain't causing no one no trouble. We both got one foot in the grave."

"So an old git like me could put you straight in the hole with a good hard kick in the arse."

"I don't go in for rough stuff these days but that don't mean I forgot how, Wallace."

"You know better than to get my brother het up," Mike warned. "And can you blame him? Here we are, minding our own business, trying to enjoy our retirement. We don't need coppers breathing down our necks."

"So you understand the point I'm making, Mike. If you don't want the police trailing your coffin around right to the cemetery gates—"

"All right, Wallace. We got nothing to hide no more, my brother and me. Not talking to coppers gets to be a habit. When you asked us about Ronny at the cemetery we said we didn't know nothing. But being as you're going to buy the next round we'll tell you what you want to save you the trouble of having to ask somebody else."

Wallace obliged. Mike took a few gulps, gathering his thoughts. Matthew glared threateningly.

"I'm thinking Ronny knew we'd be here," Mike began, "just like you did. He come in with a pair of blokes from the old days, treated us all to a drink. We was catching up on the news when in comes Charlie Gibson, mad with power, shouting light was getting out into the street. You'd have thought the war was going to be lost then and there if somebody didn't straighten out the blackout curtains.

"Then he spies Ronny and forgets all about winning the war. He got after Ronny about the kid. Things got a bit heated before Charlie shoved off, and then after a bit Ronny left."

"What do you mean by heated?" Wallace asked. "Did they fight?"

"Only yelling and cursing. Ronny can out-curse Charlie in his sleep. They couldn't very well fight. A man with only one good arm could hardly take on Ronny, and it wouldn't look good for Ronny to beat up a cripple."

"And to think someone said there was no honour among thieves. Did Ronny's friends go with him?"

"Don't remember."

"Do you think Ronny went out after Charlie?"

"Nay. It was a few minutes after Charlie left before Ronny went out."

Wallace finished his drink and stood up. "Thanks, boys. If you think of owt else, any information will be appreciated. Now you're retired an extra quid here and there might help you make ends meet."

Chapter Thirty

When Grace arrived at the station the next morning Robinson was going through reports, and Wallace was ensconced behind Sergeant Baines' makeshift desk in the kitchen, sipping from a cup.

"You've made tea?" Grace asked. "I could use something warm."

"This will warm you up faster than tea." When Baines raised his cup Grace smelled whiskey.

"The drinks are on Sergeant Baines this morning." Wallace glanced toward the cupboard under the sink.

"Should you be drinking that? What will the sergeant say?"

"Probably 'I hope you've saved some for me.'"

Grace tended to the kettle. Then she stuck her head out the doorway. "Robinson? Tea?"

The constable started before turning his head. "Um...yes, miss. Thanks. If you don't mind."

"What's the matter with him?" Grace wondered.

"He fancies you," Wallace replied.

"What?"

Wallace stared contentedly into his cup. "No, seriously."

Just what she needed. The other constables had already decided to send the upstart woman to Coventry. If Robinson felt that way about her it would only make things worse.

Wallace told Grace what he'd learned from the Anderson brothers about the encounter between Charlie Gibson and

Ronny. Grace took tea to Robinson, being careful not to smile at him before sitting across from Wallace with her own cup.

"Our Ronny was a busy lad the night he died," Wallace said. "Fought with his wife, threatened his wife's fancy man—meaning the Dutchman—at the Dying Swan, and got into an argument with Charlie Gibson at the Duke's Arms."

"Are Hans van der Berg and Charlie Gibson being viewed as the main suspects?"

"Suspects certainly."

"Why Hans? Because of the gossip that he's having an affair with Mavis?"

"It doesn't matter what I think. It's what Ronny thought. In connection with him, consider Charlie Gibson. He may only have full use of one arm, but that's enough if you have a grudge and a cosh. And then there's Phyllis, who has good reason to hate Ronny."

Wallace got up and took a step toward the sink. Grace gave him a warning look and he sat down again. "Yes, I wouldn't count Phyllis out, knowing what she was like growing up," he continued. "But I mostly suspect it was someone with a criminal background, the sort of company Ronny ran with before the war. People like the Anderson brothers."

Grace described her visit to Rutherford and their conversation.

Wallace gave her a bleak smile. "You won't let go of that supernatural nonsense, will you?"

"The circumstances suggest a strong link between the murders, don't they?" Grace argued. "My feeling is we'll find Ronny's murderer more easily if the young woman is ever identified."

"When she's identified—which she would have been by now if headquarters wasn't so far behind with everything—I'm pretty certain we'll find out she was a tart, killed by a client we'll have no way of tracking down."

"And the fact she and Ronny were both laid out the same way in the same place?"

"It's only in your imagination, Grace. You aren't living in the countryside any longer. I know people can have strange ideas when they're surrounded by dark woods and nothing for miles but fields and cows and what have you, but there's nothing supernatural about crime in Newcastle. We don't have devils here, just human monsters."

Grace forced herself to bite her tongue. "Mr. Rutherford told me his former group is holding a séance tonight," she said. "I was thinking—"

"Do you seriously think Rutherford would or could kill two people? He's a harmless old fool. Been living here for years."

"I believe he's more than a simple eccentric. It's not so much that he's our murderer, it's just I sense he's connected to the murders, though I'm not sure how."

Wallace got up, took Baines' whiskey bottle from its hiding place beneath the sink, and poured more into his cup. "I hate to see you wasting valuable time on wild goose chases, Grace. These murders have the whole area in a panic. Is it surprising? You can't be watching the skies for bombs and your back for knives at the same time."

He sighed. "If you really think attending a séance will further the investigation, I suppose it's worth a try. Go home early today and get some rest. You never know how long these things will go on."

• ● ● ● •

Returning to her lodgings, Grace was startled to find Hans there.

"I took the day off," Mavis explained. "Feeling under the weather. So Hans came over to keep me company."

"I see. Too much dancing last night?" The two looked comfortable together. Grace felt intensely uncomfortable. Had she barged in on something?

She went into the bedroom to change. Mavis' bed was still unmade. Grace had a sick feeling in her stomach. Maybe Mavis and Hans were, in fact, having an affair. She felt jealous and was ashamed of being jealous, angry at herself for her feelings. Was she a schoolgirl?

Her gaze dwelled on the rumpled bed. How could Mavis carry on as she did? Going out dancing the same week her husband was murdered, entertaining Hans as usual. And Hans…what was he thinking, continuing to visit a woman newly widowed? He had struck her as simple and straightforward. Had she misjudged the man so badly?

She could hear Hans and Mavis speaking in low tones in the kitchen. It sounded like an intimate conversation, one not meant for other ears. Well, Grace was back and she refused to cloister herself in the bedroom. Taking a deep breath, she went out to form the third party in the crowd.

• • ● • •

After Grace left the office, Wallace reluctantly settled down to a long day of paperwork. He had no qualms about requisitioning his superior's desk and whiskey for the task. Baines had been virtually useless for months and it had fallen to Wallace as the only experienced officer to keep the sub-station functioning. Wallace, who had retired and was looking forward to a future from which piles of paperwork were blessedly absent, now faced reports that hadn't existed before the war. The police were expected to keep track of blackout violations, monitor enemy aliens, trace deserters, and endless other war-related matters, each accompanied by its own forms. Perhaps the bureaucrats wanted to generate enough paperwork to smother the Nazis.

If the truth were told, Wallace had already grown bored with retirement. His only marriage had been to his job. He lived alone and his interests did not extend far beyond his work. He'd never grasped the attraction of books. Why read about other people's experiences or imaginings? And how many dog races could you go to, especially if you needed to be frugal with your betting?

The doorbell jingled and, to Wallace's amazement, in came a familiar figure wearing a flat cap.

"Bloody hell, Sefton, I never thought I'd see you walk into a police station voluntarily! Have a seat."

"You're not as young as you used to be, Wallace. I thought I'd save you a trip to the Whistling Chicken. It's perishing out there."

"You mean you don't want to risk being seen there with me. Fair enough." He noticed Sefton's gaze wandered to the cup on the paper-strewn desk. "A drink to warm you up?"

"Never refuse a drink. Me old man's best advice."

Wallace stood, shut the kitchen door, got another cup, and poured out a generous measure of whiskey. "This one's on Sergeant Baines."

Sefton emptied his cup. "A man's never too old to enjoy a drink…or two."

Wallace took the hint. "What have you found out?"

"Ronny was a busy bugger after he arrived back on leave."

"Says who?"

Sefton looked nervous. He'd opened his overcoat and was adjusting his gold watch chain. "Let's just say Ronny and me have mutual acquaintances who like to gossip over drinks if someone else is buying."

"What did they tell you?"

"Ronny planned to get into the black market."

"Did he expect the war to end in six months?"

"He planned to get discharged on medical grounds. Got hold of a doctor he squared so he could find out how to fake being what they call a psychiatric casualty."

Wallace loosed a string of ripe oaths, then grudgingly admitted Ronny was a clever bugger, if not clever enough to avoid getting himself killed. "Strange it would come practically on his own doorstep and not on the high seas," he mused.

"Aye, so it is. Bad luck. He'd already lined up a number of what he called overseas contacts."

"But how the hell could he, Sefton? It's not like he could send a postcard to Paris asking for a crate of French perfume to be shipped over."

"Me friends reckoned he meant he'd got hold of some of these foreign refugees swarming the city right now and there was bound to be a fiddle in it somewhere, but none of us could work out what it was."

"Who else was involved?"

"His usual mob, apparently."

"People like the Anderson brothers?"

Sefton raised his eyebrows. "They admitted he met with them?"

"I see you've heard I was talking to them."

"Word gets around. Old Wallace's back."

"So Benwell will soon see a drop in crime?"

"Do you expect me to disagree, Wallace? Here's another tidbit. Ronny let slip he was off to stay with his kid's mother in Gateshead for a while and then he might get round to calling on his wife or he might not."

Had he in fact visited Phyllis? She had denied it but then she wouldn't want to get involved in a murder investigation. "What else can you tell me? What about the shouting match Charlie Gibson had with Ronny at the Duke's Arms?"

Sefton looked peeved. "I've been putting myself at risk for nowt. I can't surprise you."

"Keep trying."

"Seems Charlie was doing a bit of work for the Andersons. Needs must. Just enough to help make ends meet. Nothing big."

"Surprise me again."

"Ronny had Stu McPherson in tow. He was following Ronny around with stars in his eyes."

"And a knife in his pocket."

"Oh, aye. He thought Ronny was a Tyneside Robin Hood. Only with him it would be Robbing Ronny and the poor wouldn't see a penny of his ill-gotten gains."

"Did Stu actually talk to the Andersons or just watch what was going on?"

Sefton fiddled with his watch chain while he thought. "Can't remember anyone saying anything about that. I wouldn't be surprised if Stu's talked to every…um…businessman in Benwell. Looking for career advice, like."

"Aye. If this bloody war doesn't let me retire again quick, I'll be arresting him sooner or later."

Sefton had little more to offer. Was he withholding information? But he'd always been a reliable informant as well as an occasional business partner.

Sefton got up and buttoned his overcoat.

"How about a bit of chocolate?" Wallace asked.

"What makes you think I carry around——?" Seeing the way Wallace was glaring at him, Sefton reached into a pocket and brought out a small parcel.

"Keep your ears open, Sefton. See if you can find out more about Ronny's plans and his movements."

Wallace sat back, unwrapped the parcel, broke off a bit of chocolate, and popped it into his mouth.

Sefton nodded and left.

Wallace scanned the shambles on Baines' makeshift desktop, papers and folders piled higgledy-piggledy. The in and out boxes were buried. Rather than filling in reports he sorted the debris, gathering files to return to the proper cabinets. If the sergeant returned to an orderly desk he might be tempted to actually work.

When Wallace reached the bottom of the largest stack he stopped abruptly.

Buried there sat the request for details of people reported missing which might have enabled them to establish the identity of the woman found dead at the temple.

No wonder they'd never heard back from headquarters.

Sergeant Baines had never sent the request out.

Chapter Thirty-one

Hans was still lounging in the kitchen when Grace set off for Jesmond to attend the séance. She had to admit she was annoyed that Hans had visited Mavis. He'd been Mavis' friend since before Grace arrived. She was an interloper and their relationship—whatever it might be—was no business of hers, even if contemplating the possibilities depressed her.

Her journey was delayed by the need to navigate the city streets slowly. In places barricades blocked the way where bombs had fallen, forcing detours. The Jesmond area, northeast of Benwell, had been hit hard by a Luftwaffe raid in the spring. Grace glimpsed scenes which would not have been out of place in London—water-filled craters, a row of houses that simply stopped, giving way to rubble, halfway down a street.

Mrs. Llewellyn's address proved to be in one of the streets running off Osborne Road. Her home was a detached red brick house that would have dwarfed every house in Noddweir. Mrs. Llewellyn herself was less imposing, a plump motherly woman dressed in black. She took Grace's proffered note, read it, and chuckled.

"Mr. Rutherford is an old friend. Happy to meet you, Miss Baxter. We're waiting for the last of our little group to arrive. Mr. Starling. A widower, you know. He never misses a meeting. He keeps hoping for a message from his wife."

She took Grace's scarf and coat and hung them on the oak

hall-stand. Grace had worn a nondescript blouse, cardigan, and skirt. She felt as if she was in disguise.

"Come into the front room," Mrs. Llewellyn said. "I hope Mr. Starling won't be much longer or we'll have to start without him."

"I appreciate your letting me attend, Mrs. Llewellyn," Grace said as she followed her hostess into a room retaining much of its Victorian elegance. A central light fixture descended from a decorative moulding, while a dark wood picture rail around the walls displayed a collection of framed sepia photographs. Grace wondered if they depicted Llewellyn family members or had been hung there for effect. The room looked the sort in old photographs of séances, where stiffly posed figures in nineteenth-century dress stared in the general direction of blurry apparitions.

Several women, ranging from middle-aged to elderly, sat around a large round, well-polished cherry table. They would not have looked out of place in those old photographs. There was only one man present. He was elderly and appeared uncomfortable.

"Really, my dear," one of the women addressed Mrs. Llewellyn, "I do wish we could devote this session to finding that murderer. Benwell's practically right next door. Any one of us could be next."

"We've already discussed that," Mrs. Llewellyn replied. "We are seekers of knowledge, not searchers for criminals. And we have a visitor, Miss—" She paused to consult the note again, "Miss Baxter. She is interested in the matter to which we have been devoting our studies and I have here her introduction from Mr. Rutherford."

The note was passed round the table. A stout woman whose clothing was too tight looked over her glasses at Grace and then at Mrs. Llewellyn. "I thought we had banished Mr. Rutherford from our group? He really went too far when he expected us to dance around naked for his cone of power business. How do we know this young woman is not a spy for him, begging your pardon, miss."

A low murmur of agreement rustled round the table.

"And really the man always makes me uncomfortable," she continued. "There was a strange look in his eyes all the time. I do wonder if he is, well, you know, all there."

Mrs. Llewellyn flushed. "Mr. Rutherford himself is not attending our séance, Jane, and since I've known him for over twenty years I am willing to accept his recommendation Miss Baxter be admitted to our circle."

"Mr. Starling is late again," Jane pointed out. "We ought to start now. I don't like trying to get home in the blackout on my own."

"Very well," Mrs. Llewellyn replied. "I shall put out the light after the circle joins hands." She turned toward Grace. "The spirits don't like light and won't manifest if conditions are not right. Everyone ready? Start the music box, please, Emily."

She dowsed the lights and as the music began the room was plunged into darkness.

Grace felt foolish as she joined hands with Jane and her other neighbour, the elderly man. The woman's pudgy hand felt warm and gripped Grace's tightly. The man's cool, bony hand held hers diffidently, almost reluctantly.

The tinkling music continued, its notes sounding louder than Grace would have expected but not quite drowning out Mrs. Llewellyn's regular breathing.

Don't be silly, Grace told herself. The next thing she knew bedsheets on strings would be flying through the air.

Even as she was telling herself how ridiculous the whole thing was, the sudden loud knocking startled her.

"The spirits are speaking to us already!" one of the ladies cried.

"Nonsense, Miss Abbott! It's just someone at the door," Mrs. Llewellyn replied. "Luckily, I have not entered the trance state yet, given how dangerous it is to be brought out from one suddenly."

She went out into the hall, letting light into the room and returning with a man who on seeing Grace faltered in his stride.

The newcomer had a wide forehead and wore spectacles. As he took off his hat he revealed himself to be prematurely balding.

Grace suppressed a gasp. It was Joe Baines.

To Grace's surprise and confusion he was greeted as Mr. Starling.

Baines gave a slight shake of the head to her as he took his seat in the circle. It did not take a spirit message for Grace to grasp he did not want her to recognise him. Her mind was racing. Had Baines followed her here?

Mrs. Llewellyn had seated him directly across from Grace, who tried to avoid staring at him. She had the impression he was gazing fixedly into space to avoid looking at her.

Again the light was switched off and the helpful Emily wound up the music box once more. Perhaps it was the shocking and inexplicable presence of Baines but now the music sounded almost sinister to Grace.

A cold draught began to play on the table.

The members of the Tyneside Scientific and Literary Circle clearly did not realize the risks they were taking. Grace knew. She had grown up with a keen awareness of a spirit world imping-ing on our own where the shadows at the edge of the woods deepened, just beyond the meadow, on the other side of the hill. There dwelt her mother's angels but also the unseen beings that made cats bristle and would come if called. Her grandmother had warned her for that reason never to take part in a séance, for who knew whether the spirits which responded would be benign or the reverse.

Once they were there it was too late.

She tried to put the recollection out of her mind.

Mrs. Llewellyn, it turned out, did not indulge in manifesta-tions of flitting white shapes, spirits tapping on tambourines or blowing toy trumpets, strange lights circling the table, or any of the usual trappings that went with attempts to penetrate the veil. All she did was sit quietly a few feet away from the circle round the table.

A voice began to whisper in Grace's head, telling her she would make a far better medium than Mrs. Llewellyn. It was in her blood, the voice told her. The blood of generations of wise women. Why was she not using her gift, it asked. Think of the power she could wield.

Who was speaking to her?

Surely it was her imagination.

Grace tried to concentrate on her surroundings. Jane's hand, moist now, squeezed ever more tightly, the elderly man's a dead weight. And although she could not see him, she could sense Baine's presence on the other side of the table.

The mental whisper continued, but now it was drowned out by her grandmother's warning.

Grace began to feel panic as the cold draught grew stronger.

Suddenly Mrs. Llewellyn said in a low voice "Spirits are here. We are fortunate tonight!"

"Eeee!" someone whispered. "Isn't this exciting!"

A muffled giggle was the reply. The music box tinkled to a stop.

"Which one of us is favoured tonight?" Mrs. Llewellyn asked. "A man or a woman?"

"Man."

Grace had spoken without realising it.

Or had something spoken through her? Her lips had moved without her volition.

A loud communal gasp. Mrs. Llewellyn asked for quiet. "His name?"

"Ba—" This time Grace bit the name off. What was talking through her? She felt dizzy, wanted to vomit the thing out.

"Bannister!" the man on Grace's right interrupted. "It's a message for me!"

"Most encouraging! What is the message for Mr. Bannister?" Mrs. Llewellyn asked.

Silence, then Mrs. Llewellyn continued, speaking now in a broad Yorkshire accent. "Nowt went on wi' Tom. "

Bannister thanked God for that.

Grace leaned back in her chair. Thank God. Whatever the intruder in her head was it had moved to Mrs. Llewellyn. Could Jane and Mr. Bannister feel her hands trembling?

Mrs. Llewellyn, seemingly unperturbed at serving as mouthpiece for the dead, went on to deliver cryptic messages from a couple of deceased relatives to members of the circle and even one from Emily's pet dog, who assured her he was proud to have been euthanized, aiding the war effort by not having to be fed. Or so Emily interpreted its declaration it had died happy.

Grace was shaking, what with the cold air flowing over her and her horror at having spoken in such an odd way.

After a moment of silence, Mrs. Llewellyn declared "A message for the young lady! Who is speaking?"

Grace had a sinking feeling in her stomach. Then abruptly she felt furious. She was acting like a fool. She was tired and nervous in this new, strange city. Did all these silly women think she was a country bumpkin to be taken in by this charade?

"You have advice for your granddaughter?" Mrs. Llewellyn was asking.

How dare the woman pretend to be her grandmother communicating from beyond? Grace struggled to control her temper, reminding herself she had gained entrance to this group by subterfuge and that they might prove to be valuable to her investigation.

"Home," came the message.

Of course. Come home. Come back to the countryside where you belong. Forget the big city and this nonsense about working in the police force.

Grace forced herself to offer a word of appreciation

Mrs. Llewellyn announced the next message was for a man whose name began with an S. "Mr. Starling, it must be for you. The message is 'forgiven.'"

The words had hardly left her mouth when sirens began to wail and the Tyneside Scientific and Literary Circle's meeting broke up in confusion.

"Eccc!" cried the woman Mrs. Llewellyn had addressed as Emily. "You'd think the spirits could have warned us."

Grace looked around for Baines. She felt a hand on her arm.

It was Mrs. Llewellyn. "My dear, my dear, Cyril was right. You have the power. You are a true medium…the spirits spoke through you." Mrs. Llewellyn's face was flushed and she stared at Grace in awe. "We must speak again. But right now—"

"Yes, certainly, at a more convenient time." Grace tried to persuade herself the words she had blurted out had been a nervous reaction, rising up from her subconscious due to surprise at seeing Baines.

Baines had slipped away. Bannister, the other man in attendance, was determined to go home despite a long walk, rather than spend the night trapped in the local shelter with a bunch of panicked old women, as he put it to Grace. He would be passing through Benwell. Of course he'd escort her if she didn't mind chancing the walk since, as he pointed out, a moving target was harder to hit than a stationary one.

Chapter Thirty-two

They arrived at the temple after dark, a dozen teenagers looking bemused or skeptical. Surely this was nothing but foolishness. They had only agreed to be there because Stu had asked them to do so. Was he playing a prank on them? On Rutherford?

Stu was aware of their doubts. Even Jim had been giving him sidelong glances.

Rutherford looked on, dimly illuminating the proceedings with a discreetly handled torch. He had positioned himself before the altars and now began speaking. Stu, who had never heard his talks at the church hall, was surprised by the old man's assured tone.

"My young friends," Rutherford was saying, "we have gathered this evening to form a cone of power, or at least an approximation of one, given we cannot have a fire and must keep on our clothes. Even so, we shall use our intention and best efforts to attempt to create magical energy and use it to direct a message toward Hitler and his murderous minions, telling them to keep away, thus protecting this green and pleasant land."

"What green land is that, then?" someone put in with a snigger.

Rutherford ignored the comment. "This energy will be augmented a hundred times over by the power of one who protected and still protects this space—the great god Antenociticus, within whose sacred enclosure we stand. Do you not sense its ghostly ancient walls rising around us?"

Mabel Greene, standing next to Stu, whispered, "He's scaring me."

"How shall we call forth this power?" Rutherford went on. "We shall create the base of the cone by joining hands and forming a circle. That's right."

Rutherford paused for a moment as the teenagers shuffled awkwardly into place. "What a wonderful night this is, my friends," he continued. "For years I have been laughed at when I spoke of the power of the ancient mysteries. Tonight I speak to those who seek to use that knowledge."

Suddenly Stu felt uneasy. Did the loony old man really think him and a dozen kids were going to stop Hitler's armies?

In his room, grieving for Rob, Stu had been able to convince himself he believed in Rutherford's cone of power. Here, with marrers with whom he talked and joked and argued at school and on the prosaic streets of Newcastle, magic and ancient gods just seemed stupid, a fairy tale for bairns.

"Look at the sky!" cried Rutherford. "Focus your thoughts there! Do you feel energy forming?"

The teenagers tilted their heads as instructed.

"Come, great Antenociticus! Assist us in our hour of need! Add your power to our plea!" A pause and then, "He is with us! See his shadow! Now we send our message to Berlin. Shout as loud as you can! Listen well, Hitler! You cannot cross the channel. You cannot set foot on our shores! You cannot come here!"

Rutherford's shouting brought Stu back to his senses.

What did Rutherford think he was doing? Stu had anticipated revenge. Was this all the old man had in mind? Not retribution or a total defeat of the Nazis, but just some kind of defense?

Even as the heavy weight of dashed hopes settled into the pit of his stomach, sirens started up.

●　●　●　●　●

Grace arrived to find the church on Chandler Street on fire.

She ran to the blaze, crunching over broken glass and avoiding pieces of burning wood. The air reeked of brick dust and smoke, carrying the crackling sound of flames and hoarse shouts from firemen already attempting to put out the flames. Several local residents milled across the street.

It wasn't just St Martha's that was undergoing a baptism of fire. Houses on either side had had their front walls sliced off as neatly as if by a giant knife and what remained tottered out over the pavement, displaying pieces of furniture still in place.

Casting her gaze around the gathered crowd, Grace spotted the vicar comforting a woman who alternated between sobbing and shrieking about losing her ration book and now what would she do?

Another woman clutched a small dog and shouted curses to the sky. The woman looked familiar to Grace. It was the woman who had wished the temple could be destroyed.

Two men carried a girl out of the swirling smoke. One was Charlie Gibson. He took off his coat and they laid the girl down on it. Dark rivulets of blood trickled down her leg. Grace ripped strips from her scarf, using them as a makeshift bandage.

Mavis appeared at Grace's elbow. "There you are, safe and sound. Thank God Hans left half an hour ago and missed all the excitement."

Neither of them voiced the thought he could be meeting it elsewhere.

A burly fireman wiped his brow as he crossed the street to address the small group. "There's a man trapped round the back of that house on the far side of the church. It's unstable, so keep well back. It'll fall soon."

As he spoke the front wall of the house in question crumbled in a rain of bricks and a cloud of dust. A double bed, undamaged by some freak of circumstances, slid after it, ending up perched on top of the heap of rubble on the pavement and road.

"It's not too late to try for him," the fireman said. "Any volunteers?"

Charlie Gibson and a couple others immediately followed the fireman.

"The vicar, he said it was a miracle," a woman remarked to Grace.

"A miracle?"

"Aye. See, my bairn and me come round to get down into the crypt as usual but there was no one to let us in, else we would have been roasting right now. The vicar only arrived a few minutes ago. Said he'd come straight from the hospital 'cos some man there asked for him. Turned out he wanted to see another vicar with a name that sounded the same. Ellison, I think it was. But if the vicar had not gone we'd all have been in the crypt."

She didn't need to say more. Clearly anyone in the church would not have survived what must have been a direct hit.

Above the blazing edifice hungry flames mounted to the sky. Grace and Mavis stood well back and gazed at the conflagration. It was hard to believe that out beyond the reach of the fire's light and heat lay a bitterly cold December night.

"Charlie and them are going to get themselves killed," Mavis observed.

Grace feared she was right. She couldn't see how the men could possibly rescue anyone so close to the inferno without being burnt or crushed as more walls fell, and said so.

It was the vicar, who had joined them, who provided the solution. "They're going through a house a few doors down, into its backyard, down the back lane, and then over the backyard wall and into the rear of the house where the poor man's trapped."

"I don't see how Charlie can climb over a wall with that bad arm," Mavis said.

"He won't have to. Someone will get over first and unlock the backyard door," the vicar replied. "I wish I'd had the chance to go with them, but one of my flock needed comforting. Now it's too late."

"I daresay there won't be any lack of opportunities to help out in similar situations in future, Mr. Elliott," Grace observed grimly.

The church was enveloped in a boiling cloud of inky smoke illuminated from within by flames. There was a roar as its walls gave way. Grace felt the ground tremble under her feet. A pillar of dust, colored a strange pink by the fire, rose high into the sky. When the dust dissipated the church was gone.

The vicar stared at it in silence with that peculiar askance look of his. Grace would have described his expression as serene, almost contemplative. But how could he remain so calm seeing the center of his life changed into a pile of rubble?

"The Germans have saved the church authorities from needing to act. St Martha's is being cleansed by fire," he finally said.

"What do you mean, Mr. Elliott?" Mavis asked.

"A nasty business with a rat. It was on the same day I talked with a parishioner who imagined someone had stolen the host and committed evil acts with it at those wretched ruins. I'm sure you remember me telling you about it, Constable Baxter." His gaze remained fixed on the flames. "This, however, this is real evil."

"Aye," Mavis replied. "These fires are good beacons for the Huns, makes it much easier to come back and drop a bit more death and destruction. Let them get the waterworks and..." She broke off, coughing.

Mr. Elliott excused himself and hurried off to comfort a crying woman some way down the street. Grace instructed those who were not needed to assist operations to go to the nearest public shelter until the all-clear sounded, wondering why they had not already left the scene.

Glancing down the street she saw figures emerging from the house they had used as a way to get to the trapped man. A ragged cheer died away as the men approached. The limp burden slung over one man's shoulder told its own story.

Another mirror would have been turned to the wall, another clock stopped, were it not that both lay shattered in the roadway.

They said it was seven years' bad luck to break a mirror. But what, after all, could be worse luck than a man killed in his own home as the result of enemy action?

Grace decided to go home, put on her uniform to demonstrate her right to give orders, and return to assist in whatever way she could. Leaving Mavis, who had decided to remain on the scene to help as much as she could, Grace walked down the street to where the destruction ended in houses whose back walls had collapsed but which had not, yet at least, caught fire. Passing by the entrance to the lane behind the destroyed houses, she saw two bicycles leaning against a backyard wall.

She knew who owned a red bicycle.

Chapter Thirty-three

"So you never took that cone of power business seriously? It was all a joke?" Jim asked. "What were you going to do to Rutherford if the Luftwaffe hadn't arrived?"

The two boys were standing on a pile of rubble in a backyard.

"I'd brought me tin of paint. I was going to get the others to help tie him to one of them altars and paint him red. A sort of poke in the eye of this god he was going on about, see. But let's get on with business."

"I don't think we should, Stu. You said we was only going to take a gander."

The end of Stu's cigarette flared red. He blew a ghostly cloud of smoke into the cold air. "Long as we're here we might as well help ourselves to a few souvenirs. Nothing wrong with bringing souvenirs home from the war, is there?"

"I'm not sure about that."

"Yer soft, Jim. Look, old Mrs. Fenwick lives there." He pointed to the house in front of them. The back had been peeled off like the lid of a sardine tin, revealing the interior. "Me mam says she's richer than the Queen of Sheba."

"Why's she living in Benwell then, if she's so rich?"

Stu ignored him. He scrambled up a slope of brick and masonry from which timbers jutted like broken bones. Lurid light from the church fire flickered across the scene, illuminating stairs leading up from the backyard to the space where a back door had once been. The stairway railing was gone, and the stairs themselves were covered in bricks and bits of wood.

"We can't get up there, it's too dangerous," Jim said.

Stu sneered at him. "You can't, you mean."

He put his foot on the first step. It felt solid enough. He started to climb.

Halfway up he came to a spot where several steps were piled with debris, forcing him to step sideways with his back to the yard and pull himself across the gap. For a moment his legs swung over jagged masonry lying half a story below. He felt giddy and almost lost his grip on the step he was attempting to reach. "Bloody hell!" he muttered.

"Come back down before you fall, Stu," Jim called.

"Too late for that, now I'm up here!"

Stu's heart was pounding and he was sweating despite the cold. He'd never had reason to give it any thought but now he realized he didn't have much use for heights. He'd rather face a man with a knife than a long drop. He forced himself to continue. Shadows flickering across the rubble suggested a blind man's hand groping for him, waiting to grab him and throw him to his death.

Stop that, yer fool, he told himself. It's just shadows thrown by the burning church, even if they do look like fingers.

It occurred to him the Huns had destroyed a church but left the temple alone. He paused, contemplating the thought for a moment, then forced himself to continue.

He couldn't have said how many times the rattle as bricks fell into the yard or a subtle movement of those he was crawling over forced the breath out of him as he anticipated the inevitable fall. But finally he reached what was left of the scullery, cursing himself for his cowardice.

He looked around. The floor was littered with broken dishes and glass. Exploring further he found a bedroom. The ceiling had fallen in. The air smelled of the plaster that crunched under his feet, its ghostly mantle over everything.

The jewelry box sat on top of the chest of drawers. He brushed the dust off it, opened the lid, shone his torch on the contents, and whistled to himself.

"It's the bloody crown jewels!"

• • ● • •

Grace, now in uniform, stood in Stu McPherson's bedroom. Stu slouched as far away from her as possible in the cramped space. Mrs. McPherson occupied the doorway. In her dirty pinny she looked both outraged and beaten down. "Oh Stu, looting houses before the smoke's cleared! I would never have believed it."

"I didn't do nothing," Stu said, not for the first time. "I was delivering messages."

"To a bombed house?"

"You got me mixed up with another bloke, miss. Maybe you're thinking of that Jim Charles."

"It was you who climbed up to Mrs. Fenwick's bedroom, not the other boy. And he didn't take that box of jewelry home. I was watching you the whole time."

"Spying on us," Stu said bitterly.

The jewelry—the cheapest and gaudiest imaginable—was spread out on his eiderdown, along with a set of cutlery, two photo frames, several books, a handbag, and a binder holding gramophone records.

Grace picked up the handbag and looked into it.

There wasn't much inside. A handkerchief, a comb, a couple of sweets, and an envelope containing a photo. Grace glanced at the photo. A man in uniform stood beside a young woman. The picture had been taken in a park. There was a kind of fairy-tale castle building in the background and nearer to the couple a column surmounted by an angel holding a wreath out at arm's length. Her gaze moved down from the angel to the young woman's face.

It was the woman found dead in the temple ruins.

Stu's mother must have seen how Grace's expression suddenly hardened. "He was a good boy before his brother was killed, miss. Will he get into much trouble?" Her voice quavered.

"A great deal," Grace replied. "Please go into the kitchen until I call you."

Stu's mother shuffled away as Grace turned back to Stu.

"We are going to have a talk, Stu, and I advise you to tell the truth. Where did you get this handbag?"

Stu gave her a look of innocence mixed with insolence, a look he would probably have numerous occasions to employ in later life. "I didna kill her, honest. I'd been out visiting me marrers and on the way home stopped at the ruins, see, so I could catch this cat what hangs about there. Then I seen the tart on the ground."

"Why did you want to catch a cat?"

"I wanted it for a pet."

Grace thought it more likely he wanted something small to torment. "Go on."

"Well, I sees she's out of it, so I takes her bag. There was only a few bob in it. But there's this girl I like, Mabel Greene, and I thought she might like a handbag for a present, so I—"

"Did you touch the woman's body?"

"Never! I never did! I thought she was drunk. But next morning I seen she hadn't moved, so I went and told the police." He wiped his nose on the back of his hand and gave Grace a sly look she pretended not to notice.

"She died from a head injury, Stu. Did you knock her down so you could steal her handbag? Maybe she tried to hold onto it and you pulled her over in the struggle?"

"No, miss. I'd never rob anyone like that."

An all but imperceptible shift in his demeanor told Grace she'd hit upon the truth. "So you only rob bombed houses and drunks?"

Stu shrugged. "That's different, isn't it?"

"You're out a lot after dark. Darkness is good cover for a boy up to no good," Grace observed.

Stu glared at her in defiance but he couldn't keep his mouth from twitching into a smirk. "It's fun following people in the blackout, scaring silly buggers like Rutherford. He's afraid to turn around to look. But try proving I said that."

The boy was baiting her, she realised. "And the blackout is handy for hiding people painting swastikas on back doors and throwing paint over cemetery angels."

"Got no proof of that either, have you? Just guessing," the boy sneered.

"I don't need to guess who nailed a rat to the church altar, Stu. But right now I'm more interested in the woman you robbed. Why did you arrange her the way you did?"

"I told you already, miss. I never touched her."

Grace felt he was telling the truth. After all, the swastika on Mavis' door had been the familiar German symbol. Was it possible then that the way the bodies had been laid out might have been a simple mistake, that whoever carried out the unpleasant job had meant to form a Nazi swastika?

Now Stu had begun to smirk without any effort at concealment. Grace restrained her anger. "It's no secret you wished the Dutchman dead. Did you try to kill him?"

The smirk vanished. "If I'd tried to kill him, miss, I would've killed him and I'd make sure everybody knew it was me done him in! They give you medals for killing Huns, don't they?"

"You don't get a medal for killing the wrong man."

Stu's composure wavered. "What do you mean?"

"He and Ronny Arkwright are about the same size. Leaving the Arkwrights' home in blackout conditions, they might well be mistaken for one another."

"I know Ronny. I wouldn't mistake him for a Hun!" He abruptly bent toward the bed and grabbed the record binder. "Look, I'll give you this if you like, miss. It's Mrs.. Arkwright's. You can give it to her."

Mavis hadn't mentioned stolen records to Grace. "You have just admitted breaking into Mrs. Arkwright's home, Stu."

"If she gets them back she won't care about making a complaint, will she? See, she wrote her name on them."

Stu opened the binder and pulled a record from its sleeve, bringing a ration book with it.

He tried to grab the small book but Grace was too quick. Examining it, she saw blank spaces where a name and address should have been entered.

"A blank ration book is worth something on the black market. Where did you get it?"

"Honest, miss, I never seen it before. Must be Mrs. Arkwright's."

Grace pulled another record from its sleeve. Mavis had, indeed, written her name on the label. Since these records belonged to her, why hadn't she reported them as missing? Maybe she hadn't noticed, she had so many.

Grace found more ration books tucked into binder sleeves. "This is much more serious than frightening people in the blackout—"

"I didn't get them anywhere," Stu interrupted, "and I never pinched them either."

"Then who gave them to you? Were you keeping them for someone?" Grace began to replace the handbag's contents and paused.

When she'd dumped the items out she'd missed the identity card in a pocket stitched to the lining.

Pulling the card free, she opened it.

The handbag belonged to Mona Collingwood. She had lived in Gateshead.

At the same address as Phyllis Gibson.

● ● ● ● ●

So the dead woman was the housemate Phyllis had complained had left her to pay the rent alone. The tarts who had told Grace they didn't recognize Mona's photograph had been truthful. Mona probably didn't spend much time on the Benwell side of the river. Had Phyllis lied? Did she know, in fact, that Mona Collingwood was dead, murdered?

Grace returned to her lodgings, having taken Stu and the stolen property to the police station and leaving both with the night shift. Stu would be charged and released.

The maisonette was dark. Evidently Mavis was still assisting at the scene of the fire.

A record had been left beside the gramophone. It was "She Had to Go and Lose it at the Astor," an ironic coincidence, given the ration books Stu claimed to have known nothing about. Nevertheless, feeling guilty about suspecting Mavis, Grace picked up the record and looked in its sleeve.

Nothing extra there.

She examined a random selection of record binders piled here and there around the maisonette and found nothing unusual. There was only what would be expected in the chest of drawers, in a wardrobe stuffed with garments. Mavis must spend half her pay on clothes, Grace thought. Either that or she'd had generous boyfriends.

Chapter Thirty-four

It was mid-morning when Wallace followed Baines into the station kitchen. "Now you've here, sir, I'd like to talk to you about the contents of this file." He slapped a folder on the cluttered table.

Baines sat down without glancing at the folder. "Don't be insubordinate, Wallace. Got a terrible headache. Keep it short."

"It won't take long. I say contents but there isn't any. Where's all the paperwork on the case? Have we been robbed by a burglar who only took the records about the girl found dead but didn't bother with a tea caddy which actually has tea in it?"

Baines leaned back in his chair, rubbed his forehead, and grimaced. "Oh, that. Not a problem, Wallace. I shoved the papers into an envelope and took them home to study. Left them on the tram. Reported the loss to the company and expect them to produce them any minute."

"You didn't leave the request for missing persons information you were supposed to send to headquarters on the tram. I found it at the bottom of a pile of paperwork on your desk."

"Bloody hell, Wallace, you know the force is undermanned and things take time to—"

"That's as may be. I've asked headquarters for copies of anything they have relating to the case, so some of the missing paperwork at least can be replaced quickly. But the big news is we've got a real break. Grace was telling me about it. She had reason to search Stu McPherson's bedroom and found the handbag belonging to our mystery woman. She's a mystery no longer. There was a photo of her in the handbag, taken at Saltwell Park over in Gateshead. Her identity card shows she was Phyllis Gibson's housemate Mona Collingwood."

Baines sat up. "Phyllis Gibson?" There was an edge to his voice that Wallace guessed was more than mere irritation.

"The very same. Yet when Grace and I interviewed Phyllis the other day she only mentioned that her housemate had scarpered. Made it sound as if she'd left to avoid helping with the rent."

"Probably thought she had. Nothing strange about it, Wallace. These girls are always going missing for a few days. Then they come back with a grin and more pounds than usual in their purses."

Wallace thought Baines seemed at pains to defend the former Benwell resident.

• • ● • •

Grace spent the morning and part of the afternoon patrolling the area, hearing complaints about looting—Stu had not been alone in his endeavors—exchanging words with emergency workers placing barricades around the more dangerous points, redirecting an occasional vehicle that wandered into the partly blocked streets, and generally "showing bobbies were on the beat," as Wallace had put it.

The air, smelling of smoke and ash, seemed corrosive. She exchanged a few words with Mr. Elliott, who was gingerly picking through the remains of his church. His cardboard box so far held only a few severely twisted candlesticks.

All the time Grace couldn't help worrying over what she'd found in Stu's bedroom and what Wallace had been told by Sefton. They'd exchanged information before she left the station for her patrol.

Wallace was gratifyingly impressed at everything Grace had discovered, particularly the dead woman's identity. According to Wallace, Ronny had been planning to set himself up as a black marketeer. What interested Grace more was that it appeared Phyllis had lied about not seeing Ronny, who had mentioned his intention to visit her in Gateshead.

Did all this new information put the solution of the cases nearer or only complicate them further?

Grace was asking herself that question when Wallace, looking agitated, unexpectedly joined her on the street and threw the situation into further chaos.

When he finished telling her about his confrontation with Sergeant Baines she stared at him, almost speechless. "How peculiar!"

"Peculiar? That's one word for it. The dead woman turns out to be living with a girl from the area. Meantime Baines suddenly starts showing an interest in the case and takes the paperwork home to study after letting work slide so long and expecting us to cover up for him. And this after not bothering to send out a request for missing persons information. Then he loses the paperwork on the tram, or so he says.

"It's suggestive, don't you think?" Wallace continued. "If the woman came all the way over here, she must have expected to meet someone. It would have to be a regular and well-paying arrangement, though, given the distance to travel and in the blackout to boot."

"And here's another thing," Grace replied, "why was he attending that séance under a false name to begin with? Could he be trying to find out if Mrs. Llewellyn charges fees? That would leave her open to obtaining money by false pretenses. So he concealed his identity and hoped no one recognised him as a policeman, given the group used to meet around the corner in the church hall."

"None of those people would recognize him, Grace. Respectable persons never see the inside of a police station, unless they're burgled and their silver tea service is stolen."

They went around the barricades where the bombing had exposed a shop cellar to the sky.

"Regular Aladdin's Cave down there for the criminally minded," Wallace remarked. "I've been thinking, and it looks as if we may have another possible suspect in our first murder. Stu McPherson. You say he denied touching the woman. But can you believe him? He wouldn't think twice about knocking her down to get her bag."

"His mother says he's only been like that since his brother was killed in the war."

"She would, wouldn't she? Did you ever wonder about Rob McPherson, Stu's role model? He was a career criminal in the making. Knew Ronny, which is how Stu knew him. Ran errands for the Andersons. The war started and now he's a dead hero. Otherwise he'd be alive and serving time."

Chapter Thirty-five

Rutherford lay on his bed. His attempt to form an approximation of a cone of power had failed. If only the Luftwaffe hadn't chosen last night to attack, who knows what might have happened. Then again, what remained of the temple had been spared. So perhaps, after all, the ritual had had some effect.

He had lain awake for some time. The concoction he'd prepared had not helped, nor had his attempts at self-hypnotism. The book he had consulted dated to the earliest days of mesmerism and had, perhaps, not been reliable.

Now he attempted to rest, draped in gently purring cats, pondering the fiasco at the temple.

Lucifer snored against his neck and kneaded his chest. Rutherford finally dozed.

A thud made him open his eyes

There was another.

Had the Luftwaffe returned?

He climbed off the bed, spilling cats everywhere.

He heard it again.

Going into the front room and peering around the edge of the blackout curtain he saw a man lift a sledgehammer and bring it down against the remains of a temple wall.

A knot of people had gathered. Several looked familiar, but Rutherford and the neighbors had little to do with one another so he could not connect faces with names, except for Agnes Cooper in her familiar tartan headsquare.

The group obviously intended to attack the temple and reduce its remains to rubble.

Rutherford threw on a coat, stumbling in his haste to cross the street.

"Stop this! What do you think you're up to?" he cried.

"We're removing an evil from the world," Agnes Cooper informed him.

"This is public property!"

"It's the devil's property!" Agnes flourished a hammer at him.

Frantically Rutherford plunged into the group, grabbing the arm of a man to prevent him using his crowbar. The arm might as well have been a metal bar for all the effect Rutherford's grasp had on it. "Harraway, man, or you'll get yourself hurt," the man growled at him.

"You'll be sorry," Rutherford yelled impotently. "You don't understand, there's power here that can save us!"

"Like it saved us last night? All it saved was itself. The Lord saves us, Mr. Rutherford," Agnes Cooper shouted back.

"Then why did he allow Hitler to be born? Where is your god when you need him? The old gods, they will come if you summon them properly, not like yours!"

The man he had attempted to stop thrust his crowbar under the corner of an altar and heaved.

Rutherford felt tears filling his eyes. He tried to halt this ultimate sacrilege and felt a sharp pain in his shoulder blade. As he turned, another rock hit him in the chest.

The women were stoning him.

He lifted his arm barely in time to deflect a piece of broken brick from his face.

They've gone mad, Rutherford thought. They are going to kill me.

He saw Agnes Cooper bend down and reach into the grass to pick up another stone.

She let out a scream and began shaking her arm. Rutherford's rat trap had fastened its jaws to her hand.

Demolition efforts and rock-throwing came to a halt as everyone stared at Agnes, who managed to extract her hand from the trap as Rutherford staggered away, shaken, certain his execution was about to resume.

But before it could, a familiar voice drew the group's attention.

"What is going on here?" Mr. Elliott had come trotting down the street. "You have no business doing what you're doing. And you, Miss Cooper, need to go inside and attend to that hand."

He looked around at the gathering. "You're all good Christians, aren't you?" He fixed his gaze on the big man standing by the altar with a crowbar. "How many gods are there?" he asked him.

The man looked at his feet like an embarrassed schoolboy. "One, vicar."

"That's right. So this temple is of no account, is it? Whatever god its builders might have imagined they were honoring doesn't exist. If you truly believe it would be best to tear it down, then you must believe that there are other gods who wield power in this world."

At that moment, alerted by the commotion, Grace and Wallace arrived. Whether or not the crowd would have been swayed by Mr. Elliott's theological argument, they took police orders to disperse seriously.

As they began to leave, Rutherford, furious and emboldened, shouted after them. "How can you be so ignorant, trying to destroy our only protection? Antenociticus will save us from the Germans if we approach him in the proper fashion!"

Then Rutherford, too, returned home. He resolved to make a suitable offering to the Egyptian cat goddess Bast. After all, his feline friends had saved him. If he had not set out rat traps to feed them, he would doubtless have been seriously injured before the vicar arrived.

He believed in the power of the old gods. As he had declared, they would come if you summoned them properly.

Chapter Thirty-six

Grace caught up to Rutherford as he opened his front door. "May I have a word with you?"

Wary, he invited her into his cluttered front room. From corners came the thump, thump, thump of cats leaving their perches to swarm around the master's ankles. He lit the gaslight and Grace again noted how much her surroundings resembled a disordered museum full of antiquities.

"I attended the séance," she told him. "It was interesting."

"There'll be time enough to chat with spirits when the Germans are defeated," Rutherford replied, bending to stroke his furred acolytes one by one as if bestowing benedictions. He gave her a searching look as he straightened up

"Just now at the temple you said its gods would save us if they were approached in the proper fashion," Grace said. "I hear you attempted to engage their aid last night without success."

"The conditions were not exactly right, but I'm hoping we produced sufficient energy for the message to reach Berlin."

"I know your former group wouldn't assist you in the effort but could you approach these gods by yourself to ask them for help? Had you in fact already begun to seek their aid on your own?"

"Why do you say that?"

"Keep in mind, Mr. Rutherford, I also possess this kind of knowledge. To me it appears as if a plea for help was made with an offering at the altars."

Rutherford's stooped shoulders sagged. "I don't understand."

"An offering consisting of two bodies, Mr. Rutherford, each laid at the base of an altar with their limbs arranged as left-handed swastikas."

Rutherford collapsed into the chair by his desk. Two cats immediately jumped into his lap. "I knew it," he muttered. "When you kept knocking at my door, when you surprised me at my fire-watching post. The police want to make me the scapegoat for the murders."

"Why would a murderer arrange his victims the way they were found? There had to be a reason for it, and how many people even know the significance of a reversed swastika? You told me yourself you thought being the opposite of theirs, such a symbol would be effective against the Germans."

"To think that I trusted you." Rutherford fell silent, the cats purring contentedly in his lap.

"You never trusted me, Mr. Rutherford. You don't trust anyone. You thought with my background, my special knowledge, I might be of use to you."

Rutherford laughed bitterly. "The old gods can be cruel and capricious, even when they are approached carefully. I didn't kill either of those people, but it's obvious you don't believe me."

"Both died from head injuries. Injuries easily delivered by surprise from behind in the blackout."

"You have it all worked out, don't you? I should have realized." Rutherford pulled himself together. He gently removed the cats from his lap and stood. "You are going to have to leave. I have nothing else to say."

Unaccustomed to waiting for their dinner, the cats were becoming restless. There were mewlings of complaint.

"How do you feed all these cats, Mr. Rutherford?"

He looked startled and suddenly defensive. "What do you mean?"

"It is against the law to waste food fit for human consumption. You could feed a family with what it must take to feed so many cats."

"My pets eat rats. I set out traps."

"You can't possibly catch enough rats."

"But I do. I leave traps along my route to work and check them coming and going."

"I have the authority to have all these cats removed, Mr. Rutherford."

Rutherford looked around at his milling charges. "You wouldn't do that, would you?" His voice came out in a weak gasp.

"I can and I will, unless you are more forthcoming."

There was another long silence during which the cats' squalling became louder. "All right," Rutherford finally said. "I moved the dead woman's arms and legs. I admit it. She was lying there when I went over to see if my traps had caught anything before I set out for the waterworks. In fact, I tripped over her. But I'm not a murderer!" He put his hand on the desk to steady himself, then sat back down.

"Only someone who tampers with dead bodies and doesn't report them to the police."

Rutherford looked at her, his eyes shining with tears. "It was an opportunity. How could I ignore it? I believe it was an invitation from Antenociticus to call out to him for aid."

He paused for a moment. "Who can say how the gods think? Do you suppose it was easy, moving the poor woman? It was horrible, horrible. I had to force myself to touch her. Before I got to the waterworks I vomited more than once."

"I fail to see why you considered this arrangement a cry for help, Mr. Rutherford."

"He is a purely local god. The arrangement of her limbs was a plea to Antenociticus that he defend us against those who are attacking his people under the banner of a perverted form of the sacred symbol, do you see?"

It made a certain amount of sense, Grace admitted to herself. At least for someone who thought like Rutherford. In his way the man was a patriot, if somewhat unhinged by normal standards. "But you didn't notify the police as you should have done."

"It wouldn't have been a proper offering if I had. They would have had the woman removed immediately, wouldn't they?"

"And what about Ronny Arkwright? Do you expect me to believe you didn't arrange his body as well and failed to report it to the police, to boot? Even though you claim you didn't kill him either?"

Rutherford shook his head violently. "You think I'm lying but I've told you the truth. I didn't kill the woman but I did arrange her limbs. I never touched Ronny or his corpse."

Chapter Thirty-seven

After leaving Rutherford, Grace returned to the police station. She considered going back to her lodgings but the moment Mavis arrived home she'd be playing foxtrots on the gramophone and what Grace needed was a less noisy place to think. The station was quiet except for the eternal laboured clicking of Constable Robinson at the typewriter.

Grace sat beside the shelves where the gas masks were kept and began making notes on a pad. Turning her thoughts into writing helped her think. She was confused. How could she believe Rutherford had tampered with one of the bodies at the temple but not the other, and had not murdered either one?

She began with the first victim, who had finally been identified as Mona Collingwood and who had been, strangely enough, the housemate of Phyllis Gibson. Or perhaps not so strange. Phyllis had moved to Gateshead from Benwell and may well have introduced Mona to one or more of her old clients.

Stu McPherson had confessed to robbing Mona after her handbag was found in his room but denied killing her.

Still, it wasn't the only possibility.

Rutherford could have killed her for ritualistic use.

What about Ronny, who had planned to visit Phyllis upon returning to the area? Could he have had a dispute with his former lover's housemate?

Grace penciled a dark line underneath her Mona Collingwood list and wrote down Ronny Arkwright.

The fact he'd also been found dead at the temple, his limbs arranged in the same fashion as Mona's, pointed to Rutherford with his wild, necromantic schemes as the culprit, even if Rutherford wouldn't admit it.

Then, too, Charlie Gibson had plenty of reason to hate Ronny. Impregnating his daughter, deliberately breaking his arm and crippling him. And he had got into a shouting match with Ronny the night Ronny died. He could have waited outside the pub for Ronny, followed him, and caught up to him near the ruins.

Phyllis, who had borne his child, also had a grievance against Ronny. Constable Wallace had mentioned her vicious temper.

So might Ronny's widow. Despite Mavis' denial, it was obvious to Grace it was Ronny who'd bloodied her nose.

What about Hans? Could he have been searching for Ronny that night trying to protect his friend Mavis? Hans had outbursts and Joop had wondered what he might do during one.

Then there were any number of unsavoury acquaintances. Ronny planned to move into the black market after he'd bribed a doctor to get a medical discharge. Had one of those acquaintances been afraid that Ronny might interfere with his business?

She heard Baines' phone ring. A moment later Baines rushed out, pulling on his jacket, and was gone almost before the door's bell stopped jingling.

Grace grabbed her coat, stuffed the pad in her pocket, and followed after Baines.

For a constable with barely a week on the job to be shadowing her superior was highly irregular, but some second sense had urged her to do so.

Despite a dying sun filling windows with blood, Grace felt dangerously exposed. All Sergeant Baines needed to do was look over his shoulder and he would see her.

Baines walked in the direction of the river. His progress was unsteady, reaching Scotswood Road as a tram was pulling up to the kerb. "Shop at Binns" advised the advertisement on the front of the tram.

Baines boarded the tram.

Grace had no time to think. She raced to the tram and got on as it started into motion.

Baines could hardly miss seeing her. "Miss Baxter, where are you going?"

He'd seated himself near the front. Not wanting to appear suspicious, Grace plumped down next to him. "Wallace asked me to deliver papers to headquarters." She patted the pocket holding the note pad.

"A bit late, isn't it? You ought to be on your way home now."

"I'm going shopping afterward."

"Oh?"

"At Binns," she added, then realised she had no idea where Binns was located.

Luckily Baines wasn't really paying attention. As the tram clattered on he lapsed into silence. Once he frowned. "Miss Baxter, you don't have your gas mask with you!"

"Neither do you, sir."

After that he was silent, leaving the tram at the Central Station. When they parted Grace did her best to lose herself in the crowd. As she looked back, he caught a Gateshead tram, just as she and Wallace had when they visited Phyllis Gibson.

Could Baines be going to interview Phyllis? Why?

Because Mona Collingwood had been Phyllis' housemate. But why would Baines suddenly involve himself with a case he'd been ignoring?

Grace couldn't very well follow Baines on the same tram after having claimed she was on her way to headquarters. She waited and took the next tram instead, having resolved to go straight to Phyllis Gibson's home.

This time, crossing the High Level Bridge, Grace began to get nervous. What if her superior was there? Then what? It was reasonable for him to interview someone who knew the victim, although he shouldn't be doing it in an impaired state.

Yet she didn't think it was an official visit. There was that phone call before he departed the police station in a hurry.

There was really no way to know what was going on, nothing to do but take the leap or not.

Grace decided to leap.

• • ● • •

Phyllis wore curlers and a flowered dress similar to the one she'd worn during Grace's first visit. This time the flowers were bright yellow. She didn't seem surprised to see Grace. She looked too exhausted for surprise or any other emotion. She had obviously been crying.

"You might as well come in, miss."

Baines sprawled in an armchair facing the front window, sunlight framing him in a bright square. His eyeglasses were askew. "Good God, Phyllis!" He slurred her name. "What do you think you're doing letting—?"

Phyllis told him to shut up, invited Grace to take a seat, and offered her tea.

Baines rose laboriously, steadying himself on the chair arm, and went to the table where he sat slumped forward, not looking at the women.

Grace glanced at him and then at Phyllis.

"Yes, we know each other," Phyllis confirmed. "We've known each other for years. We met on the job. He was on his and I was on mine. A regular workplace romance, it was."

She fetched a cup for Grace. "I hear you gave my daughter, Veronica, a nice Christmas present, miss. Thanks. I couldn't do as much as usual for her this year. Things have been a little tight since my housemate vanished. Only found out today you bluebottles know she was the woman found at the temple. Took the local coppers coming round to tell me." She turned to Baines. "Why didn't you tell me, you bloody bastard?"

"I would have told you. You didn't need to call me at the station."

"When? When would you have told me, Joe?"

"Soon. I didn't want to worry you. Tried to keep the police out of it," he muttered.

"So you say," Phyllis replied. "Seems like you failed, seeing as the police are here."

"If you hadn't rung up the station all hysterical insisting I get over here right away, she wouldn't have followed me!"

Since she expected at the very least a reprimand on her record for following Baines and on the principle of in for a penny, in for a pound, Grace seized the opportunity Phyllis offered. "The lost paperwork, sir. Does that mean you didn't want us investigating Mona's death in case it led us here?"

Baines gave her a grim smile. "Oh, but I did want you investigating. You personally, Miss Baxter. Why do you think I'd put a raw newcomer on a murder case? And a woman, to boot? I was sure you and that broken down old fool, Wallace, would never find anything out."

"Shows what you know, Joe," put in Phyllis. "Women aren't so stupid as you suppose. Was Mona blackmailing you? It wouldn't do your career any good if it came out you were having an affair with me, a prostitute."

Abruptly there was a gun in Baines' hand.

"You looked in my handbag when I answered the door!" Phyllis shouted in outrage. "What else did you steal, you swine?"

Baines shrugged. "Illegal weapon. Shouldn't have it. Useful for a personal quick exit, though."

"But why?" Grace demanded, horrified.

"Do you think I haven't felt like it ever since the night of the bombing? I killed her, her and the kids."

"Joe, stop!"

The gun swung toward Phyllis.

Grace flung her cup at Baines' head. Throwing up his hands to protect his face from hot tea, he dropped the weapon. Grace retrieved it from under the table.

"It's mine," Phyllis said, holding out her hand. "Like I said, my line of work is dangerous. These days I feel safer carrying it when I go out in the blackout. You never know who you might meet on a dark street."

Baines got up abruptly and left the house, slamming the door.

"I would feel a lot safer if I actually had any bullets for it," Phyllis continued after a moment.

"What does he mean he killed his wife and family?"

"He wasn't at home at the time they died. It was a direct hit. He was with me at the time, you see, and feels so guilty about it he's gone to pieces. He can't forgive himself."

Forgiven. That's what the message at the séance must have meant, Grace thought. If it had indeed been sent by Baines' wife.

Phyllis stared at her. "I love him," she went on. "What in bloody hell's wrong with me?"

• • ● ● •

Grace sat propped up on her bed, the bedroom door shut. She needed to be alone. She liked to think while walking, but the streets of Newcastle were too dark and cold for that, so she sought solitude, telling Mavis she wasn't feeling well.

She heard Hans come in. She should have gone into the kitchen to say hello but she didn't have the energy. Instead she picked up her mother's Bible and leafed through its pages, searching out colloquies between her mother and grandmother.

Pausing at their lengthy duel over the witch of Endor, she thought of the séance.

What would the vicar say about attending such meetings? She recalled Mr. Elliott staring into the flaming church. This is real evil, he had said. Worse than the sacrilege committed with the rat, worse than any imagined rituals carried out at the temple with a stolen host.

From the kitchen came the sound of Geraldo and his Gaucho Tango Orchestra.

She set the Bible down on the chest of drawers, next to a couple of Mavis' crisp bars.

Whether it was her wise woman's blood or her subconscious at work, Grace could not say, but whatever the cause, the solution to the dual mystery came in a sudden silent explosion of realization, blowing everything else she had imagined away with the force of a bomb.

Chapter Thirty-eight

"I could just fancy a bit of one of those crisp bars of yours, Hans." Grace took a seat at the kitchen table where Mavis and Hans were sitting talking.

"Certainly, Miss Grace." Hans pulled an opened packet from his shirt pocket, as he had on the night of the dance, and snapped off a piece of the chocolate-covered wafer.

"Thanks." Grace took a bite. "I would have thought these were hard to come by."

"He's a canny shopper and he knows I like them," Mavis replied with a wink.

"At least Stu didn't take any the night he broke in."

Mavis looked perplexed. "What's this, then? I told you I made a mistake about that."

"You were right the first time, Mavis. You were burgled, but I suppose you wouldn't miss one record binder with so many scattered around. Stu had taken it. You came back too early and interrupted him, so it was all he could get."

"So he really did break in, the little swine? Well, no harm done."

"I've been thinking," Grace said slowly.

"You're acting very mysterious, Grace," Mavis observed.

Hans frowned in concern. "Is it because you are feeling unwell?"

"Worried rather than ill. Did anyone from the station come round to see you today, Mavis?"

"No. Why would they?"

"To interview you about the ration books hidden in the stolen record binder. Where did you get them?"

"I don't know what you're talking about! You said Stu had it. So obviously it was Stu who hid them."

"That makes sense, I admit, but from his reaction when we found them I could see he was genuinely surprised. Oranges. Now I'm thinking about oranges. Hard things to get, oranges."

Hans tried to smile. "Everyone buys a little extra now and then when nobody is looking. It is the custom, is it not?"

"Really, Grace!" Mavis said, flushing with anger.

"You know Ronny's old acquaintances, Mavis."

"I do but I avoid them."

"Sefton visited you," Grace pointed out.

"Couldn't stop him paying his respects to me dead husband, could I?"

"Sefton told Wallace Ronny planned to get into the black market using foreign refugees in some way. As I said, I'm thinking about oranges." She glanced at Hans.

"You're not accusing Hans?"

Grace ignored the question. "And what about you, Mavis? Extra money from dealing on it would be very useful."

Mavis leaned back in her chair. "What are you getting at, Grace? If I was involved in illegal goings-on why would I have a bluebottle for a lodger?"

"Camouflage. And perfectly safe. It would be easy to pull the wool over the eyes of a simple woman from the countryside, wouldn't it?"

Hans cast a worried look at Mavis as Grace continued. "Let us say you contacted some of Ronny's former associates and recruited Hans to help you. Whatever the details might be, you both profited. Then Ronny came home and he wasn't happy to find you in the same line of business he intended to take up, particularly since your partner was someone he thought was your fancy man."

"So what if I happened to get hold of a few ration books? Which I'm not admitting by any means, mind, so don't think I am."

"They don't leave ration books lying around at Vickers," Grace pointed out. "More importantly, not everyone dealing in the black market ends up so close to murder."

"You mean Ronny and the dead woman? Isn't it obvious she and Ronny were murdered by the same person?"

"The woman's name is Mona. Give her that much respect, Mavis. Stu robbed her and it appears possible he killed her by accident, pushing her over when he grabbed her bag. Seems to me if he meant to kill her, given his character, he would be far more likely to stab her. Cyril Rutherford's admitted he arranged Mona's limbs and claims it was a sort of cry for help to the god of the temple."

"Well, there you have it. Rutherford's mad. Obviously he attacked Ronny while he was wandering about after visiting every pub in Benwell, if I know Ronny."

"Ronny never went to the temple. He came back here to resume his argument with you. Hans returned just in case things got out of hand," Grace replied. "Stu told me he saw him hanging around the night Ronny was killed."

"Stu!" Mavis spat the name out. "You're quick to believe that little bugger!"

"It seems to me it fits together." Grace paused, feeling she had come to the edge of the precipice.

She looked at Hans in silence.

"No, Miss Grace!" Hans shook his head. "I would not kill anyone!"

"Not deliberately, Hans, but you have episodes when you're not right. Joop told me about them and I saw one myself at the cinema."

Mavis laughed bitterly. "Hans? A murderer? Next you'll be accusing me of helping him!"

"Mavis, you forget I saw Ronny threatening you, saw your bloody nose. Right now I am speaking as a friend, pointing out what will weigh heavily with the authorities, which is that Hans fled that night. It was suspicious behaviour, to say the least."

"They might also consider what I just said about where Ronny was found," Mavis emphatically pointed out. "And furthermore you can start looking for new lodgings tomorrow. Accusing us of black marketeering and murder!"

"It wouldn't be hard for Hans to carry Ronny to the place he was found," Grace continued relentlessly. "It's barely a step up the back lane and across Chandler Street, and in the blackout nobody could see him anyway. And Hans knew, because I told him myself, Mona's body was laid out in the form of a swastika. A left-handed swastika. Arranging Ronny like Mona would make the authorities think Ronny's murderer was the same person."

"But Miss Grace, how can you possibly think that?" Hans protested.

"The vicar told me a parishioner found what she thought was a piece of the host over there. Those crisp bars you carry around in your shirt pocket have wafers in them. One must have dropped out, while…while…" Grace's voice broke.

"You're a bloody fool, Grace! What kind of proof is that? Anyone could have dropped it, and you damn well know it!" Mavis was scarlet with anger. "I don't care how late it is, we're going over to the station right now and you can tell them what you have to say. See what good it does you. And when we get back, you can start packing."

They got their jackets.

• • ● •• •

Stu waited, hiding in a doorway on Carter Street. The blackout was so impenetrable he could have stood in the middle of the street without being seen, but he wasn't taking chances. Now that bloody meddling policewoman had caught him out he'd be spending time in the borstal. He might not get another opportunity to avenge his brother, Rob.

His feet were blocks of ice. He kept blowing on his hands to keep them warm. He needed warm hands to be able to grip his knife properly.

He ran his thumb along the blade. How many hours had he spent lovingly honing that sharp edge on the back doorstep?

They all thought he wouldn't do it. Jim at least had feared he might and tried to discourage him.

By tomorrow morning they'd all know better.

Stu McPherson was no coward. Sometimes justice had to be taken into yer own hands instead of relying on some old god who probably never existed in the first place.

Soon at least one Hun would pay for Rob's death.

Down the street, a torch flickered.

• • ● • •

Hans strode on ahead. Grace wondered if he would run off as he had before. She half hoped he would run and try to escape. She tried to push aside the memory of the dance, how Hans had offered her a crisp bar and later kissed her, how he had held her hand in the darkness of the cinema.

No one spoke. They moved through what might have been an endless abyss of darkness, their tiny world defined by the dim light of shaded torches.

As they picked their way across the pitch black street, there was a sudden rush of footsteps.

Grace whirled, the gleam of her torch finding only house-fronts and empty pavement.

Mavis screamed.

Grace swung her torch back round and saw a figure darting at Hans.

Stu!

A knife blade glinted.

Grace lunged forward, swinging her torch upwards. It clanked against a knife raised for a second stab, sending it flying into the darkness.

Hans fell to the ground, blood on his chest.

Stu stood over him and kicked him in the ribs. "Got you at last, you Hun bastard!"

Grace pushed the boy aside and knelt down. "Hans! Hans!"

"Miss Grace," he gasped painfully. "It was just as you said. Miss Mavis had nothing to do with it...."

Epilogue

"I've made a right mess of things," said Grace.

Constable Wallace had offered to show her around Saltwell Park. It was the sort of winter day when warmth and greenery were part of a half-forgotten dream. A January sun, sharp and cold as a reflection in polished steel, illuminated the fairy-tale turrets, towers, and chimneys of the mansion Grace and Wallace faced. Saltwell Towers, Wallace had called it.

"Nowt you could have done to stop Stu springing out of the dark, Grace. It happened too fast," Wallace replied. "Since he's still a minor they'll only put him away for a while in a place where he can study for his future criminal career.

He paused. "I happen to know a member of the staff where Stu is currently held and he told me over a pint the lad got into a fight the night he arrived. Attacked another boy for making shadow pictures on a wall. You know, rabbits and elephants and such. Needless to say, some of the other boys started making them to start fights. He's already been in sick bay several times because of such brawls, but all they can get out of him is something about shadows with knives being after him. Apparently he's terrified of them, not that anyone else sees them."

"That's ironic, given his penchant for following people around in the blackout to frighten them," Grace replied.

The thought of Hans' death did not bring forth the feeling of grief Grace imagined it should. Rather she felt anger at how he had deceived her. "Hans didn't have to kill Ronny to protect Mavis, did he?"

"No. But the situation offered a good excuse to get Ronny out of the way."

The conversation turned to the repercussions of recent events.

Grace had taken a temporary room while seeking other lodgings. Mr. Elliott was holding church services in a school in Benwell. Sergeant Baines was in hospital.

"The doctors call it a mental breakdown," Wallace mused. "I hope headquarters finds someone to replace him soon. If I have to deal with one more frightened woman demanding we demolish what remains of that bloody temple I'm going to have a breakdown meself."

"I gather Mr. Rutherford isn't going to be treated too harshly?"

Wallace shrugged. "He's a old man who thought he was doing his bit for Blighty. Mona was a tart, so he'll likely just get a slap on the wrist for tampering with a corpse. He's already paying a fine for his mystical nonsense in the shape of smashed windows. I advised him to move but he won't leave his temple, as he put it.

"Mavis Arkwright isn't being charged for black marketeering," he went on. "We can't make a convincing case. She not only insisted those ration books weren't hers, you yourself confirmed none could be found in her maisonette. The only evidence we have they belonged to her is Stu's word and what's the word of a murderer worth?"

"Then there'll be no further investigation into that?"

"There's not the time or manpower to look further into it, Grace. Nothing to be gained. Courts have bigger fish to fry when it comes to black marketeers."

It struck Grace that Wallace was oddly vehement that the matter would be pursued no further.

"Besides," Wallace went on, "she helped clear up Ronny's death."

"You mean she blamed it on Hans! There's nobody to contradict what she said happened that night, is there? That he came back through the unlocked back door, saw Ronny beating her, had some sort of murderous fit, picked up the kitchen poker, and whacked him on the head. Hans disposed of the body in the way I had guessed. After that she was too afraid to come to us in case Hans turned on her too. Or so she claims," Grace replied, angry with herself for saying too much and giving her former landlady valuable information she had used to protect herself.

"Not much we can do about it, Grace, especially given your own statement concerning what the Dutchman told you practically in his dying breath."

I didn't step into a fairy tale in Newcastle, Grace thought, as she stared at Saltwell Towers. Then she realized she and Wallace were standing near the spot where Mona and her friend had been the day they'd had their photo taken, the snapshot the young woman had carried in her handbag.

The thought gave her a chill.

Was it a coincidence?

What about the séance? Baines had been told he was forgiven. About what? His absence when his family were killed, his being unfaithful to his wife?

Hadn't Grace's grandmother's communication said "home"? Grace's lodgings with Mavis were, indeed, where she had located Ronny's murderer. Or by home, assuming the message was genuine, had she been advising her to return to Shropshire?

Had the messages been contrived by Mrs.Llewellyn? The words "forgiven" and "home" would mean something to everyone.

The apparent concentration of evil happenings around the temple must surely have been coincidental.

"Cat got your tongue, eh?"

Wallace's question made Grace realize she had been standing silent, lost in a brown study.

"You've had a terrible introduction to Newcastle," he continued. "I expect you'll be wanting to return to the countryside where things are familiar and quiet."

Grace looked away from Saltwell Towers and toward Wallace. "You still underestimate me, don't you, Arthur?" She pulled up her collar against the wind. "It's time we should be gannen. It's parky out and I'm clamming."

Afterword

Many World War II mysteries are set in London, often during the Blitz. So it was only natural for us (the husband-and-wife team of Mary Reed and Eric Mayer, writing as Eric Reed) to send our protagonist, Grace Baxter, up to Newcastle-on-Tyne at the opposite end of England. Why keep repeating what's been done so many times before? Especially when one of the coauthors spent her early life in Newcastle. The northeastern city did not suffer the amount of bombing other large industrial centres endured, perhaps because Hitler hoped to preserve its factories for his own eventual use. In 1941, however, residents must have gone to sleep every night wondering whether they would wake up under an all-out attack by the Luftwaffe.

We have taken poetic license—or perhaps we should say poetic building permit—to place two imaginary streets, Chandler and Carter, just south of Newcastle's West Road and west of Condercum Road. Today easily accessible census records show who lived in every house on every street in the area. By placing characters at a precise location we feared inadvertently press-ganging real World War II city residents into service on the fictional ship Ruined Stones.

Otherwise the city is depicted as it was in 1941 and the scanty ruins we describe still exist. During the 1930s, casts of the temple altars replaced the originals now displayed in the Great North Museum in Newcastle. Antenociticus was a Celtic god, unknown aside from the Benwell temple, although in 2013 a sculpted head with similarities to the one discovered in Benwell was excavated at Binchester Roman Fort in County Durham.

We admit to not being able to verify any deaths at the ruins. These must be chalked up to that invaluable trait of historical mystery writers, sheer bloody cheek.

We did not, however, invent the Cone of Power which Cyril Rutherford so patriotically attempted to perform. It has been claimed that such a ritual was performed in August 1940 in the New Forest. It was intended to prevent the Nazis from invading Britain and, judging by history, it succeeded.

Finally, the reader will notice a smattering of Geordie dialect, as much a part of Newcastle's atmosphere as its sooty fogs in the period in which the book is set. We have included just enough words and phrases to provide a bit of ambience. The American half of the writing team can attest that to an outsider Geordie sounds like a foreign language.

Concise Geordie Dictionary

The development of Tyneside's Geordie dialect is considered to have been heavily influenced by the language of Anglo-Saxons and Scandinavians who arrived in the area centuries ago. Some terms given here are also shared with Scotland.

There is an ongoing argument about who can be classified as a Geordie. Purists maintain only those born in Newcastle-on-Tyne are true Geordies, while others claim the nickname also applies to residents of Gateshead (across the River Tyne from Newcastle) and other towns lying along the river, both north and south of it.

Bairn: Baby or toddler

Bonny: Good-looking, attractive.

Braying: Hitting or smacking

Broon: Local nickname for Newcastle Brown Ale

Bubbling: Crying.

But: Verbal full stop to a sentence.

By: Single word often beginning a sentence

Canna: Can't

Canny: Nice, pleasant, good; can also refer to large amount of something

Chare: Narrow riverside alley

Clamming: Hungry

Crack on, cracking on: Talk, talking

Didna: Did not

Divn't: Don't

Eeee: Exclamation of surprise, excitement, or other strong emotion

Eeyem: Home

Fash: To be bothered about or annoyed by

Gan, gannen: Go, going

Gan canny: Go carefully, mind how you go

Harraway: Get away.; also an expression of disbelief

Howay: Come on

Hoy: Shout used to attract attention; can also mean to throw something

Hinney: Term of endearment

Ken: Know

Lops: Fleas

Man: General term used to address either gender

Marrer: Friend; sometimes used to mean a work-mate

Netty: Backyard outhouse

Nowt: Nothing

Owt: Anything

Parky: Cold

Sneck: Latch

Stotting: Downpour of rain

Tab: Cigarette

Wor: Our

To see more Poisoned Pen Press titles:

Visit our website: poisonedpenpress.com/
Request a digital catalog: info@poisonedpenpress.com